Fri

MW01010710

Nick, age 2 months

Frindle

Andrew Clements

Illustrated by Brian Selznick

ATHENEUM BOOKS FOR YOUNG READERS

New York   London   Toronto   Sydney   Singapore

First Aladdin Paperbacks edition February 1998

Text copyright © 1996 by Andrew Clements
Illustrations copyright © 1996 by Brian Selznick

Atheneum Books for Young Readers
An imprint of Simon & Schuster Children's Publishing Division
1230 Avenue of the Americas
New York, NY 10020

Also available in a Simon & Schuster Books
for Young Readers hardcover edition.

The text of this book is set in 14-point Revival.
The illustrations are rendered in pencil.

Manufactured in the United States of America
76 78 80 79 77 75

The Library of Congress has cataloged the hardcover edition as follows:
Clements, Andrew, 1949–
Frindle / by Andrew Clements; illustrations by Brian Selznick.
p. cm.
Summary: When he decides to turn his fifth grade teacher's love of the dictionary around on her, clever Nick Allen invents a new word and begins a chain of events that quickly moves beyond his control.
ISBN-13: 978-0-689-80669-8 ISBN-10: 0-689-80669-8 (hc.)
[1. Teacher-student relationships—Fiction. 2. Words, New—Fiction.
3. Schools—Fiction.] I. Selznick, Brian, ill. II. Title.
PZ7C59118Fr 1996 95-26671
[Fic]—dc20

ISBN 978-0-689-81876-9 (pbk.)
ISBN 978-0-689-83250-5 (eBook)

0119 OFF

For Becky, Charles, George, Nate, and John
—A. C.

one

Nick

IF YOU ASKED the kids and the teachers at Lincoln Elementary School to make three lists—all the really bad kids, all the really smart kids, and all the really good kids—Nick Allen would not be on any of them. Nick deserved a list all his own, and everyone knew it.

Was Nick a troublemaker? Hard to say. One thing's for sure: Nick Allen had plenty of ideas, and he knew what to do with them.

One time in third grade Nick decided to turn Miss Deaver's room into a tropical island. What kid in New Hampshire isn't ready for a little summer in February? So first he got everyone to make small palm trees out of green and brown construction paper and tape them onto the corners of each desk. Miss Deaver had only been a teacher for about six months, and she was delighted. "That's so *cute*!"

The next day all the girls wore paper flowers in their hair and all the boys wore sunglasses and beach hats. Miss Deaver clapped her hands and said, "It's so *colorful*!"

The day after that Nick turned the classroom thermostat up to about ninety degrees with a little screwdriver he had brought from home. All the kids changed into shorts and T-shirts with no shoes. And when Miss Deaver left the room for a minute, Nick spread about ten cups of fine white sand all over the classroom floor. Miss Deaver was surprised again at just how *creative* her students could be.

But the sand got tracked out into the hallway, where Manny the custodian did not think it was creative at all. And he stomped right down to the office.

The principal followed the trail of sand, and when she arrived, Miss Deaver was teaching the hula to some kids near the front of the room, and a tall, thin, shirtless boy with chestnut hair was just spiking a Nerf volleyball over a net made from six T-shirts tied together.

The third-grade trip to the South Seas ended. Suddenly.

But that didn't stop Nick from trying to liven things up. Lincoln Elementary needed a good jolt once in a while, and Nick was just the guy to deliver it.

About a year later, Nick made the great blackbird discovery. One night he learned on a TV show that red-wing blackbirds give this high-pitched chirp when a hawk or some other danger comes near. Because of the way sound travels, the hunter birds can't tell where the high-pitched chirp is coming from.

The next day during silent reading, Nick glanced at his teacher, and he noticed that Mrs. Avery's nose was curved—kind of like the beak of a hawk. So Nick let out a high, squeaky, blackbird "peep!"

Mrs. Avery jerked her head up from her book and looked around. She couldn't tell who did it, so she just said, "Shhh!" to the whole class.

A minute later Nick did it again, louder. "Peeep!" This time there was a little giggling from the class. But Mrs. Avery pretended not to hear the sound, and about fifteen seconds later she slowly stood up and walked to the back of the classroom.

Without taking his eyes off his book, and without moving at all, Nick put his heart and soul into the highest and most annoying chirp of all: "Peeeeep!"

Mrs. Avery pounced. "Janet Fisk, you stop that this instant!"

Janet, who was sitting four rows away from Nick, promptly turned white, then bright crimson.

"But it wasn't me . . . honest." There was a catch in Janet's voice, as if she might cry.

Mrs. Avery knew she had made a mistake, and she apologized to Janet.

"But someone is asking for big trouble," said Mrs. Avery, looking more like a hawk every second.

Nick kept reading, and he didn't make a peep.

At lunchtime Nick talked to Janet. He felt bad that Mrs. Avery had pounced on her. Janet lived in Nick's neighborhood, and sometimes they played together. She was good at baseball, and she was better at soccer than most of the kids in the whole school, boys or girls. Nick said, "Hey Janet—I'm sorry you got yelled at during reading. It was my fault.

I was the one who made that sound."

"You did?" said Janet. "But how come Mrs. Avery thought it was me?"

So Nick told her about the blackbirds, and Janet thought it was pretty interesting. Then she tried making a peep or two, and Janet's chirps were even higher and squeakier than Nick's. She promised to keep everything a secret.

For the rest of Nick's fourth-grade year, at least once a week, Mrs. Avery heard a loud "peeeep" from somewhere in her classroom— sometimes it was a high-pitched chirp, and sometimes it was a *very* high-pitched chirp.

Mrs. Avery never figured out who was making that sound, and gradually she trained herself to ignore it. But she still looked like a hawk.

To Nick, the whole thing was just one long—and successful—science experiment.

And Janet Fisk enjoyed it, too.

Mrs. Granger

FIFTH GRADE WAS different. That was the year to get ready for middle school. Fifth grade meant passing classes. It meant no morning recess. It meant real letter grades on your report cards. But most of all, it meant Mrs. Granger.

There were about one hundred fifty kids in fifth grade. And there were seven fifth-grade teachers: two math, two science, two social studies, but only one language arts teacher. In language arts, Mrs. Granger had a monopoly— and a reputation.

Mrs. Granger lived alone in a tidy little house in the older part of town. She drove an old, pale blue car to school every morning, rain or shine, snow or sleet, hail or wind. She had a perfect attendance record that stretched back farther than anyone could remember.

Her hair was almost white, swept away from her face and up into something like a nest on the back of her head. Unlike some of the younger women teachers, she never wore pants to school. She had two skirt-and-jacket outfits, her gray uniform and her blue uniform, which she always wore over a white shirt with a little cameo pin at the neck. And Mrs. Granger was one of those people who never sweats. It had to be over ninety degrees before she even took off her jacket.

She was small, as teachers go. There were even some fifth graders who were taller. But Mrs. Granger seemed like a giant. It was her eyes that did it. They were dark gray, and if she turned them on full power, they could make you feel like a speck of dust. Her eyes could twinkle and laugh, too, and kids said she could crack really funny jokes. But it wasn't the jokes that made her famous.

Everyone was sure that Mrs. Granger had X-ray vision. Don't even think about chewing a piece of gum within fifty feet of her. If you did, Mrs. Granger would see you and catch you and make you stick the gum onto a bright yellow index card. Then she would safety-pin the card to the front of your shirt, and you'd have to wear it for the rest of the school day. After that, you had to take it home and have your mom or dad sign the card, and bring it back to Mrs. Granger the next day. And it didn't matter to Mrs. Granger if you weren't in fifth grade, because the way she saw it, sooner or later, you would be.

All the kids at Lincoln Elementary School knew that at the end of the line—fifth grade— Mrs. Granger would be the one grading their spelling tests and their reading tests, and worst of all, their vocabulary tests—week after week, month after month.

Every language arts teacher in the world enjoys making kids use the dictionary: "Check your spelling. Check that definition. Check those syllable breaks."

But Mrs. Granger didn't just enjoy the dictionary. She *loved* the dictionary—almost worshipped it. Her weekly vocabulary list was thirty-five words long, sometimes longer.

As if that wasn't bad enough, there was a "Word for the Day" on the blackboard every morning. If you gave yourself a day off and didn't write one down and look it up and learn

Mrs. Granger loved the dictionary

the definition—sooner or later Mrs. Granger would find out, and then, just for you, there would be *two* Words for the Day for a whole week.

Mrs. Granger kept a full set of thirty dictionaries on a shelf at the back of the room. But her pride and joy was one of those huge dictionaries with every word in the universe in it, the kind of book it takes two kids to carry. It sat on its own little table at the front of her classroom, sort of like the altar at the front of a church.

Every graduate of Lincoln Elementary School for the past thirty-five years could remember standing at that table listening to Mrs. Granger's battle cry: "Look it up! That's why we have the dictionary."

Even before the school year started, when it was still the summer before fifth grade for Nick and his friends, Mrs. Granger was already busy. Every parent of every new fifth grader got a letter from her.

Nick's mom read part of it out loud during dinner one night in August.

Every home is expected to have a good dictionary in it so that each student

can do his or her homework properly.
Good spelling and good grammar and
good word skills are essential for
every student. Clear thinking
requires a command of the English
language, and fifth grade is the ideal
time for every girl and boy to acquire
an expanded vocabulary.

And then there was a list of the dictionaries that Mrs. Granger thought would be "acceptable for home study."

Mrs. Allen said, "It's so nice to have a teacher who takes her work this seriously."

Nick groaned and tried to enjoy the rest of his hamburger. But even watermelon for dessert didn't cheer him up much.

Nick had no particular use for the dictionary. He liked words a lot, and he was good at using them. But he figured that he got all the words he needed just by reading, and he read all the time.

When Nick ran into a word he didn't know, he asked his brother or his dad or whoever was handy what it meant, and if they knew, they'd tell him. But not Mrs. Granger. He had heard all about her, and he had seen fifth graders in the library last year, noses stuck in their dictionaries, frantically trying to finish their vocabulary sheets before English class.

It was still a week before school and Nick already felt like fifth grade was going to be a very long year.

three

The Question

THE FIRST DAY of school was always a get-acquainted day. Books were passed out, and there was a lot of chatter. Everyone asked, "What did *you* do over the summer?"

Periods one through six went by very smoothly for Nick.

But then came period seven. Mrs. Granger's class was all business.

The first thing they did was take a vocabulary pretest to see how many of the thirty-five words for the week the kids already knew. *Tremble, circular, orchestra*—the list went on and on. Nick knew most of them.

Then there was a handout about class procedures. After that there was a review paper about cursive writing, and then there was a sample sheet showing how the heading should look on every assignment. No letup for thirty-seven minutes straight.

Nick was an expert at asking the delaying question—also known as the teacher-stopper, or the guaranteed-time-waster. At three minutes before the bell, in that split second between the end of today's class work and the announcement of tomorrow's homework, Nick could launch a question guaranteed to sidetrack the teacher long enough to delay or even wipe out the homework assignment.

Timing was important, but asking the right question—that was the hard part. Questions about stuff in the news, questions about the college the teacher went to, questions about the teacher's favorite book or sport or hobby—Nick knew all the tricks, and he had been very successful in the past.

Here he was in fifth grade, near the end of his very first language arts class with Mrs. Granger, and Nick could feel a homework assignment coming the way a farmer can feel a rainstorm.

Mrs. Granger paused to catch her breath, and Nick's hand shot up. She glanced down at her seating chart, and then up at him. Her sharp gray eyes were not even turned up to half power.

"Yes, Nicholas?"

"Mrs. Granger, you have so many dictionaries in this room, and that huge one especially . . . where did all those words come from? Did they just get copied from other dictionaries? It sure is a big book."

It was a perfect thought-grenade—KaPow!

Several kids smiled, and a few peeked at the clock. Nick was famous for this, and the whole class knew what he was doing.

Unfortunately, so did Mrs. Granger. She hesitated a moment, and gave Nick a smile that was just a little too sweet to be real. Her eyes were the color of a thundercloud.

"Why, what an interesting question, Nicholas. I could talk about that for hours, I bet." She glanced around the classroom. "Do the rest of you want to know, too?" Everyone nodded yes. "Very well then. Nicholas, will you do some research on that subject and give a little oral report to the class? If you find out the answer yourself, it will mean so much more than if I just told you. Please have your report ready for our next class."

Mrs. Granger smiled at him again. Very sweetly. Then it was back to business. "Now, the homework for tomorrow can be found on page twelve of your *Words Alive* book. . . ."

Nick barely heard the assignment. His heart was pounding, and he felt small, very small. He could feel the tops of his ears glowing red. A complete shutdown. An extra assignment. And probably a little black mark next to his name on the seating chart.

Everything he had heard about this teacher was true—don't mess around with The Lone Granger.

word Detective

IT WAS A BEAUTIFUL September afternoon, bright sun, cool breeze, blue sky. But not for Nick.

Nick had to do a little report for the next day. Plus copy out all the definitions for thirty-five words. For Mrs. Granger. This was not the way school was supposed to work. Not for Nick.

There was a rule at Nick's house: Homework First. And that meant right after school. Nick had heard his older brother, James, groan and grumble about this rule for years, right up until he graduated from high school two years ago. And then James wrote home from college after his first semester and said, "My grades are looking great, because when I came here I already knew how to put first things first." That letter was the proof Nick's mom and dad had been

Homework First

looking for. "Homework First" was the law from September to June.

This had never bothered Nick before because he hardly ever had homework. Oh sure, he looked over his spelling words on Thursday nights, and there had been a few short book reports in fourth grade, but other than that, nothing. Up to now, schoolwork never spilled over into his free time. Thanks to Mrs. Granger, those days were gone.

First he looked up the definitions in the brand-new red dictionary that his mom had bought—because Mrs. Granger told her to. It took almost an hour. He could hear a baseball game in John's yard down the street—yelling and shouting, and every few minutes the sharp crack of a bat connecting with a pitch. But he had a report to do. For Mrs. Granger.

Nick looked at the very front of the dictionary. There was an introduction to the book called "Words and Their Origins."

Perfect! Nick thought. It was just what he needed to do his report. It would all be over in a few minutes. Nick could already feel the sun and the breeze on his face as he ran outside to play, homework all done.

Then he read the first sentence from the introduction:

> *Without question this modern American dictionary is one of the most surprisingly complex and profound documents ever to be created, for it embodies unparalleled etymological detail, reflecting not only superb lexicographic scholarship, but also the dreams and speech and imaginative talents of millions of people over thousands of years—for every person who has ever spoken or written in English has had a hand in its making.*

What? Nick scratched his head and read it again. And then again. Not much better. It was sort of like trying to read the ingredients on a shampoo bottle.

He slammed the dictionary shut and walked downstairs.

Nick's family did a lot of reading, so bookshelves covered three of the four walls in the family room. There were two sets of encyclopedias—the black set was for grown-ups, and the red set was for kids. Nick pulled out the

D volume from the red set and looked up *dictionary*. There were three full pages, with headings like Early Dictionaries, Word Detectives, and Dictionaries Today. Not very exciting. But he had to do it, so Nick just plopped down on the couch and read all of it.

And when he was finished with the kids' book, he opened up the black encyclopedia and read most of what it said about dictionaries, too. He understood only about half of what he read.

He leaned back on the couch and covered his eyes with his arm, trying to imagine himself giving a report on all this boring stuff. He'd be lucky to have three minutes worth. But because Nick was Nick, he suddenly had an idea and it brought a grin to his face.

Nick decided that giving this report could actually be fun. He could make it into something special. After all, Mrs. Granger had asked for it.

five

The Report

BY LUNCHTIME the next day, Nick had a bad feeling in the pit of his stomach. Seventh period was coming. He was going to have to stand up in front of Mrs. Granger's class. The eyes of everyone in the class would be glued to his face. And Mrs. Granger's eyes would be cranked up to maximum punch power.

He looked over his notes again and again— the first English dictionary, the growth of the English language, William Shakespeare, words from French and German, new words, old words, new inventions, Anglo-Saxon words, Latin and Greek roots, American English—it all became a big jumble in his mind. And his grand plan from the night before? In the harsh fluorescent light of the school day, it seemed impossible.

What is it with the clocks in school? When you're planning to go to the carnival after school, the clocks in every class practically run backward, and the school day lasts for about three weeks. But if you have to go to the barber or go shopping for clothes after school, zzzzip—the whole day is over before you can blink. And today? After lunch, periods five and six went by in two ticks.

As the seventh-period bell rang, Mrs. Granger walked into the classroom, took four steps to her desk at the side of the room, flipped open her attendance book, glanced out at the class, and made two little check marks. Then looking up at Nick, she said, "I think we have a little report to begin our class today. Nicholas?"

Fifteen seconds into seventh period, and Nick was onstage. *This lady plays for keeps*, thought Nick. He gulped, grabbed his crumpled note cards and his book bag, and walked to the front of the room. He stood next to the giant dictionary on its little table, and Mrs. Granger walked to the back of the classroom and sat primly on a tall stool next to the bookcases. She was wearing her blue uniform.

Taking a deep breath, Nick began. "Well, the

first thing I learned is that the first English dictionary—"

Mrs. Granger interrupted. "Excuse me, Nicholas, but does your report have a title?"

Nick looked blankly at her. "A title? N-no, I didn't make a title."

"Class, please remember to include a title whenever you prepare an oral or written report. Now, please go on, Nicholas," and she smiled and nodded at him.

Nick began again. Looking right at Mrs. Granger he said, "The Dictionary." A couple of kids thought that was funny, but Nick played it straight, and just kept talking. "A lot of people think that the first English dictionary was put together in the 1700s by a man named Samuel Johnson. He lived in London, England. He was real smart, and he wrote a lot of books, and he wanted all the other smart people to have a good dictionary to use, so he made one. But there were other dictionaries before his. The thing that was different about Johnson's dictionary was its size, first of all. He had over forty-three thousand words in it."

The class made a bunch of noise at this big number—"Ooh," and "Wow!" and stuff like that—and Nick lost his concentration. He glanced up at Mrs. Granger, expecting to see those eyes drilling a hole in him. But they weren't. They were almost friendly, in a teacher-y kind of way. She shushed the class and said, "Go on, Nicholas. That's a fine beginning."

Nick almost smiled, but he saw all the kids staring at him, so he gripped his note cards even tighter, and jumped back in.

"The other thing that Samuel Johnson did that was special was to choose the words he thought were most important, and then give lots of examples showing how the words got used by people. For example, he showed how the word *take* could be used in one hundred thirteen different ways. . . ."

Nick's report went on smoothly for twelve minutes. Nick was surprised at how easy it was to stand there and talk about this stuff. At the end of the first five minutes Mrs. Granger had had to stop Nick again to say, "Class, it is not good manners to yawn out loud or to put your heads down on your desks when someone is giving an oral report." No one in the class cared one little bit about the report. Except Mrs. Granger.

Every time Nick glanced up, she was smiling.

And her eyes were not the least bit icy or sharp. She was eating this stuff up, listening, and nodding, and every once in a while she would say, "Very good point" or "Yes, that's exactly right."

But the next time Nick looked up, he saw Mrs. Granger sneaking a look at her watch. Eighteen minutes gone. Maybe his idea was going to work after all. Time for phase two.

Reaching into his book bag, Nick pulled out the red dictionary he had brought from home, the one most of the kids had—the one Mrs. Granger said they should use. Nick said, "This is the dictionary that I use at home for my vocabulary work, and . . . and I opened it up last night to the very front, and right there I found out a lot about how the dictionary was made . . . right in this book. So I thought some of the ideas would be good as part of my report. It says here . . ."

"Nicholas?" Nick looked up. Mrs. Granger got off her tall stool, and its wooden legs made a screech on the linoleum. Heads snapped to attention, and the class was alert again. Mrs. Granger smiled, raised her eyebrows and pointed at her watch. "Nicholas, I think the class should read that at home themselves. Now . . ."

John's hand was up in the air, and at Mrs. Granger's nod he said, "But I don't have that dictionary at home, Mrs. Granger. I have the blue one." And several other kids immediately said, "Me, too."

Mrs. Granger tried not to show that she was annoyed. "Very well, Nick, but it shouldn't take too long. We have other things to do today."

Nick kept his eyes open wide and nodded, adjusted his glasses on his nose, and began to read.

> *Without question this modern American dictionary is one of the most surprisingly complex and profound documents ever to be created, for it embodies unparalleled etymological detail, reflecting not only superb lexicographic scholarship, but also the dreams and speech and imaginative talents of millions of people over thousands of years—for every person who has ever spoken or written in English has had a hand in its making. . . .*

It was a long article, and the kids were bored to death. But no one looked bored at all. Every kid in the room knew now that the period was more than half over, and that Nick's report wasn't just a report. It was one of the greatest time-wasters he had ever invented.

Mrs. Granger knew it, too. She had edged around from the back of the room to the side near the windows. Nick glanced up at her now and then as he read, and each time, Mrs. Granger's eyes clicked up to a new power level. After eight minutes of Nick's best nonstop reading, her eyes were practically burning holes in the chalkboard behind him. There were only ten minutes left in seventh period.

When he took a breath to start a new paragraph, Mrs. Granger cut him off. "That's a fine place to stop, Nicholas. Class, let's all give him a round of applause for his report." The applause didn't last long.

As Nick took his book bag and notes and sat down, Mrs. Granger's eyes went back to almost normal, and she actually smiled at him. "Although your report was a little long—"she paused to let that sink in—"it was quite a good one. And isn't it fascinating that English has more different words than any other language used anywhere in the world?" She pointed at her large dictionary. "That one book contains the definitions of more than four-hundred fifty thousand words. Now, wasn't I right, Nicholas? All this will mean so much more since you learned about it on your own."

Mrs. Granger was beaming at him. Nick sank lower in his chair. This was worse than writing the report, worse than standing up to give it. He was being treated like—like the teacher's pet. And he had the feeling she was doing it on purpose. His reputation was in great danger. So he launched another question.

He raised his hand, and he didn't even wait for Mrs. Granger to call on him. "Yeah, but, you know, I still don't really get the idea of why words all mean different things. Like, who says that d-o-g means the thing that goes 'woof' and wags its tail? Who says so?"

And Mrs. Granger took the bait. "Who says *dog* means dog? You do, Nicholas. You and I and everyone in this class and this school and this town and this state and this country. We all agree. If we lived in France, we would all agree that the right word for that hairy four-legged creature was a different word—*chien*—it sounds like 'shee-en,' but it means what d-o-g means to

Who says dog *means dog?*

you and me. And in Germany they say *hund*, and so on, all around the globe. But if all of us in this room decided to call that creature something else, and if everyone else did, too, then that's what it would be called, and one day it would be written in the dictionary that way. *We* decide what goes in that book." And she pointed at the giant dictionary. And she looked right at Nick. And she smiled again.

Then Mrs. Granger went on, "But of course, that dictionary was worked on by hundreds of very smart people for many years, so as far as we are concerned, that dictionary is the law. Laws can change, of course, but only if they need to. There may be new words that need to be made, but the ones in that book have been put there for good reasons."

Mrs. Granger took a look at the clock, eight minutes left. "Now then, for today you were to have done the exercises beginning on page twelve in your *Words Alive* book. Please get out your papers. Sarah, will you read the first sentence, identify the mistake, and then tell us how you corrected it?"

Mrs. Granger jammed the whole day's work into the last eight minutes, a blur of verbs and nouns and prepositions, and yes, there was another homework assignment.

And Nick didn't try to sidetrack Mrs. G. again. He had slowed her down a little, but had he stopped her? No way.

She was unstoppable . . . at least for today.

six

The Big Idea

THREE THINGS HAPPENED later that same afternoon.

Nick and Janet Fisk had missed the bus because of a school newspaper meeting, so they walked home together. They were seeing who could walk along the curb without falling. It took a lot of concentration, and when Janet stepped off into the street, Nick said, "That's three points for me."

But Janet said, "I didn't fall. I saw something. . . . Look." She bent down and picked up a gold ballpoint pen, the fancy kind.

That was the first thing—Janet finding the pen.

They got back on the curb, and Nick followed Janet, putting one foot carefully in front of the other on the narrow concrete curb.

And while he stepped along, he thought back over the school day, especially about his report. And what Mrs. Granger had said about words at the end of the period finally sank in.

That was the second thing—understanding what Mrs. Granger had said.

She had said, "Who says *dog* means dog? You do, Nicholas."

"You do, Nicholas," he repeated to himself.

I do? Nick thought, still putting one foot in front of the other, following Janet. *What does that mean?* And then Nick remembered something.

When he was about two years old, his mom had bought him one of those unbreakable cassette players and a bunch of sing-along tapes. He had loved them, and he played them over and over and over and over. He would carry the tape and the player to his mother or his big brother or his father and bang them together and say, "Gwagala, gwagala, gwagala," until someone put the cassette in the machine and turned it on.

And for three years, whenever he said "gwagala," his family knew that he wanted to hear those pretty sounds made with voices and instruments. Then when Nick went to preschool, he learned that if he wanted his teacher and the other kids to understand him, he had to use the word *music*. But *gwagala* meant that nice sound to Nick, because Nick said so. Who says *gwagala* means music? "You do, Nicholas."

"No fair!" yelled Janet. They were at the corner of their own street, and Nick had bumped into her, completely absorbed in his thoughts. Janet stumbled off the curb, and the gold pen in her hand clattered onto the street.

"Sorry . . . I didn't mean to, honest," said Nick. "I just wasn't watching. . . . Here . . ." Nick stooped over and picked up the pen and held it out to her. "Here's your . . ."

And that's when the third thing happened.

Nick didn't say "pen." Instead, he said, "Here's your . . . frindle."

"Frindle?" Janet took her pen and looked at him like he was nuts. She wrinkled her nose and said, "What's a *frindle*?"

Nick grinned and said, "You'll find out. See ya later."

It was there at the corner of Spring Street and South Grand Avenue, one block from home on a September afternoon. That's when Nick got the big idea.

The big idea

And by the time he had run down the street and up the steps and through the door and upstairs to his room, it wasn't just a big idea. It was a plan, a whole plan, just begging for Nick to put it into action. And "action" was Nick's middle name.

The next day after school the plan began. Nick walked into the Penny Pantry store and asked the lady behind the counter for a frindle.

She squinted at him. "A what?"

"A frindle, please. A black one," and Nick smiled at her.

She leaned over closer and aimed one ear at him. "You want *what?*"

"A frindle," and this time Nick pointed at the ballpoint pens behind her on the shelf. "A black one, please."

The lady handed Nick the pen. He handed her the 49¢, said "thank you," and left the store.

Six days later Janet stood at the counter of the Penny Pantry. Same store, same lady. John had come in the day before, and Pete the day before that, and Chris the day before that, and Dave the day before that. Janet was the fifth kid that Nick had sent there to ask that woman for a frindle.

And when she asked, the lady reached right for the pens and said, "Blue or black?"

Nick was standing one aisle away at the candy racks, and he was grinning.

Frindle was a real word. It meant *pen*. Who says frindle means pen? "You do, Nicholas."

Half an hour later, a group of serious fifth graders had a meeting in Nick's play room. It was John, Pete, Dave, Chris, and Janet. Add Nick, and that's six kids—six secret agents.

They held up their right hands and read the oath Nick had written out:

> *From this day on and forever, I will never use the word PEN again. Instead, I will use the word FRINDLE, and I will do everything possible so others will, too.*

And all six of them signed the oath—with Nick's frindle.

The plan would work.

Thanks, Mrs. Granger.

word wars

SCHOOL WAS THE PERFECT place to launch a new word, and since this was a major historical event, Nick wanted it to begin in exactly the right class—seventh-period language arts.

Nick raised his hand first thing after the bell rang and said, "Mrs. Granger, I forgot my frindle."

Sitting three rows away, John blurted out, "I have an extra one you can borrow, Nick."

Then John made a big show of looking for something in his backpack. "I think I have an extra frindle, I mean, I told my mom to get me three or four. I'm sure I had an extra frindle in here yesterday, but I must have taken it . . . wait . . . oh yeah, here it is."

And then John made a big show of throwing it over to Nick, and Nick missed it on purpose.

Then he made a big show of finding it.

Mrs. Granger and every kid in the class got the message loud and clear. That black plastic thing that Nick borrowed from John had a funny name . . . a different name . . . a new name—*frindle*.

There was a lot of giggling, but Mrs. Granger turned up the power in her eyes and swept the room into silence. And the rest of the class went by according to plan—her plan.

As everyone was leaving after class, Mrs. Granger said, "Nicholas? I'd like to have . . . a word with you," and she emphasized the word *word*.

Nick's mouth felt dry, and he gulped, but his mind stayed clear. He walked up to her desk. "Yes, Mrs. Granger?"

"It's a funny idea, Nicholas, but I will not have my class disrupted again. Is that clear?" Her eyes were lit up, but it was mostly light, not much heat.

"Idea? What idea?" asked Nick, and he tried to make his eyes as blank as possible.

"You know what I mean, Nicholas. I am talking about the performance that you and John gave at the start of class. I am talking about—this," and she held up her pen, an old maroon fountain pen with a blue cap.

"But I really didn't have a frindle with me," said Nick, amazed at his own bravery. And hiding behind his glasses, Nick kept his eyes wide and blank.

Mrs. Granger's eyes flashed, and then narrowed, and her lips formed a thin, hard line. She was quiet for a few seconds, and then she said, "I see. Very well. Then I guess we have nothing more to discuss today, Nicholas. You may go."

"Thanks, Mrs. Granger," said Nick, and he grabbed his backpack and headed for the door. And when he was just stepping into the hallway, he said, "And I promise I won't ever forget my frindle again. Bye."

eight

Mightier than the Sword

TWO DAYS LATER the photographer came to take class pictures. The fifth-grade picture would be taken last, right after lunch.

That gave Nick and his secret agents plenty of time, and they whispered something into the ear of every fifth grader. All the individual pictures had been taken, and finally it was time for the group picture. Everyone was lined up on the auditorium stage, everyone's hair looked great, and everyone was smiling.

But when the photographer said, "Say cheeese!"—no one did.

Instead, every kid said, "Frindle!" And they held one up for the camera to see.

The photographer was out of film. So that

shot was the only fifth-grade group picture he took. Six of the fifth-grade teachers were not pleased. And Mrs. Granger was furious.

No one had really wanted to make the teachers mad. It was just fun. It also got all the kids in the school talking about the new word. And when people pick up a new word, they say it all the time. The kids at Lincoln Elementary School liked Nick's new word. A lot.

But not Mrs. Granger. The day after the class picture she made an announcement to each of her classes, and she posted a notice on the main bulletin board by the office.

> *Anyone who is heard using the word* frindle *instead of the word* pen *will stay after school and write this sentence one hundred times: I am writing this punishment with a pen.*
>
> *—Mrs. Granger*

But that just made everyone want to use Nick's new word even more. Staying after school with The Lone Granger became a badge of honor. There were kids in her classroom every day after school. It went on like that for a couple of weeks.

One day near the end of seventh period, Mrs. Granger asked Nick to come talk to her after school. "This is not detention, Nicholas. I just want to talk."

Nick was excited. It was kind of like a conference during a war. One side waves a white flag, and the generals come out and talk. General Nicholas Allen. Nick liked the sound of it.

He stuck his head in Mrs. Granger's doorway after school. "You wanted to talk with me?"

"Yes, Nicholas. Please come in and sit down."

When he was settled she looked at him and said, "Don't you think this 'frindle' business has gone far enough? It's just a disruption to the school, don't you think?"

Nick swallowed hard, but he said, "I don't think there's anything wrong with it. It's just fun, and it really is a real word. It's not a bad word, just different. And besides, it's how words really change, isn't it? That's what you said."

Mrs. Granger sighed. "It *is* how a word could be made up brand new, I suppose, but the word *pen*? Should it really be replaced by . . . by that other word? The word *pen* has a long, rich history. It comes from the Latin word for feather, *pinna*. It started to become our word *pen* because quills made from feathers were some of the first writing tools ever made. It's a word that comes from somewhere. It makes *sense*, Nicholas."

"But *frindle* makes just as much sense to me," said Nick. "And after all, didn't somebody just make up the word *pinna*, too?"

That got a spark from Mrs. Granger's eyes, but all she said was, "Then you are not going to stop this?"

And Nick looked right in her eyes and said, "Well, me and . . . I mean, a bunch of my friends and I took an oath about using the word, and we have to keep our promise. And besides, I don't think there's anything wrong with it. I like my word." Nick tried to look brave, like a good general should.

"Very well then. I thought it would end up this way." Mrs. Granger pulled a fat white envelope from her desk drawer and held it up. "This is a letter I have written to you, Nicholas."

Nick held out his hand, thinking she was going to give it to him. But she didn't.

"I am not going to send it to you until all this is over. I want you to sign your name and put

Like a conference during a war

today's date across the back of the envelope. When you read it, whenever that may be, you will know it is the same letter, and that I have not made any changes to it."

"This is weird," Nick said to himself. But to Mrs. Granger he said, "Sure," and he signed his name in his best cursive, and put the date under it.

Then Mrs. Granger stood up abruptly and said, "Then that is all for today, Nicholas. And may the best word win."

There was a frown on her face, but her eyes, her eyes were different—almost happy.

And Nick was halfway down the hall before it hit him—"She likes this war, and she wants to win real bad!"

Walking to school the next day, Pete had a great idea. "How 'bout we see if we can get every kid in the whole fifth grade to go up and ask Mrs. Granger, 'Can I borrow a frindle?'"

"You mean 'Mrs. Granger, *may* I borrow a frindle?'" said Dave. "Got to use good grammar. Don't wanna upset Dangerous Grangerous."

"Sounds good to me," said Nick. "She can't keep everyone after school, can she?"

Almost eighty kids stayed after school with Mrs. Granger that day. They filled her room and spilled out into the hallway. The principal had to stay late to help, and they had to arrange two special late buses to get all the kids home.

And the next day, all the fifth graders did it again, and so did a lot of other students—over two hundred kids.

Parents called to complain. The school bus drivers threatened to go on strike. And then the school board and the superintendent got involved.

And about this time the principal of Lincoln Elementary School paid a little visit to the home of Mr. and Mrs. Allen. She wanted to talk to them about their son. The one in fifth grade. The one named Nick.

nine

Chess

MRS. MARGARET CHATHAM had been principal of Lincoln Elementary School for eighteen years. She knew Mr. and Mrs. Allen, because they had all served together on the building committee when the old Lincoln School was torn down and the new one was built six years ago.

When she telephoned on the afternoon of October first to set up the meeting, Mrs. Chatham had asked Nick to be there, too. It was 6:30 when she knocked, and Nick opened the door.

"Good evening, Nick," she said. No smile.

"Hi, Mrs. Chatham," said Nick, backing away as she filled the doorway. She was a large person, as tall as Nick's dad, with wide shoulders. Nick guessed she would play linebacker on

The game was not over

a football team, because that's what his dad had played in college.

"Hello, Mr. and Mrs. Allen," she said, stepping into the living room. She was wearing a long black raincoat with a red silk scarf tied loosely around her neck. She kept her coat on, but took off the scarf and tucked it into her left pocket. She shook hands stiffly with both of Nick's parents before sitting down on the chair to the left of the couch. Nick's mom and dad sat on the couch, and Nick sat on the rocking chair that faced Mrs. Chatham across the low coffee table.

"This is not an easy visit for me. We are having some trouble at school, and it appears that Nick is in the middle of it."

Then while Nick's parents listened, Mrs. Chatham laid out the story as she saw it—Nick encouraging the other kids to use his new word, Mrs. Granger forbidding it, the ruined fifth-grade class picture, hundreds of kids staying after school, and a general feeling that there was a rebellion at school, with no one respecting the rules anymore.

Nick watched his mom and dad while Mrs. Chatham talked, looking from one face to another. His dad was listening carefully, nodding and frowning. He looked embarrassed about the trouble. But his mom looked—kind of annoyed.

And when Mrs. Chatham finished her story, Nick's mom was the first one to speak. "But doesn't all this seem like a lot of fuss about something pretty silly?"

Nick sat quietly, but in his mind he shouted, *Hurrah for mom, hurrah for mothers everywhere!* His mom wasn't annoyed with him! She was annoyed with Mrs. Granger, maybe even annoyed with Mrs. Chatham. This was getting interesting.

Mrs. Allen was still talking to the principal. "I mean, is there really any harm in the children making up a funny word and saying it? Does there have to be a rule that a word like this may not be used?"

Mrs. Chatham sighed and said, "Yes, I suppose it does seem silly. But Mrs. Granger thinks that it's rather like keeping children from saying 'ain't'—there have to be standards. That's why we have dictionaries. And really, the problem isn't so much the word itself. It's the lack of respect for authority."

Mr. Allen said, "Mrs. Granger's right about

that. There have to be standards. We can't have kids walking around saying 'ain't,' can we?"

And that's when Nick piped in. "You know that big dictionary in Mrs. Granger's room? The word *ain't* is right there in the book. I looked it up, and there it was. I don't see why I can't use a word if it's in the dictionary. Mrs. Granger even said that her big dictionary was the law." Nick looked from face to face to face. That stumped them all. He had just launched a first-class thought-grenade.

"Well, yes . . . but . . . well, as I said, the word *ain't* and even the word *frindle*—these are not the real issue here," said Mrs. Chatham.

Mrs. Allen said, "Well, I think the real issue is Mrs. Granger's reaction to a harmless little experiment with language—it's an overreaction, don't you think so, Tom?" And Mrs. Allen looked at her husband.

It was Mr. Allen's turn to look from face to face to face. He was lost. "Yes, well sure . . . I—I guess so . . . I mean, it's not like anybody's been hurt . . . umm . . . I mean, it's not like vandalism or stealing or something like that . . ." His sentence trailed off, and he rubbed his chin and stared thoughtfully through the window on the wall behind Mrs. Chatham.

And while the three grown-ups sat there in an uncomfortable moment of silence, Nick had a sudden vision of what was really going on here. It was a chess game, Nick against Mrs. Granger. Mrs. Granger had just tried to end the game by using her queen—Mrs. Chatham in her black raincoat, the black queen.

Nick didn't know it until the attack was under way, but he had a powerful defender of his own—good old Mom, the white queen. And the game was not over. It would go on until there was a winner and a loser.

Mrs. Chatham didn't stay much longer. There was a little more talk back and forth across the chessboard about how children have a right to explore new ideas, about the importance of respecting teachers and the work they do, about everybody needing to keep up standards and make school a safe place to learn.

Then Mr. Allen offered Mrs. Chatham some coffee and banana bread, but she said, "No thanks, I really must be going now."

She thanked Nick's parents and they thanked her. Nick opened the door, and said, "Good night, Mrs. Chatham." Then the black queen put on her red scarf and walked off into the October twilight.

"Nick, I think we'd better talk a little more about this," said his mom, sitting back down on the couch. "If I find out that you have been disrespectful to Mrs. Granger or any other teacher at school, then you really will be in big trouble."

"I haven't been disrespectful. Honest. I did get everybody started using my word, but like you said, it's not hurting anybody. And I'm sorry if me and Dave and Pete got everybody to ask Mrs. Granger to borrow a frindle. That was mean, I guess . . . but she started it by making kids stay after school and write a hundred sentences just for saying my word once. All the kids like to use my word. It's just fun, that's all."

"Well," said Nick's dad, "if it gets everyone upset and makes the principal come talk to your mother and me, then it must not be fun for everybody, is it? And I think you should just tell all your friends to knock it off, right now . . . I mean, tomorrow."

Nick shook his head. "I can't, Dad. It won't work. It's a real word now. It used to be just mine, but not anymore. If I knew how to stop it, I think I probably would. But I can't." And Nick looked at both of their faces to see if that idea was sinking in. It was. "Like I said, I won't be disrespectful, but I do like my word. And I guess now we're just going to have to see what happens."

And the chessmen—Nick's king and queen—had to agree.

The game would go on.

ten

Freedom of the Press

JUDY MORGAN WAS a reporter for *The Westfield Gazette*, the local newspaper. Westfield was a quiet little town. There was the occasional burglary, the teenagers got rowdy once in a while, and there was some shouting at the town council or the planning board now and then. But mostly, things were calm and orderly in Westfield, and every Thursday *The Westfield Gazette* proved it.

Ted Bell sold advertisements for the paper, and he had a daughter in fourth grade at Lincoln Elementary. He told Judy that a bunch of fifth graders were making trouble and were not obeying teachers anymore, that there was something about a secret code word they were all using.

And half the students had been kept after school one day last week—including his own little girl.

The only other story Judy was working on was about eighteen new trees that were going to be planted along East Main Street. The trees could wait. This thing at the elementary school sounded like a real story.

So Judy Morgan showed up at Lincoln Elementary School at three o'clock the day after Mrs. Chatham had been to visit Nick's parents. The sign on the door said, "All Visitors Must Report to the Office," and she did.

On the bulletin board outside the office, Judy saw Mrs. Granger's notice about the punishment for using the word *frindle*. She stepped back two paces, aimed her camera at the notice, and snapped a photo. She read the notice once more, and then stepped into the office.

Mrs. Freed, the school secretary, looked up and smiled. "May I help you?"

"Yes, I'm sure you can. My name is Judy Morgan, and I work for *The Westfield Gazette*. I'd like to know about that poster outside the office, the one about this word *frindle*. Who should I talk to?"

Mrs. Freed stopped smiling. She was sick and tired of anything to do with that word. For the past week her phone had been ringing off the hook. If it wasn't a parent complaining about a child who had to stay after school, it was someone from the school board trying to get in touch with Mrs. Chatham or Mrs. Granger. Mrs. Freed pursed her lips and narrowed her eyes. She said, "You'll have to speak with the principal. Let me see if Mrs. Chatham is free."

She was. There isn't a principal alive who won't find the time to talk to someone from the local newspaper. The reporter was invited into Mrs. Chatham's office.

Judy noticed right away that the principal was not comfortable talking about this stuff. When asked about the poster outside the office door, Mrs. Chatham laughed and said, "Oh, that? It's nothing really. Some kids have been playing a prank, and it was time to put a stop to it."

The principal's laugh sounded phony to Judy Morgan. "And did that notice put an end to the prank? I heard that a lot of children were kept after school last week. Would you tell me a little about that? Parents would like to know what's going on."

Mrs. Chatham looked like . . . well, like a kid who had been sent to the principal's office. She squirmed a little in her chair and tried to smile. She said, "Well, we do still have a little problem, but it's under control. Mrs. Granger may have overreacted a bit. I don't think the children have really been trying to be disrespectful. They are just having some fun, and it's more like a difference of opinion . . ." And then Mrs. Chatham went on to tell the reporter what she knew about the word *frindle*, and how it had become popular among the students. Judy Morgan took careful notes.

And when the principal had finished Judy said, "Would you mind if I asked Mrs. Granger a few questions?"

Mrs. Chatham said, "No, not at all." But Judy could tell that the principal wished she would just go away. What could she say, though? Mrs. Chatham couldn't very well keep the reporter away from Mrs. Granger because, after all, America is a free country with a free press. If Judy really wanted to, she would talk to Mrs. Granger sooner or later.

It was sooner. In three minutes Judy Morgan was standing at the doorway of Room

12, looking in at Mrs. Granger. There were about fifteen children sitting at desks scattered around the room, busy writing out their one hundred sentences. She knocked and the teacher and students looked up from their work. "I'm Judy Morgan from *The Westfield Gazette*, Mrs. Granger. May I have a word with you?"

Mrs. Granger stood and came out into the hallway and closed the door. Judy could see past her and saw that every kid in the room was straining to listen. Judy noticed Mrs. Granger's eyes right away—gray, maybe flecked with a little gold, and very sharp, but not hard or mean. Just bright, and strong.

The reporter didn't waste words. "So I hear that you plan to stop the students from using their new word. How goes the battle?"

Mrs. Granger did not smile, and her eyes got even brighter. "First of all, it is not a battle. I am merely helping my students to see that this foolishness should stop. Such a waste of time and thought! There is no reason to invent a new and useless word. They should each learn to use the words we already have. But of course, all of this is just a silly fad, and when you add an *e* to *fad*, you get *fade*.

And I predict that this fad will fade."

Judy looked up from her note pad and asked, "Any idea how it all got started?"

Mrs. Granger's eyes seemed to almost catch on fire at that question, and she said, "Yes, I have a *very* good idea how it all got started. It was one young man's idea, a fifth-grade student named Nicholas Allen. And now you will have to excuse me, Ms. Morgan, for I have papers I must grade." And with a brief, firm handshake, Mrs. Granger ended the interview.

The reporter didn't leave right away. She walked back through the hallway and sat on a bench outside the office so she could look over her notes to make sure they made sense. It took her about five minutes. Then Judy stood up, put her notebook into her large black purse, waved good-bye to a frowning Mrs. Freed, and headed out the door.

As she walked to the parking lot, five or six kids who had just finished writing their sentences for Mrs. Granger came out another door. Judy walked beside them, listening to them laugh and joke. Then she asked them, "Why do you kids keep saying 'frindle'? Don't you hate staying after school?"

A boy who was almost falling over from the weight of his backpack looked up at her and smiled. "It's not so bad. There's always a bunch of my friends there. I've written that sentence six hundred times now."

And then the kids said Mrs. Granger didn't even look at their punishment papers anymore. They were sure, because where you were supposed to write "I am writing this punishment with a pen," everyone was writing the word *frindle* every fourth or fifth sentence. And Mrs. Granger hadn't said anything. One girl bragged that she had written the word *frindle* forty-five times on her sheets today. She grinned and said, "That's a new record."

"And this boy named Nick," Judy asked, "has he had to stay after school, too?"

The kids giggled, and a tall boy with reddish-brown hair and glasses said, "Mrs. Granger has kept Nick after school so much that everyone thinks she wants to adopt him."

The reporter smiled and said, "Do you think I could find Nick and talk to him this afternoon?"

The boy looked at Judy for a second, and then said, "I don't think Nick would want to

That's a new record

talk to you right now. He might say something stupid and get himself in trouble." Then he grinned at his friends. The kids laughed and poked and punched each other, and headed off down the block. Judy drove back to her office and started writing.

The next morning a brown envelope arrived at the *Gazette* offices addressed to Judy Morgan, and below her name was written "Frindle Story." When Judy opened it, there was a class picture, the fifth grade at Lincoln Elementary School. Mrs. Granger and the six other teachers were standing at the ends of the rows and the kids were dressed neatly, hair all combed. But there was something odd about the picture.

The reporter looked closely and saw that each kid was holding up a pen, and each little mouth was puckered in the same way. She was puzzled for a second, but then she said softly, "Of course! They're all saying 'frindle'!"

Written on the back of the picture in neat cursive was "3rd row, 5th from left."

Judy looked at the picture, and there she saw the same grinning red-haired boy with glasses that she had talked to in the school parking lot yesterday. She chuckled and said, "Well, well, well. Pleased to meet you, Mr. Nicholas Allen."

eleven

Extra! Extra! Read All About It!

ON THURSDAY MORNING, *The Westfield Gazette* was delivered to all 12,297 homes and post office boxes in Westfield. The story about Lincoln Elementary School was the first item on the front page. And the headline?

Local 5th Grader Says, "Move over, Mr. Webster"

It was quite an article. Not that Judy Morgan didn't tell the truth—every statement in the article was completely true. It was the particular way she told the truth that got things hopping around town.

For example, take this sentence about Mrs. Granger: "Mrs. Granger, champion of the forces of order and authority, is battling hundreds of young frindle-fighters. Neither side is giving in."

Or this bit about Nick: "Everyone agrees that Nick Allen masterminded this plot that cleverly raises issues about free speech and academic rules. He is the boy who invented the new word."

Or this last sentence in the article: "One thing is sure: the kids at Lincoln Elementary School love their frindles, and no one seems to be backing off in this war of the words."

And of course *The Westfield Gazette* published the class picture, too. And Mrs. Granger and Nick were identified for all the world to see.

"What is the meaning of this?!" That's what Nick's mother said, putting the article in front of Nick's nose when he got home from school. "Did you talk to this reporter? She seems to know an awful lot about you and your new word, young man!"

"What is the meaning of this?!" That's what the school superintendent said to Mrs. Chatham, slapping a copy of the article onto her desk. "Why did you have to talk to that reporter? Don't we have enough trouble getting the taxpayers to pay for the schools without articles like this banging around town?!"

"What is the meaning of this?!" That's what Mrs. Chatham said to Mrs. Granger, shaking the newspaper in front of her face. "I know you had to talk to that woman, but did you have to say all these things? It'll be a wonder if we don't all get fired!"

It was quite a Thursday for everyone. And no one could figure out how Judy Morgan had gotten that fifth-grade class picture.

twelve

Airwaves

WITHIN A WEEK after the article was published in *The Westfield Gazette*, the kids at the junior high and the kids at the high school had stopped using the word *pen* and had started using the word *frindle*. They loved it.

Nick became sort of a hero for kids all over town, and he quickly learned that being a hero—even if you're only a local hero—isn't a free ride. It has a price.

People noticed Nick when he walked into his dad's hardware store or when he stood in line at the Penny Pantry to buy a candy bar. He could feel it when someone recognized him, and it made him shy and awkward.

Kids at school started expecting him to be clever and funny all the time, and even for a kid as smart as Nick, that was asking a lot. Every teacher, the office secretary, the principal, even the school nurse and the custodian, all seemed to be watching, always watching.

His parents were great about everything. True, his mom had been upset when the article first came out, and so had his dad. Nick had said, "But I didn't do anything wrong, Mom. And neither did that lady from the newspaper." And his parents could see that he was right. The things in the article were true, and the truth is the truth, and nothing could be done about it now. Even though it made them uncomfortable to have their boy talked about all over town, secretly, Nick's mom and dad were pleased. After all, a brand-new word is a pretty amazing thing. Their Nicholas was quite a fellow—no getting around it.

Someone else in town thought this brand-new word was pretty amazing, too. Bud Lawrence had lived all his life in Westfield, and when he was only nineteen years old, he had saved enough money to make an investment. He looked around for a good idea, and then bought the first Dairy Queen in the state. After a few years he bought a McDonald's restaurant. That was almost thirty years ago, and these two restaurants had made him rich, one of Westfield's leading citizens.

When Bud Lawrence saw the article about the new word, he had his lawyer file a preliminary trademark claim on the word *frindle*. Within four days he had set up a small company that was selling cheap plastic ballpoint pens specially imprinted with the word *frindle*. He sold three thousand *frindles* the first week, and they sold so fast that stores all over Westfield couldn't keep them in stock. Then just as quickly, kids stopped asking for frindles. The sales slowed down, and Bud Lawrence started thinking about other projects.

A week later it was Halloween, the leaves started falling, and it seemed like the town was going to quiet down.

And it would have—if it hadn't been for Alice Lunderson. Alice lived in Betherly, a town seven miles away from Westfield, and she worked part time for the local CBS-TV station in Carrington, a town of about 75,500 people.

When there was important area news— disasters like floods or tornadoes—or sometimes if she came across little stories that seemed cute or original, Alice would call the station news manager in Carrington. If it was a good story or if it was a day when not much else was happening in the world, then the TV station would send out a van with a camera crew to shoot some videotape.

Alice subscribed to all the small-town newspapers in the area to keep up with local events. Most of them were published on Thursday, and they arrived at her house by Monday or Tuesday. Then it took her a day or so to look through them all. On Wednesday morning she finally saw the article in *The Westfield Gazette* about the word war. She read it through twice, and looked carefully at the class photograph. She was sure that this story was a winner.

The TV station manager in Carrington agreed with her. He called the CBS station in Boston, because sometimes Boston picked up stories from the Carrington newsroom. The woman in Boston thought the story had some real zip to it, so she called the network news editor in New York.

When the fax of *The Westfield Gazette* article got to New York, the staff there loved it. They looked over the schedule sheet for the week and decided it would be the perfect closing story for the CBS evening news for the next day, Thursday. Orders flew back through the telephone links from New York to Boston to Carrington to Betherly. By Wednesday at noon, Alice had a "go" order to take the story all the way. It was her first piece to get onto the national news, and twenty million viewers would see it.

Alice Lunderson and her camera crew stood on Mrs. Granger's front porch Wednesday after school. Mrs. Granger was not impressed at all by the lights and the microphones. She looked right into the camera and said, "I have always said that the dictionary is the finest tool ever made for educating young minds, and I still say that. Children need to understand that there are rules about words and language, and that those rules have a history that makes sense. And to pretend that a perfectly good English word can be replaced by a silly made-up word just for the fun of it, well, it's not something I was ready to stand by and watch without a fight."

"And have you lost that fight, Mrs. Granger?" asked the reporter.

Mrs. Granger turned her eyes up to nearly full power as she looked into the camera, and with a pale smile she said, "It's not over yet."

When Alice and the crew showed up at Nick's house, the Allen family was ready for them. Mom and Dad sat on the couch with Nick between them. Nick squinted into the lights. His mom had worked out with Nick what he could say and what he couldn't say. "You remember, young man," she had told him as she combed his hair, "these reporters are just looking for a quick story that will make some excitement. But you have to stay here and live in this town. So mind your Ps and Qs."

As they sat there on the couch, Mrs. Allen had her foot on top of Nick's under the coffee table, and if she pushed down, it meant that the reporter had just asked a question that she was going to answer for him. Mrs. Allen did not trust reporters.

"So tell me, Nick, why did you make up this new word, *frindle*?" asked Alice Lunderson.

Nick gulped and said, "Well, my teacher Mrs. Granger said that all the words in the dictionary were made up by people, and that they mean what they mean because we say they do. So I thought it would be fun to just make up a new word and see if that was true."

"And were you surprised when Mrs. Granger got mad about that?" asked Alice with a smile.

There was a push on Nick's foot and his mother said, "We never felt that Mrs. Granger got angry. When everyone started using the word *frindle*, it just got to be a disruption, that's all. She's really a very fine teacher."

"Yeah," said Nick. "I mean, I learned a lot about words, and without her, I wouldn't have."

"So what's next for you and the new word?" Alice was wrapping it up. She could see that Nick and his parents were not going to be pushed into saying anything controversial. So she just kept it light and happy.

"Well," said Nick, "the funny thing is, even though I invented it, it's not my word anymore. *Frindle* belongs to everyone now, and I guess everyone will figure out what happens together."

Alice also had a short chat with a worried looking Mrs. Chatham, and a smiling Bud Lawrence, maker of the official *frindle*. Then she shot her opening bit and her closing bit, and the camera crew drove back to Carrington to edit all the pieces and put them together into a two-minute news story.

The next night, when all the serious news about wars and oil prices and world food supplies had been talked about on the CBS evening news, the anchorman looked into the camera and smiled.

He said, "It is believed by many that the word *quiz* was made up in 1791 by a Dublin theater manager named Daly. He had bet someone that he could invent a brand-new word in the English language, and he chalked up the letters *q-u-i-z* onto every wall and building in town. The next morning, there it was, and within a week people all over Ireland were wondering what it could mean—and a new word had been created. *Quiz* is the only word in English that was invented by one person for no particular reason—that is until now. Now there is a new word, *frindle*, and here is Alice Lunderson in Westfield, New Hampshire, with the story."

Alice came on the screen with a short introduction. Then, right there on TV, Mrs. Granger and Nick and Bud Lawrence and Nick's mom were talking to twenty million people about frindles.

One of those twenty million people was a producer for the *Late Show with David*

Letterman. And another one of those twenty million people was a staff writer for *People* magazine, and another one was a writer for *3-2-1 Contact* magazine for kids. Dozens of other writers and producers and marketing people saw that story on the news—and all of them smelled a great story.

During the next three weeks every man, woman, and child in America heard about this funny new word that kids were using instead of the word *pen.* And kids in Ohio and Iowa and New York and Texas and California started using it, too.

Bud Lawrence was suddenly flooded with orders for anything with the word *frindle* on it, and he quickly got interested again. But there were complications.

Bud's lawyer said, "You see that stack of orders there? Trouble. That's what that is. We got a trademark filed, but it's only like an application. The whole country knows that that little kid made up the word, and unless you make a deal with his dad, you're going to end up with nothing—maybe even a big fat lawsuit. That kid owns that word."

When Mr. Allen came home at lunchtime,

America heard about this funny new word

his wife told him that he had to call Bud Lawrence. "It's something about the new word."

This was not good news to Tom Allen. He was sick and tired of all the fuss. And being away from the hardware store so much while all this nonsense was happening had put him weeks behind on his paperwork. He'd be lucky now to get his Christmas order in time.

Even though he didn't really want anything to do with it, Bud was an old friend. So on the way back to the store, Nick's dad went to Bud Lawrence's office.

"Tom—good to see you," said Bud. He stood up and walked around his desk to shake hands. "Have a seat." Tom sat down uneasily, and Bud pulled another chair over. "Ever seen Westfield so stirred up about anything in your life? You and Ginny must be pretty proud of . . . that boy of yours." Bud couldn't remember Nick's name.

Tom shifted in his chair and nodded. "Yes, he's quite something, that's for sure. But I tell you, Bud, I'm ready for it all to just die down and blow away—too much fuss."

Instantly, Bud saw how to get what he wanted. "Well, Tom, I'm afraid it's not really going to go away. Looks like something's started up, and people are real interested. You probably saw those bright red ballpoints around town with the word *frindle* on 'em? That was my doing. Just testing the waters. But your boy, he owns that word. I got my lawyer to apply for a trademark a few weeks back, because that's just the way I am. New thing comes along, I like to be right there in the middle of it." He grinned at Tom Allen, and Tom smiled back weakly.

"Right now, I got a shirt printer in Massachusetts and another one in Chicago and another one in Los Angeles making T-shirts with the word *frindle* above a picture of a pen—I mean a frindle. Each supplier has orders so far for over twenty thousand shirts. Profit on every one of those is going to be two, maybe three dollars. And I'm talking with some big pen and pencil companies in Hong Kong and Japan about a deal that could be worth some really big money. They've seen this frindle thing in the media, and they want to buy the rights to the trademark and make a new line of frindles for kids. I'm not kidding—this is a hot, hot idea!"

Bud guessed right. Just the thought of all this made Tom shrink back uncomfortably in his chair. It was way too much fuss.

"Tom, let me be direct with you. As the boy's guardian, you need to do the right thing about all this. I'd like to see where all this is going to go. I'm going to take some risks, spend some money, see what happens. But I need your permission. I need your signature on these trademark papers, and I need to strike a deal with you about permission to use that trademark. I know it seems like a big ruckus about a word, but we just can't tell what's to come of it unless we take some steps." Bud pointed at the papers on his desk. "That's a contract, and it's fair and honest. It gives your boy thirty percent of whatever profits I might make. That's a fair royalty, generous for this kind of deal. So what do you say—make sense? Let me take care of all the fuss, and see if some good doesn't maybe come of it all?" The papers and a pen were there on the desk next to Tom.

He looked at Bud, then reached over, picked up the pen, and signed both copies of the trademark papers and three copies of the contract. "I've got no reason to doubt you one bit, Bud, and I sure don't want to mess with any of this myself. Is that it?" he asked, standing up.

"Not quite, Tom. Here." Then Bud Lawrence

handed Nick's dad a check for $2,250.

"What's this for?"

"That's what I owe Nick for the sales of frindles from the first three weeks," explained Bud with a smile.

Tom looked at the check and said, "This is terrific, Bud, and I'm really glad about it because it'll sure help with Nick's college. But I wish you'd just keep this between us. If Nick knew, he'd probably stop mowing lawns and I'd never get him to save another penny. So just between us, okay?"

Bud said, "Sure, Tom, I understand. Just between us." And they shook hands.

Mr. Allen left Bud's office and walked across the street to the savings bank. He set up a trust account for Nick, and the bank manager said he could make arrangements with Mr. Lawrence so any other money would be deposited automatically. That sounded good to Tom Allen. If he never heard another word about it, that would be fine.

As Nick's dad walked slowly back to the hardware store, he wondered if things were ever going to be the same again in his quiet little town.

thirteen

Ripples

BUT LIFE DID SETTLE back to normal in
Westfield. More leaves fell, Thanksgiving came,
then the first snow, then Christmas, and more
snow. Fall and winter seemed to calm everything
down and drive everyone into their own houses.

Things were calmer at Lincoln Elementary
School, too. Frindle-mania was over. But that
didn't mean the word was gone. Not at all.

All the kids and even some of the teachers
used the new word. At first it was on purpose.
Then it became a habit, and by the middle of
February, *frindle* was just a word, like *door* or
tree or *hat*. People in Westfield barely noticed it
anymore.

But in the rest of the country, things were
hopping. Frindle was on the move. In hundreds
of little towns and big cities from coast to coast,

kids were using the new word, and parents and teachers were trying to stop it. What had happened in Westfield happened over and over and over again.

Bud Lawrence couldn't have been happier. There were frindle shirts and sunglasses and erasers and notebooks and paper and dozens of other items. The new line of frindles imported from Japan were a big hit, and now there was talk of selling them in Japan and Europe, as well. The checks that went into Nick's trust fund got bigger and bigger.

Bud opened his own factory in Westfield to make frindle baseball caps, which created jobs for twenty-two people. And in March the town council voted to put up a little sign on the post below the town's name along Route 302. It said, "Home of the Original Frindle."

And Mrs. Granger? She seemed to have given up, or perhaps she had been ordered to. No one knew. Her poster about the forbidden word had quietly disappeared from the bulletin board, and kids were not staying after school writing sentences anymore. It was business as usual.

Except for one thing.

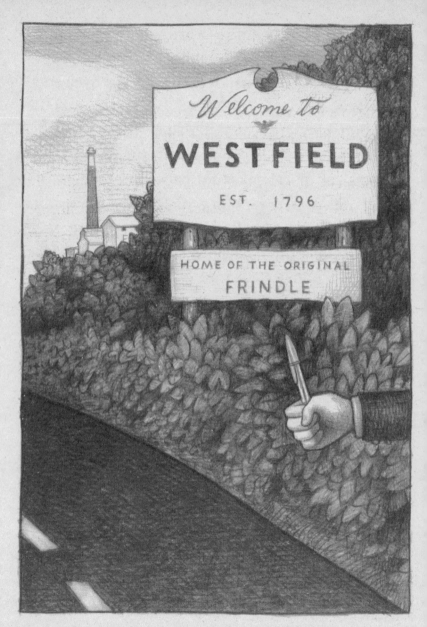

But life did settle back to normal

Everyone in fifth grade got at least one word wrong on his or her spelling test each week. Every week, the first word at the top of Mrs. Granger's list was *pen*. And each Friday during the spelling test, every kid spelled it *f-r-i-n-d-l-e*.

Nick was sort of a celebrity for a while. Everyone had seen him on *The Late Show*, and on *Good Morning, America* and two or three other TV shows. John and Chris and all his friends kept asking about what it was like to ride in a limousine. After a week or two, though, it was old news, and everyone seemed to forget it and move on.

The only person who couldn't quite forget about everything was Nick.

fourteen

Inside Nick

ON THE OUTSIDE, Nick was still Nick. But inside, it was different. Oh sure, he still had a lot of great ideas, but now they scared him a little.

For instance, Nick learned in social studies class that people who buy stuff are called *consumers*. If consumers stop buying, stores and shops and restaurants go out of business.

Then—boom—a new idea hit him.

All the kids loved lunchtime. But the awful part about lunch was the eating part—school food. And the food was never a surprise—you had to smell it all morning and then go eat it. The food was always bad.

Well, thought Nick, *the school cafeteria is sort of a restaurant, isn't it? And the students are the consumers, right? And we don't really have to buy our lunches there, do we?*

Nick could see it all: He would get all the kids to bring their lunches from home every day until the ladies who made the lunches cooked better food. He was sure those women didn't cook food like that for their own families. The kids were the consumers with $1.35 in their pockets, and until the food was better, that's where their money would stay.

Great idea! Nick was sure it would work, and he got all excited about it.

But then Nick remembered what had happened with *frindle*. It stopped him cold. He was sure that if all the kids stopped buying lunch, sooner or later someone would figure out that it was all Nick Allen's idea. He would get in trouble. People would write about it in the newspaper. The principal would call his parents—anything could happen.

So for the first time in his life, Nick kept a good idea to himself. He never even told John or Chris.

And that changed Nick.

His mom was the first to notice. "Are things okay at school, honey?" she asked one day in early March. He had seemed kind of down, a little sad. It worried her.

"Sure," said Nick. "Everything's fine."

"Everything's okay with your friends? They haven't been hanging around here very much."

"Mom, honest. Everything's fine. It's winter. Everyone's really busy with hockey and basketball—that's all." And Nick went to his room and shut the door.

Mrs. Granger noticed the change, too. The clever little rascal who had looked her in the eye and said, "But I really didn't have a frindle with me—" that boy wasn't in her class anymore. Now a quieter, more careful Nicholas Allen came into class every day. He did all his work perfectly, didn't speak unless she called on him, and didn't laugh and joke with his friends like he used to. School would be over in a few months, and it seemed like there was nothing she could do to help him.

Toward the end of the year, Nick remembered the letter that Mrs. Granger had asked him to sign on the back when the frindle business was just getting started. The chess game was over, so he was expecting to get that letter from Mrs. Granger any day. But all spring it didn't come, so he thought she must have forgotten about it. Nick was afraid to bring it all up again, but he was dying of curiosity.

So on the last day of school, Nick knocked on Mrs. Granger's classroom door. She was straightening up the textbooks on the bookcases below the windows. Without turning around she sang out, "Come in."

Nick said, "Hi, Mrs. Granger."

Mrs. Granger stood up and turned to face him. "Oh, it's you, Nicholas. I'm so glad you stopped by. I've been meaning to talk to you, and this will save me having to send you a letter this summer."

Nick gulped and said, "That's what I came for—the letter."

Mrs. Granger looked puzzled for half a second, and then she said, "Oh! That letter." Then she paused. "You will recall, Nicholas, that I said I would send you that letter when all this was over . . . and it's not over."

"It's not?" Nick tilted his head to one side, and asked, "When will it be over?"

Mrs. Granger smiled and said, "Oh, believe me, Nicholas. You'll know when it's over. I wanted to talk to you about something else."

She walked across the room and stood about two feet from him. Nick had grown during the year, and their eyes were almost on the same level. Nick noticed that the eyes were softer, but just as powerful. "I've noticed that you've been very quiet for the past few months. You know, Nicholas, you didn't do anything wrong this year. I know a lot of things happened, and a lot of things were said, and you must have had some difficult days here and there. But your idea was a good idea, and I have been very proud of the way you behaved—most of the time."

Nick was embarrassed, but Mrs. Granger kept on talking. "And Nicholas, you have great things to do in this life. I'm absolutely sure you do, and you mustn't let a few hard days trick you into clamming up."

Then Mrs. Granger reached out and shook Nick's hand, and looked him in the face. Her eyes were turned up brighter than Nick had ever seen them before. She said, "Nicholas Allen, I have enjoyed having you as a student. Now you go out there and have a wonderful summer. And I expect to hear remarkable things about you, young man. "

Mrs. Granger watched Nick start to leave. But before he got to the door, he turned and said, "Thanks, Mrs. Granger. You have a great summer, too." Then he grinned and said, "And don't forget to buy some new frindles for next year."

Thanks to his little talk with Mrs. Granger—along with a healthy dose of summer vacation—Nick made a full recovery. He was proud that he had made up a new word, and he enjoyed thinking about all the commotion it had stirred up. That one little word had made fifth grade a year to remember.

Before he started sixth grade Nick was Nick again, and all through junior high and high school and college, he proved it.

For example, two years later, all the school cafeterias in town were serving delicious food at least four days a week, all because of Nick the Consumer. And the state superintendent of schools had made a special trip to Westfield to learn why this little town had the most successful school lunch program in the state.

And in high school, well, the stories about Nick's other adventures could go on and on and on. But that would delay the end of this story, the one that started when Nick was in fifth grade.

Because the end of this story came later—ten years later.

And what was happening to Nick's word during those ten years? Nothing fancy, nothing exciting. Words don't work that way. Words either get used, or they don't. And *frindle* was being used more and more. It was becoming a real word.

fifteen

And the winner
Is . . .

TEN YEARS LATER, Nick Allen was a junior in college. And during November of his junior year, two important things happened.

First, Nick turned twenty-one years old, and the frindle trust fund set up by his father became legally Nick's.

Nick was rich. Nick was very rich. Nick was so rich he couldn't even begin to imagine how rich he really was.

Nick wanted to give his parents some of the money, which they said they did *not* need and would *not* accept. But Nick reminded them that they had always wanted to travel, and they should just think of this as a big birthday present or something. So they accepted.

And Nick also wanted to give some money to his big brother, James—who said he did *not* need it and would *not* accept it. But Nick reminded James that his two-year-old daughter would grow up and go to college someday—and besides, hadn't James once given Nick his whole baseball card collection? So James accepted the gift.

After that Nick went out and bought himself a fast new computer. And about ten new games. And a mountain bike. Then he tried to forget about the money, which is a hard thing to do. But he managed pretty well and kept working on his college degree as hard as ever.

The second important thing that fall was the arrival of a package at the door of Nick's apartment one day—a large, heavy package. It was from Mrs. Granger.

There were three things in the package: 1) a brand-new eighth-edition *Webster's College Dictionary*; 2) a short handwritten note taped to the cover of the dictionary; and 3) a fat white envelope. Turning the white envelope over, Nick saw the name—his name. He had written it there one September afternoon in Mrs. Granger's room after school. Ten years ago.

Nick set the envelope down and gently peeled the note off the front of the dictionary.

My dear Nicholas:

Please turn to page 541 of this book.

Nick grabbed the dictionary and leafed to page 541, his heart pounding. And there between *Friml* and *fringe* he read:

> **frin•dle** *(frin' dl) n. a device used to write or make marks with ink [arbitrary coinage; originated by Nicholas Allen, American, 1987– (see* **pen***)]*

Nick went back to the note from Mrs. Granger.

This is a brand-new dictionary, the one I recommend that my students use for their homework. And now when I teach them how new words are added to the dictionary, I tell each and every one of them to look up the word frindle.

And, of course, I have sent along that letter I promised to give you when our little battle was over.

And now it's over.

Your teacher,

    Mrs. Lorelei Granger

Nick's head was spinning. With shaking hands, he opened the fat white envelope. He pulled out the ten-year-old letter and began to read.

Dear Nicholas:

If you are reading this letter, it means that the word frindle *has been added to the dictionary. Congratulations.*

A person can watch the sunrise, but he cannot slow it down or stop it or make it go backward. And that is what I was trying to do with your word.

At first I was angry. I admit that. I was not happy to see the word pen *pushed aside as if it did not matter. But I guess that if the Latin word for feather had been* frindilus *instead of* pinna, *then you probably would have invented the word* pen *instead. Like the sunrise, some things just have to happen—and all you can really do is watch.*

The word frindle *has existed for less than three weeks. I now see that this is the kind of chance that a teacher hopes for and dreams about—a chance to see bright young students take an idea they have learned in a boring old classroom and put it to a real test in their own world. I confess that I am very excited to see how it all turns out. I am mostly here to watch it happen.*

But somehow I think I have a small part to play in this drama, and I have chosen to be the villain. Every good story needs a bad guy, don't you think?

So someday, I will be asking you to forgive me, and I hope you will.

Nick, I know you like to think. Please think about this: When I started teaching, no one had landed on the moon, there were no space shuttles, no CNN, no weather satellites. There were no video cassette recorders, no CDs, no computers.

The world has changed in a million

ways. That is why I have always tried to teach children something that would be useful no matter what.

So many things have gone out of date. But after all these years, words are still important. Words are still needed by everyone. Words are used to think with, to write with, to dream with, to hope and pray with. And that is why I love the dictionary. It endures. It works. And as you now know, it also changes and grows.

Again, congratulations. And I've enclosed a little present for you.

Yours truly,

Mrs. Granger

Nick remembered Mrs. Granger's eyes, and now he understood what some of those special looks had meant. The old fox! She had been rooting for *frindle* the whole time. By fighting against it, she had actually helped it along.

There was a flat, oblong case in the white

envelope, the kind of case you get when you buy a watch. Nick pulled it out and opened the lid. Inside was something else Nick had not seen for ten years. It was Mrs. Granger's favorite pen, her old maroon fountain pen with the blue cap. And under the clip was a little folded piece of paper. It was another note. A very short note. Just one word: Frindle.

About a month later, something happened over in the old part of Westfield, over where the trees are huge and the houses are small. On Christmas morning, Mrs. Granger's doorbell rang. Mrs. Granger opened the door, but no one was there.

Someone had left a package inside her storm door—a box wrapped in green paper with a red bow and a white envelope taped to one end. She smiled as she stooped down to pick it up.

As she picked up the package she noticed a red, white, and blue Express Mail envelope sticking halfway out of her mailbox next to the doorway. It must have been delivered late on Christmas Eve. She opened the storm door plucked the envelope from the mailbox, and

FRINDLE

then shut both doors and went inside with a shiver.

Mrs. Granger went across the living room and sat on the couch. The express envelope was from the Westfield School District office. It looked important, so Mrs. Granger opened it right away.

It was a letter from the superintendent of schools, a letter of congratulations. A permanent trust fund for college scholarships had been established with a donation of one million dollars "from one of your former students."

It would be called The Lorelei Granger Students' Fund.

Mrs. Granger was sure it was a mistake. Or maybe a prank. A million dollars? Nonsense! She had the urge to pick up the telephone and give the superintendent a call and straighten this out right away.

But this was Christmas morning, and even though the superintendent *was* one of her former pupils, Mrs. Granger decided to wait a day. Couldn't hurt.

Besides, the other package was sitting next to her on the couch, waiting impatiently with its red bow. She opened the envelope first.

It was a little Christmas card with a sloppy note—obviously the work of a fifth-grade boy.

Dear Mrs. Granger;

Your one of my favorite teachers. Here is somthing I want you to have.

Sincerly,

A student of yours

Mrs. Granger glared at the spelling mistakes, but then chuckled and shook her head. Kids are always the same, year after year. Here she was in her forty-fifth year of teaching, all set to retire in June. She could hardly remember a Christmas day when she didn't have a present from one of her students.

Mrs. Granger pulled off the red ribbon and tore off the paper and lifted the lid of the box. She expected to find something made of yarn and popsicle sticks, or maybe curly macaroni and glue.

But instead she found an oblong case covered with blue velvet. She opened the case and inside was a beautiful gold fountain pen. She picked it up, and it was cool and heavy in her hand. Words were engraved along the pen's shiny barrel, and Mrs. Granger had to slide down to the end of the couch and turn on her reading lamp. Then she could read the three thin lines of type:

This object belongs to Mrs. Lorelei Granger, and she may call it any name she chooses.
—With love from Nicholas Allen

What's next from the
master of the school story?

Turn the page for an excerpt from
Andrew Clements's new series!

Available now from
Atheneum Books for Young Readers

As the ship's bell clanged through the school's hall-way for the third time, Ben ran his tongue back and forth across the porcelain caps that covered his front teeth, a nervous habit. And he was nervous because he was late. Again.

When she was being the art teacher, Ms. Wilton was full of smiles and fun and two dozen clever ways to be creative with egg cartons and yarn—but in homeroom she was different. More like a drill ser-geant. Or a prison guard. Still, maybe if he got to his seat before she took attendance, he *might* not have to stay after school. Again.

The art room was in the original school building, and Ben was still hurrying through the Annex, the newer part of the school. But the long connecting hallway was empty, so he put on a burst of speed. He banged through the double doors at a dead run, slowed a little for the last corner, then sprinted for the art room.

Halfway there, he stopped in his tracks.

"Mr. Keane—are you okay?"

It was a stupid question. The janitor was dragging his left leg as he used the handle of a big dust mop like a crutch, trying to get himself through the doorway into his workroom. His face was pale, twisted with pain.

"Help me . . . sit down." His breathing was ragged, his voice raspy.

Ben gulped. "I should call 9-1-1."

"Already did, and I told 'em where to find me," the man growled. "Just get me . . . to that chair."

With one arm across Ben's shoulders, Mr. Keane groaned with each step, then eased himself into a chair by the workbench.

"Sh-should I get the school nurse?"

Mr. Keane's eyes flashed, and his shock of white hair was wilder and messier than usual. "That windbag? No—I broke my ankle or somethin' on the stairs, and it hurts like the devil. And it means I'm gonna be laid up the rest of the school year. And you can stop lookin' so scared. I'm not mad at *you*, I'm just ... *mad.*"

As he snarled that last word, Ben saw his yellowed teeth. And he remembered why all the kids at Oakes School tried to steer clear of old man Keane.

A distant siren began to wail, then a second one. Edgeport wasn't a big town, so the sound got louder by the second.

From under his bushy eyebrows, Mr. Keane looked up into Ben's face. "I know you, don't I?"

Ben nodded. "You helped me and my dad scrape the hull of our sailboat two summers ago. Over at Parson's Marina." He remembered that Mr. Keane had been sharp and impatient the entire week, no fun at all.

"Right—you're the Pratt kid."

"I'm Ben . . . Benjamin."

The janitor kept looking into his face, and Ben felt like he was in a police lineup. Then the man suddenly nodded, as if he was agreeing with someone.

He straightened his injured leg, gasping in pain, pushed a hand into his front pocket, then pulled it back out.

"Stick out your hand."

Startled, Ben said, "What?"

"You hard a' hearing? *Stick out your hand!*"

Ben did, and Mr. Keane grabbed hold and pressed something into his palm, quickly closing the boy's fingers around it. Then he clamped Ben's fist inside his leathery grip. Ben wanted to yank his hand loose and run, but he wasn't sure he could break free . . . and part of him didn't want to. Even though he was frightened, he was curious, too. So he just gulped and stood there, eyes wide, staring at the faded blue anchor tattooed on the man's wrist.

"This thing in your hand? I've been carryin' it around with me every day for *forty-three years*. Tom Benton was the janitor here before me, and the day he retired, he handed it to me. And before Tom Benton, it was in Jimmy Conklin's pocket for thirty-some years, and before *that*, the other janitors had it—every one of 'em, all the way back to the very first man hired by Captain Oakes himself when he founded the school. Look at it . . . but first promise that you'll keep all this secret." He squinted up into Ben's face, his blue eyes bright and feverish. "Do you swear?"

Ben's mouth was dry. He'd have said anything to get this scary old guy with bad breath to let go of him. He whispered, "I swear."

Mr. Keane released his hand, and Ben opened his fingers.

And then he stared. It was a large gold coin with rounded edges, smooth as a beach pebble.

Outside, the sirens were closing in fast.

"See the writing? Read it."

With shaky hands, Ben held the coin up to catch more light. The words stamped into the soft metal had been worn away to shadows, barely visible.

He read aloud, still whispering. "'If attacked, look nor'-nor'east from amidships on the upper deck.'" He turned the coin over. "'First and always, my school belongs to the children. DEFEND IT. Duncan Oakes, 1783.'"

Mr. Keane's eyes flashed. "You know about the town council, right? How they sold this school and all the land? And how they're tearin' the place down in June? If that's not an *attack*, then I don't know what is."

He stopped talking and sat still. He seemed to soften, and when he spoke, for a moment he sounded almost childlike. "I know I'm just the guy who cleans up and all, but I love it here, with the wind comin' in off the water, and bein' able to see halfway to England. And all the kids love it too—best piece of coast for thirty miles, north or south. And this place? This is a *school*, and Captain Oakes meant it to stay that way, come blood or blue thunder. And I am *not* giving it up without a fight. And I am *not* giving this coin to that new janitor—I told him too much already." His face darkened, and he spat the man's name into the air. "*Lyman*—you know who he is?"

Ben nodded. The assistant custodian was hard to miss, very tall and thin. He had been working at the school since right after winter vacation.

"Lyman's a *snake*. Him, the principal, the superintendent—don't trust any of 'em, you hear?"

The principal? Ben thought. And the superintendent? What do they have to do with any of this?

The sirens stopped, and Ben heard banging doors, then commotion and shouting in the hallway leading from the Annex.

The janitor's breathing was forced, and his face had gone chalky white. But he grabbed Ben's wrist with surprising strength and pushed out one more sentence. "Captain Oakes said this school *belongs* to the kids. So that coin is yours now, and the fight is yours too—*yours!*"

The hairs on Ben's neck stood up. Fight? What fight? This is crazy!

Two paramedics burst into the room, a woman and a man, both wearing bright green gloves. A policeman and Mrs. Hendon, the school secretary, stood out in the hallway.

"Move!" the woman barked. "We're getting him out of here!"

Mr. Keane let go of Ben's wrist, and Ben jumped to one side, his heart pounding, the coin hidden in his hand.

The woman gave the janitor a quick exam, then nodded at her partner and said, "He's good to go—just watch the left leg."

And as they lifted the custodian onto the gurney and then strapped him down flat, the old man's eyes never left Ben's face.

As they wheeled him out, Mrs. Hendon came into the workroom and said, "I'm glad you were here to help him, Ben. Are you all right?"

"Sure, I'm fine."

"Well, you'd better get along to class now."

Ben picked up his backpack and headed toward the art room. And just before he opened the door, both sirens began wailing again.

GREAT MIDDLE-GRADE FICTION FROM
Andrew Clements,
MASTER OF THE SCHOOL STORY

FRINDLE

THE SCHOOL STORY

NO TALKING

THE LANDRY NEWS

ROOM ONE

LOST AND FOUND

THE JANITOR'S BOY

A WEEK IN THE WOODS

EXTRA CREDIT

"Few contemporary writers portray the public school world better than Clements."—*New York Times Book Review*

From Atheneum Books for Young Readers
Published by Simon & Schuster
KIDS.SimonandSchuster.com

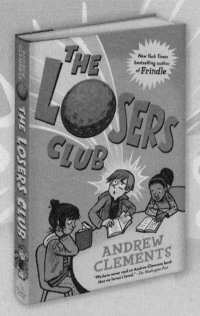

The Janitor's Boy

Also by Andrew Clements

The Landry News

Frindle

Andrew Clements

ATHENUM BOOKS FOR YOUNG READERS

New York   London   Toronto   Sydney   Singapore

First Aladdin Paperbacks edition September 2001
Copyright © 2000 by Andrew Clements
Atheneum Books for Young Readers
An imprint of Simon & Schuster
Children's Publishing Division
1230 Avenue of the Americas
New York, NY 10020

Designed by Steve Scott
The text for this book was set in Garth Graphic.
Printed and bound in the United States of America
34 36 38 40 39 37 35 33

The Library of Congress has cataloged the hardcover edition as follows:
Clements, Andrew, 1949-
The janitor's boy / Andrew Clements.—1st ed.
p.   cm.
Summary: Fifth grader Jack finds himself the target of ridicule at school
when it becomes known that his father is one of the janitors,
and he turns his anger onto his father.
ISBN: 978-0-689-81818-9 (hc.)
[1. Janitors—Fiction. 2. Fathers and sons—Fiction. 3. Schools—Fiction.]
I. Title
PZ7.C59118 Jan 2000
[Fic]—dc21
99-047457
ISBN: 978-0-689-83585-8 (pbk.)
0418 OFF

Chapter 1

The perfect crime

Jack Rankin had a particularly sensitive nose. As he walked into school in the morning, sometimes he would pause in the entryway and pull in a snoot-load of air from the flow rushing out the door. Instantly he could tell what the cafeteria lunch would be, right down to whether the Jell-O was strawberry or orange. He could tell if the school secretary was wearing perfume, and whether there was an open box of doughnuts on the table in the teachers room on the second floor.

On this particular Monday morning Jack's nose was on high alert. He was working on a special project—a bubble gum project. Today's activity was the result of about a week's worth of research and planning.

Days ago, Jack had begun the project by secretly examining the bottoms of desks and tables all over the school, trying to decide exactly which kind of discarded gum was the most unpleasant.

1

After he conducted his first few sniff tests, he didn't even have to look underneath a table or a chair to tell if there was gum. The scent of the stuff followed him from class to class. He had gum on the brain. He smelled gum everywhere—on the bus, in the halls, passing a locker, walking into a classroom.

Jack finally chose watermelon Bubblicious. It had to be the smelliest gum in the universe. Even weeks after being stuck under a chair or table, that sickly sweet smell and distinctive crimson color were unmistakable. And Bubblicious, any flavor of it, was definitely the stickiest gum available. By Jack's calculations, it was more than three times stickier than Bazooka.

The final stage of Jack's gum caper began in today's third-period gym class. Mr. Sargent had them outside in the cool October air, running wind sprints to prepare for a timed mile next week. By the end of the period Jack had four pieces of gum in his mouth, chewed to maximum stickiness. The smell of it almost overpowered him.

Carefully steering a wide path around Mr. Sargent, he went to his locker before the next class. He spat the chewed gum into a sandwich bag he had brought from home. The bag had two or three tablespoons of water in it to keep the gum from sticking to the plastic.

Jack sealed the bag, stuffed it into his pocket, and immediately jammed another two pieces of gum into his mouth and started to chew.

He processed those two pieces plus two more during science, managed to chew up another four pieces during lunch period, and even finished one piece during math—quite an accomplishment in Mrs. Lambert's classroom.

By the time he got to music, he had thirteen chewed pieces of gum in a plastic bag in the pocket of his jeans—all warm and soft and sticky.

Monday-afternoon music class was the ideal crime scene. The room had four levels, stair-stepping down toward the front. The seats were never assigned, and Mr. Pike always made kids fill the class from the front of the room backward. By walking in the door just as the echo of the bell was fading, Jack was guaranteed a seat in the back row. He sat directly behind Jed Ellis, also known as Giant Jed. With no effort at all he was completely hidden from Mr. Pike.

The only other person in the back row was Kerry Loomis, sitting six seats away. She was hiding too, hunched over a notebook, trying to finish some homework. Jack had half a crush on Kerry. On a normal day he would have tried to get her attention, make her laugh, show off a little. But today was anything but normal.

Mr. Pike was at the front of the room. Standing behind the upright piano, he pounded out a melody with one hand and flailed the air with his other one, trying to get fidgety fifth graders to sing their hearts out.

Jack Rankin was supposed to be singing along with the rest of the chorus. He was supposed to be learning a new song for the fall concert. The song was something about eagles soaring and being free and happy—not how Jack was feeling at this moment.

Bending down, Jack brought the baggie up to his mouth and stuffed in all thirteen pieces of gum for a last softening chew. The lump was bigger than a golf ball, and he nearly gagged as he worked it into final readiness, keeping one eye on the clock.

With one minute of class left, Mr. Pike was singing along now, his head bobbing like a madman, urging the kids to open their mouths wider. As the class hit a high note singing the word "sky," Jack leaned over and let the huge wad of gum drop from his mouth into his moistened hand. Then he began applying the gum to the underside of the folding desktop, just as he'd planned.

4

He stuck it first to the front outside edge and then pulled a heavy smear toward the opposite corner. Then he stretched the mass to the other corner and repeated the action, making a big, sticky X. Round and round Jack dragged the gum, working inward toward the center like a spider spinning a gooey, scented web.

As the bell rang Jack stood up and pulled the last gob of gum downward, pasting it onto the middle of the metal seat. A strand of sagging goo led upward, still attached to the underside of the desk.

It was the perfect crime.

The whole back of the music room reeked of artificial watermelon. And that gob on the seat? Sheer genius. Jack allowed himself a grim little smile as he shouldered his way into the hall.

There were two more class periods, so a kid would *have* to notice the mess today—this very afternoon. Mr. Pike would have to pull the desk aside so no one would get tangled in the gunk. Mr. Pike would need to get *someone* to clean it up before tomorrow.

So after *someone* had swept the rooms and emptied the trash cans and washed the chalkboards and dusted the stairs and mopped the halls and cleaned the entryway rugs, *someone* would also have to find a putty knife and a can of solvent and try to get a very sticky, very smelly desk ready for Tuesday morning. It would be a messy job, but *someone* would have to do it.

And Jack knew exactly who that someone would be. It would be the man almost everyone called John—John the janitor.

Of all the kids in the school, Jack was the only one who didn't call him John. Jack called him a different name.

Jack called him Dad.

Chapter 2

WHAT DO YOU WANT TO BE?

Ordinarily, no one would have imagined that Jack Rankin would vandalize a desk. But this was not an ordinary school year for Jack—or for any of his classmates, either.

The town of Huntington was growing, and more families with kids were moving in all the time. The town seemed to be playing a game of musical chairs—too many kids and not enough schoolrooms.

The kids in grades nine through twelve were all set. They had already made the move to a brand-new high school out on the west edge of town. The elementary school was still in good shape, but it was only big enough now for the kids in kindergarten through grade three.

It was Jack and the other kids caught in the middle grades who had the problem. The old junior high would work fine for grades four and five—that is, after about ten months of repair work. And the kids in grades six, seven, and eight would have a shiny, new junior high school—in about another year.

So where do you park Jack and about seven hundred other kids and all their teachers and textbooks and computers and printers and copiers and TVs and VCRs and art supplies, plus their library, for a whole school year?

Simple. You put them in the old high school.

Not simple. Not simple at all.

The old high school was . . . well, it was old.

The four-story brick building had been part of Huntington's town center for more than seventy-five years. The broad front lawn was split by a wide sidewalk leading up to the front steps. High above the front steps, a square bell tower rose another thirty feet beyond the roofline. The bell tower was capped by a green copper dome with a weather vane on top—made in the shape of an open book.

The old high school had been built back when fewer kids went on to college. It was Huntington's monument to higher education. For generations graduation from Huntington High had been the goal line.

But not for Jack and the other middle graders.

For them it was going to be an educational stopover—sort of like a long field trip. It would be nothing more than a strange world they would pass through on their way to somewhere else.

And from the second Jack heard about the move, he wished he could make the whole place just disappear.

The news of the school changes had been mailed to every home in Huntington just before spring break during Jack's fourth-grade year. His mom had read the letter aloud at supper one night.

Someone at the school superintendent's office thought it would be fun to give the transition process a cute name. The letter began like this:

Dear Student:
  Are you and your friends and family ready
for Huntington's newest adventure in learning?
Next year will be the year of
    THE BIG SWITCHEROO!

Jack was not amused.

After she finished the letter, his mom said, "Don't you think it's exciting, Jack? Those special tours in June should be fun. They want all the kids to feel comfortable, especially the fourth- and fifth-grade kids. . . . Of course, that's not a problem for you, I mean with your dad working there and all."

Jack looked quickly at his dad across the dinner table. "Won't you be going to work at the new high school, Dad? I mean, you're the high school janitor, right?"

Wiping his mouth, John Rankin smiled and said, "Nope. It doesn't work that way. What I am is the janitor for a *building*. The high school and all the high school kids are moving, but the building stays—so I stay too. No one knows that building like I do. Unless the town decides to tear it down, that'll be where I work."

Jack's mom said, "I loved going to school in that old place. It's got character, you know? And Jackie, if you don't want to take the bus some mornings, you could ride to school in the pickup with your dad."

Looking down at the pile of peas on his plate, Jack thought, *Yeah, right. Like I'm going to ride to school with the janitor.*

Jack knew he'd be on that bus every day, no matter what.

Jack remembered the first time he had been asked about his future. It was second grade, and Miss Patton had a let's-get-acquainted session on the first day of school. Jack liked Miss Patton. She wore the same kind of perfume that his grandmother wore, only a lot less. She was conducting a little public interview with each student. She asked questions like, Do you have any brothers or sisters? Do you have any pets? What's your favorite food? Do you like sports? If you could go anywhere in the world, where would you go?

The last question she asked was always, And what do you want to be when you grow up?

The answers to that question had been all over the place.

"I'm going to be a policeman."

"I want to be a doctor."

"I want to own a ranch and raise cows and chickens."

"I want to be a lawyer when I grow up."

"I'm going to be an astronaut and fly to Jupiter."

"I'm going to make computers."

Then it was Jack's turn.

Favorite color? Blue.

Brothers or sisters? One little sister.

Favorite food? Pizza.

"And what do you want to be when you grow up, Jack?"

There was no hesitation. Jack smiled with perfect second-grade certainty and he said, "I want to be a janitor, like my dad."

Before Miss Patton could say something like,

"That's great, Jack," some kids in the class began to giggle. Raymond Hollis blurted out, "A janitor? That's a job for dum-dums! Hey, Jack wants to grow up to be a dum-dum like his dum-dum daddy!"

That got the whole class laughing. Miss Patton shushed them and said, "Raymond, that was not nice, and you owe Jack an apology. Being a janitor is a perfectly good job, and I'm sure Jack is very proud of his dad."

Jack *was* proud of his dad, and he loved him very much. But laughter from kids is more powerful than words from teachers. Raymond had to stand up and say, "I'm sorry, Jack," but Jack could tell he didn't mean it.

Ever since that day in second grade, whenever the conversation turned toward parents and jobs, Jack clammed up.

But as fifth grade approached, the topic was going to be unavoidable. All summer long, whenever Jack thought about school, he felt like he was trapped in a bad dream.

Chapter 3

L Is for Loser

On his first day of fifth grade Jack had kept a lookout for his dad. He only saw him once, across the crowded cafeteria, leaning on a push broom by the main doorway. He was wearing his usual work clothes—dark green pants and a matching shirt with his name stitched in red letters on a white patch above the pocket. His dad smiled and waved. Jack barely nodded, and then looked away. He ate his lunch in a hurry and left through the side hallway door.

During the rest of September, Jack saw his dad once or twice a day. Usually they were both busy, both going somewhere in a hurry. It was like they lived in parallel universes. They passed through the same time and space without ever actually meeting. The arrangement suited Jack just fine.

Then on Monday afternoon, the fifth of October, disaster struck.

Jack was sitting in math class. Mrs. Lambert

was reviewing how to add fractions with different denominators. Two seats away, in the front row, Lenny Trumbull's stomach had a disagreement with the cafeteria ravioli. The ravioli won. Without warning, Lenny spread his lunch all over the green linoleum floor.

Mrs. Lambert hurried Lenny down to the nurse's office, and she sent Rick Arneson to get the janitor.

To escape the smell and avoid the vomit-o-domino effect, the whole math class was crowded into the back of the room by the open windows. Jack had gotten there first and practically had his whole head out the farthest window. Fortunately for his sensitive nose, the airflow was coming into the room instead of out of it. The breeze was from the direction of downtown, and Jack could smell the fries and hamburgers cooking at the diner seven blocks away.

Keeping his place by the window, Jack turned slightly and watched the doorway. There were always one or two other janitors in the building besides his dad. It didn't have to be John. Rick could find someone else. It didn't have to be John.

But it was. Jack's dad showed up with a bucket, a mop, a plastic bag of red sawdust, and a dustpan and brush. Jack cringed. He quickly ducked behind a knot of girls and turned to look out the window.

The rest of the class watched the janitor with horrified fascination. First, John shook out a few cups of sawdust to soak up the liquid. After a minute he swept the whole soggy mess into the dustpan and took it right out into the hallway. Then he shot some ammonia over the damp spot from a sprayer he pulled from his belt, and then swabbed the entire area down with the fresh mop. The smell was completely gone.

Mrs. Lambert had returned, and from the back of the room she said, "Thanks a lot, John."

John Rankin nodded and said, "All in a day's work."

Mrs. Lambert said, "All right, back to your seats, everyone. Show's over." The kids began moving toward their desks.

As John the janitor pushed the rolling bucket toward the door he glanced up and saw Jack. His face broke into a big smile.

And then he said it: "Hi, son."

Jack mumbled, "Hi," and then looked down, pretending to search for something in his notebook.

As his dad walked out into the hallway that Monday afternoon Jack felt like a giant letter had been branded on his forehead—*L*, for Loser.

Jack sat down, his ears burning red.

It was Kirk who struck first.

Kirk Dorfmann was a walking fashion ad. From shoes to cap he was a billboard of logos and trademarks—all the very latest clothes, all very expensive. Kirk grinned and leaned across the aisle toward Jack. In a voice loud enough for most of the class to hear he said, "Hey, does Daddy let you push the big broom sometimes, Jackie? Oh, I forgot—you have to get a special permit to drive one of those things. Nice outfit he's wearing today. Your dad looks great in green polyester."

It had been a long time since Jack had punched anyone. In his mind an iron fist formed, and he could feel it slamming into Kirk's soft, fleshy smirk. Jack could feel the teeth behind the lips giving way as he followed through with his full weight.

But before thought could become action, Mrs. Lambert slipped between the two boys. Her eyes flashed, and she said, "Kirk, I'll see *you* after class."

Mrs. Lambert moved back into the math lesson, and it seemed like things had returned to normal.

But they hadn't, not for Jack.

Jack sat smoldering through the rest of the class. His jaw ached from gritting his teeth. He ignored Mrs. Lambert and passed the last fifteen minutes

16

imagining how he'd get back at Kirk. He knew Kirk would never fight him. Jack had a reputation in that department. *Just let me get him alone down by the locker room,* thought Jack. *I'll mop the floor with him!* Jack said those words to himself and immediately got even angrier that he would choose that particular way to describe winning a fight.

When class ended, Jack hoped for a clean get-away, but the door clogged up with chatting girls, and the hallway was jammed with seventh graders coming back from their lunch period. Kirk went up to Mrs. Lambert's desk, and Jack edged toward the door and got in front of Marla Jenkins and Sue Driscoll. He wanted to be far enough away to be able to pretend he couldn't hear what Mrs. Lambert said to Kirk. It was just a scolding anyway, stuff about respect for others. Jack was still ten feet from the doorway when Kirk rejoined his buddy, Luke Karnes.

Luke was one of Kirk's trendy little group. Luke looked as if he followed Kirk around the Mall of America, taking notes on exactly what Kirk bought and how he put his fashion costumes together. Tall, thin, and long-legged, Luke was always a step or two behind Kirk, always trying to catch up, always trying to impress him. Luke started talking to Kirk, pretending that Jack couldn't hear him.

17

"Hey, Kirk, must take a lot of talent to clean up a bunch of puke, huh? Sure wish *I* could learn how to do that."

Kirk said, "Well, just forget about it, Luke. It's a gift, y'know? And you have to go to a special janitor's college and take a course in vomit wiping before you can even try it. Only a few special people ever learn how to do it right—and it's passed on with pride from father to son." Kirk paused, then in a voice dripping with sarcasm he said, "I sure wish *my* dad was a janitor!"

"Yeah," said Luke, "me, too!"

Jack kept his eyes straight ahead, his lips pressed together. Marla and Sue giggled as Kirk and Luke finished their little routine, and if Mrs. Lambert heard what they'd said, she pretended she hadn't.

Jack finally made it into the hallway. He bolted left toward his locker. As he got to the corner he glanced over his shoulder at Kirk and Luke, his eyes flashing with hatred. It was the wrong moment to look backward.

John Rankin had just rinsed his mop and refilled the rolling bucket at the utility closet in the fifth-grade hall. At the exact moment Jack was rounding the corner at an angry run, his dad was coming the other way with the bucket.

The collision was spectacular. The bucket didn't

tip all the way over, but the force of Jack's impact knocked the mop out onto the floor with a clatter that made everyone in the hallway turn and stare. Jack lost his footing in the water that sloshed onto the floor. His math book and papers went flying, and Jack skidded to a stop against the lockers, sitting in a puddle.

Led by Kirk and Luke, the hallway erupted into laughter and clapping.

John rushed over to his son. "You all right, Jack?" He tried to take Jack by the elbow and help him up. Jack jerked his arm away, not even looking at his dad. Ignoring the wet worksheets and his scattered homework papers, Jack scrambled to his feet, grabbed his math book, stepped around his dad, and hurried down the hall. The laughter died out amid the normal sounds of a few hundred kids passing classes. Jack jerked open his locker, grabbed his social studies book, kicked the door shut, and headed downstairs.

Six minutes later Jack was sitting on a stool in the art room at a worktable by himself. He pounded and pushed at the lump of reddish clay in front of him, both fists clenched.

Jack stared at the clay, replaying his humiliation again and again. Inside him a firestorm roared and hissed. It was impossible to keep it in.

So all of Jack's churning anger shot straight up through the art-room ceiling, a flaming tornado of hurt and embarrassment.

It hurtled through the halls of the old high school, smacking into lockers, crashing down stairwells, vaporizing doors and windows and walls.

And when his anger had reached maximum force and speed, it needed a target.

Kirk? A major annoyance, but hardly worth a full attack.

Luke? A total dweeb—not even on the radar screen.

Like a guided missile packed with deadly resentment, Jack's anger homed in on the ultimate target, the true cause of his problems, and at last it burst into hot crimson fragments above the unsuspecting head of John the janitor.

The sizzling chunks of Jack's burning rage stuck to his father—like gobs of well-chewed watermelon bubble gum.

Chapter 4

The Sweet Smell
of Victory

Sitting in English class with his heart pounding away, Jack reviewed the mission.

Just five minutes ago he had delivered a crushing blow to the enemy, a major assault—gummage in the first degree.

His music-room attack was undetected, the weapon was untraceable, and the result was unbelievably messy.

The only flaw was that Jack would not be able to watch his dad's face when he saw that desk. *If only I could be there,* he thought. *I could point at the desk and say, "Okay, Janitor John—janitor this!" Or maybe I'd say, "Go ahead, work your magic, Tidy Guy. You decided to go and become Mr. Clean—so here's a little present from your number one fan!"*

Jack grinned, savoring the imagined moment.

"Well, Jack? What is it?"

Uh-oh—battle stations. It was Mrs. Carroll in a

21

lime green pantsuit, bearing down from the front left flank. Artillery fire had already begun.

Jack straightened up in his chair, frantically scrolling through that tiny part of his brain that had been tracking the teacher, trying to recall her last two or three droning sentences. Something about parts of speech, something about—and in a flash he knew, like instant replay in his head. With the sweetest smile he could manage he said, "It's a preposition, right?"

Mrs. Carroll glared at him and edged a little closer. She'd been watching him from the corner of her eye for the past thirty seconds, and she could have sworn Jack Rankin was completely zoned out. Daydreaming was her pet peeve, and this was the fifth time she had tried—and failed—to catch Jack at it. Pursing her lips, she said, "Yes, the word *across* is a preposition." Her eyes narrowed and she edged half a step nearer. Mrs. Carroll reminded Jack of a green lizard getting ready to flip its tongue out to snap up a fly. She said, "Now, use it in a sentence."

The sentence that popped into Jack's head was, "The English teacher darted across the ceiling like a chameleon," but what he said was, "The fisherman paddled his canoe across the lake."

Lizard Woman glared at Jack an extra second or

two. She wanted to be sure he got the message that he had almost been a very dead fly.

"Yes," she said. "That's fine." Whirling away, she instantly settled on a new victim. "Jessie, in the sentence Jack just made up, what word is the *object* of the preposition?"

Surviving a direct hit from the reptile patrol was a little scary, so Jack assigned another tenth of his mind to the unpleasant job of watching out for Mrs. Carroll.

Glancing at the clock, Jack saw he had another thirty minutes of eighth period to go. With an inward smile he went back to his own thoughts, replaying his secret victory again and again—and Jack especially enjoyed thinking about that desk, sitting there like a sweet, sticky time bomb in the back row of the music room.

Chapter 5

School Justice

Mr. Pike reported the ruined desk to the office over the music-room intercom at the start of eighth period. Mr. Ackerby dropped what he was doing and hurried upstairs to take a look. He liked detective work, especially when the trail was fresh. The vice principal was on the case.

Looking at the desk with Mr. Pike, Mr. Ackerby shook his head. Then, just to be polite, he asked, "So, Dave, got any suspects for me?" Mr. Pike seemed like he was always in his own wacky little music zone, so Mr. Ackerby didn't expect him to be much help.

"Absolutely," said Mr. Pike. "Got it all figured out."

Mr. Ackerby's eyebrows shot up. "Really?" Like Jack, Mr. Ackerby didn't understand that a good choral director notices everything.

Mr. Pike nodded and said, "Clear as a bell. I've got fifty-six kids in that seventh-period class, and three on the absence list today, so fifty-three were here. I make the kids fill the room from front to back, and there are fifty-one chairs in the first four rows. I always look up to see who's late when the bell rings, and today Kerry Loomis and Jack Rankin were almost tardy. They had to be the only kids sitting in the last row today. I wouldn't think either of them would do this, but they were back there. I'm sure of that."

As he returned to the office Mr. Ackerby revised his opinion of Mr. Pike. Then he looked up the class schedules for Loomis, Kerry, and Rankin, Jack.

Five minutes later Mr. Ackerby had a quick conversation with the Loomis girl in the hallway outside her social studies class. Mr. Ackerby could tell she was innocent.

So it had to be the Rankin boy.

Someone was about to learn that there is no such thing as the perfect crime—especially at school. And he was going to learn it the hard way.

About twenty minutes into eighth period Mr. Ackerby appeared at the doorway of Jack's English class. He said, "Excuse me, Mrs. Carroll—I need to have a word with Jack Rankin."

Jack knew.

He knew why Mr. Ackerby wanted to talk with him.

As if in a fog, Jack got up from his desk and walked through the silent room, his face chalky white, his mouth dry.

One look and Mr. Ackerby was sure he had his man.

Mr. Ackerby closed the door to the classroom and glared down into Jack's pale face. Jack couldn't look him in the eye. Without raising his voice, Mr. Ackerby said, "Jack, I'd like you to walk down to the music room and bring a folding desk back to my office for me."

Jack gulped. Weakly, lamely, hopelessly, he asked, "Which desk?"

Mr. Ackerby's eyes flashed, and he said, "Hold out your hands."

Jack raised his hands up to about his waist, and Mr. Ackerby said, "Higher, and palms up." Leaning forward, Mr. Ackerby sniffed the left hand, and then the right one.

Watermelon.

Pointing at Jack's right hand, he said, "Bring me the desk that smells like *that*."

It was a long way to the music room. Jack was tempted to dash down the stairway and out the door and just keep running and running. But he knew he couldn't.

Mr. Pike was rehearsing with the seventh-grade

26

chorus. He looked up from his music stand when Jack came in. He shook his head and gave Jack a frown, but he didn't miss a beat. Jack grabbed the desk and made his way awkwardly back out the door.

As he walked to the office Jack's mind filled with images of the horrors to come. By the time he arrived at Mr. Ackerby's doorway, the desk seemed to weigh about three hundred pounds.

Mr. Ackerby was sitting on a bookcase by the window in his office, waiting. Pointing with a stubby index finger, he showed where he wanted the desk and motioned Jack into a chair. Then he walked over and tipped the folding desk onto its side so they could both get a good look at the incredible mess on the bottom. The office filled up with the heavy scent of the gum.

Mr. Ackerby shook his head. "Look at that! Unbelievable! What in the *world* could you have been thinking? Tell me, Jack. What *were* you thinking?"

Mr. Ackerby had not had time to read Jack's school record, so he didn't know that Jack was a pretty good student and had never been in any real trouble at the elementary school.

At this moment all Mr. Ackerby knew was that this kid in blue jeans and a black T-shirt had

27

worked pretty hard to destroy a desk. And whenever he caught someone damaging property, Mr. Ackerby didn't have to pretend to be angry. It was the real thing.

Jack looked steadily at the man's brown necktie and tried not to flinch. Jack could smell the man's shampoo, his shaving cream, his aftershave lotion, the ham-and-mustard sandwich he had eaten for lunch, and the mint he was sucking on.

Jack was angry at his dad, and he was angry at himself, and he hated the way things were spinning out of control. He clenched his jaw and worked very hard to keep his eyes from filling with tears.

Jack had been asked a question, and Mr. Ackerby didn't like waiting. He leaned forward and spoke even louder. "I *demand* an answer, young man. Look at this mess! What *were* you thinking?"

Jack glanced at the desk, then into Mr. Ackerby's squinty eyes, and then back to his ugly necktie. Jack couldn't quite explain that question to himself, not clearly, and there was no way he was going to open up and try to explain all his feelings to this guy.

So Jack said, "I don't know. I just . . . I just did it."

As if he could not believe what he was hearing,

Mr. Ackerby bent his face down close to Jack's and repeated, "You 'just did it'? Well, you know what, buddy boy? You're going to just UN-did it!"

He turned on his heel, and after a couple of quick steps sat down at his desk with a *thump.* Mr. Ackerby grabbed a pen and began writing a note on a stationery pad. He finished it, ripped it off, sealed it in an envelope, and began writing again. He said, "I'm sending a note home to your parents, and I'll be putting a memo in your permanent file. And starting today, you can cancel all your after-school plans."

Mr. Ackerby ripped the second piece of paper off the notepad, sealed it in another envelope, then stood up and walked over to Jack. Handing him the first envelope, he said, "This is for you to take home to your parents. Get it signed, bring it back tomorrow."

Turning around, he nudged the desk with the toe of his brown shoe. "You take this ruined desk down to the janitor's workshop in the basement by the boys gym. Then get back to your class." Mr. Ackerby paused, and handed Jack the second envelope. "Immediately after school you go back to the workshop and you hand *this* envelope to the chief custodian, and you tell him that you have volunteered for after-school gum patrol—an hour a day—for the next three weeks. Now get going."

School justice, exactly the way Mr. Ackerby liked it—swift and certain.

As Jack lugged the smelly desk through the empty hallways and then down the stairs into the workshop, he was praying no one would be there—and no one was. He set the desk in the middle of the room and ran back up the stairs. He got to his English class just as the bell was ringing. He copied the assignment off the board, picked up his books, and went to social studies.

All during ninth period Jack fretted and worried. He wondered how much his dad would yell at him. He wondered if his mom would ground him. He wondered if something like this in his file would keep him from playing football when he got to high school. And he wondered if Mr. Ackerby had any idea that "the chief custodian" was his dad.

Jack felt stupid for getting caught, and even worse, now he'd have to be the junior janitor for three whole weeks. There was no way out. If anyone in the school hadn't figured out that John the janitor was his dad, they wouldn't be left out of the secret for long.

And of course, there was only one person to blame for the whole mess. Jack clenched his teeth and pressed his lips together, barely containing an urge to spit. And he thought, *Thanks again,* Dad.

Chapter 6

REPORTING FOR DUTY

People said Jack looked like his dad, and he hated it. They said it often enough that Jack guessed it was true. Sure, he could see that they both had straight brown hair parted near the middle, and the same thick eyebrows that almost touched above the same deep-set brown eyes. Jack was a little taller than about half the other fifth-grade kids. He guessed he was on track to end up about the same height as his dad, just under six feet, and he already had the same strong arms and broad shoulders. Even Jack's real name was the same—John Philip Rankin Jr.

But the likeness went deeper than that, deeper than Jack liked to admit. It was more than the lines cut by a strong chin or a straight nose, more than a certain smile or a way of walking or a pattern of speech.

Like his dad, Jack was mostly quiet and thoughtful. He was happy to be on his own, but he could also be friendly and quick to smile. He wasn't shy, but when he spoke, he spoke carefully.

There was a steadiness about Jack most of the time—unless you got on his bad side. Jack didn't get mad easily, and neither did his dad. But when either of them *did* get mad, look out.

And as Jack went to find his dad after school he was ready for the worst.

Jack stopped on the metal stairs leading down to the shop. The shop was next to the boiler room, so it was always cozy down there during the cold months. The main boiler was running now, and the roar of the burner made the stairs tremble beneath Jack's feet. The air coming up past him was loaded with different smells, workshop smells. The air was warm, but it didn't seem cozy, not today.

Jack set his face into a hard "Who cares?" sort of look. He took a deep breath and started down the stairs.

Halfway down, Jack let out a sigh of relief. The place was empty. The folding desk was still sitting in the middle of the gray concrete floor, right where he had left it earlier. Dim afternoon sunshine from the window well on the far wall made a small patch of light on the floor. The only other light came from the lamp on his dad's desk.

Mr. Ackerby had told him to go to the shop after school, and here he was. Jack thought, *It's not my fault if Mr. Big-Shot Janitor is busy somewhere else.* So Jack crossed the workshop to his dad's desk and sat down.

Jack tipped back in the old swivel chair and slowly spun it around. As he did he looked up at the bookshelves mounted on the wall behind the desk. He didn't remember seeing them before. A row of binders on the top shelf caught his eye. Each notebook was carefully labeled. PLUMBING LOG, ROOFING SCHEDULE, GROUNDSKEEPING, BOILER MAINTENANCE, SUPPLIES & EQUIPMENT, PURCHASING, ALARM & BELL SYSTEMS, FIRE CONTROL SYSTEMS, ELECTRICAL SYSTEM—there were more than a dozen binders. The lower shelf was jammed with fat catalogs from suppliers, some of them twice as thick as the Yellow Pages.

One catalog was labeled LEWIS BROTHERS— POWER EQUIPMENT. Jack loved tools, and he was good at making things, fixing things. His dad had got him his own toolbox for Christmas when he was seven, and he'd been gradually filling it with tools—real ones, not kids' tools.

Jack stood up to reach for the tool catalog when suddenly the room flooded with fluorescent light. A booming voice said, "You looking for something?"

Jack turned around, startled, and the man halfway down the stairs saw his face. He grinned and said,

"Hey, it's Jackie boy! Look at the size of you—you must've picked up two inches since July! No wonder they sent you over to the high school this year."

Jack smiled and said, "Hi, Lou. Um . . . I've got to talk to my dad."

Lou chuckled as he came the rest of the way down to the shop. "Thought maybe you were some kid come here to check a book out of your daddy's library."

Lou Carswell was a tall, slender man with short-cropped hair and stooped shoulders. He and his wife had come to Jack's house for Sunday suppers and summer barbecues plenty of times. Lou had been working at the high school almost as long as John Rankin.

There was a poorly focused photo on his dad's dresser—four young guys in army uniforms. Jack knew one of them was his dad, and he was pretty sure one of them was Lou. He had never asked, but that's how it looked.

Lou said, "If you're waitin' for your dad, you got a long stretch ahead of you. He's up on three west in the science lab, fixing a motor in the ventilator. You'd best walk up there and find him."

Jack said, "No . . . it's okay. I can wait."

Lou shook his head and motioned toward the stairs with his thumb. "I'm not kiddin', Jackie—he's probably got another forty minutes of work on that unit, so just pick up and get up there to room 336 right now—go on. He'll be glad to see you."

With the note from Mr. Ackerby weighing him down, Jack started the long hike to the third floor, palms sweating, mouth dry. He trudged up the stairs like a convict headed for the gallows.

Jack could have found his way just by following his nose. He had noticed a strange electrical smell all over the school right after lunch. As he approached room 336 the sharp odor of burned wiring got stronger and stronger. Peeking in the doorway, Jack saw his dad bent over the ventilator by the windows, his left arm completely inside the casing. He was reaching for something. Vent covers and spools of wire, nuts and bolts, pliers, wrenches, and wire clippers were spread out all over the floor and the nearest lab tables.

Taking a deep breath, Jack walked in and said, "Hi, Dad."

John Rankin turned his head. He smiled and said, "Hey, this is a surprise—good timing, too." He straightened up and pulled a flashlight from his back pocket. "I dropped a nut down behind the new motor assembly, and I can't get my hand in there to pick it up. Thought I was going to have to go all the way down to the shop and get a magnet. Here, I'm going to shine the light down from over this side, and you see if your hand can fit behind there and get it."

Jack thought, *What makes him think that I want to get all covered with grease and dirt like he is?* But Jack took a look down into the register, and then leaned way over, threaded his hand in, and came out with the nut. "Here."

"Great! That's going to save me some time." John Rankin straightened up and smiled at his son, and tossed him a rag to wipe off his hand. Looking into Jack's face for the first time, he saw right away this wasn't a social visit. In a quieter voice he said, "What's on your mind, Jack?"

Jack looked at the floor and said, "I . . . I got myself in some trouble, Dad." And he handed his father the note from Mr. Ackerby.

John pulled a chair out from under a lab table and sat down. He took his reading glasses from his shirt pocket and perched them on the end of his nose. Then he tore open the envelope, unfolded the paper, and started to read. Jack watched his face.

John Rankin read two lines and then looked up sharply at Jack, his dark eyebrows lifted in disbelief. "It was *you*? You're the one who messed up the desk that's down in the shop?" Jack reddened, but he met his father's eyes with a sullen look and nodded.

36

His dad looked back to the note. It only took him another ten seconds to finish it. He put the paper back in the envelope and laid it on the scarred black lab table. He took off his glasses and tucked them into his pocket. Then he turned his head and looked out the window. A brisk wind was pushing the fallen leaves into heaps along the fence around the football field.

John Rankin cleared his throat. "Hard to know what to make of this, son." There was a long pause, as if he hoped Jack would offer an explanation. Jack kept silent. Then John said, "But I guess there's time." He tapped the envelope on the lab table. "According to this, seems like we've got three weeks to get to the bottom of it."

John stood up and walked over to the ventilator. He looked in his toolbox and picked up a wrench, squinted at it to read the size, and then turned his back to Jack, both arms down inside the cabinet again. He said, "You know that door to the right of my desk down in the shop?"

Jack said, "Sure," and he thought, *What, does he think I'm a dummy?*

His dad continued, "Go inside and look on the shelves to the left. There's a can of special solvent called OFFIT that's pretty good with the fresh stuff. And you'll need a roll of paper towels and some rubber gloves and a stiff-bladed putty knife for the hardened gum. Toss your supplies in a plastic bucket to carry 'em around. Easier that way. And you'll need a trash bag. The buckets and the trash bags are behind the door to the right. After that folding desk is clean and back in the music room, you can move on to the tables and chairs in the library. I'll be checking your work, and I've got a feeling that Mr. Ackerby will too."

John turned around and tossed the wrench back into the toolbox. The metallic clatter made Jack jump. His dad said, "Any questions?"

"No."

"Then get to it."

John Rankin turned back to the broken ventilator, and Jack turned and headed back to the workshop for the third time today.

Jack felt so relieved he practically skipped down the empty stairway. His dad hadn't even yelled at him. Maybe it was a sign, a good omen. Maybe his mom wouldn't ground him. And maybe Ackerby would lighten up and let him off the hook after a week or so.

Who could say? Maybe gum patrol wasn't going to be so bad after all.

Then Jack caught himself. *What, am I nuts? Gum patrol not so bad? Yeah, right.*

Chapter 7

Gum Patrol

Jack got to the shop and gathered his supplies. The folding desk was waiting for him.

Jack turned the desk upside down on the workshop floor and bent over to take a careful look, poking here and there with his finger. His research had been right on target. Fresh watermelon Bubblicious was very sticky, very disgusting.

Jack stood up, clenched his jaw, and gave the desk a swift kick. This was *supposed* to be his dad's job. Still, Jack was smart enough to appreciate the irony of getting stuck in his own trap, so he heaved a big sigh, turned the underside of the desk toward the light, and went to work.

Jack launched his attack with the putty knife. Big mistake. The gum was too fresh. It smeared around, covering more of the surface. It took him five minutes to clean the blade of the putty knife, and when he was done, he had to shake his hand until the tool clattered to the floor, its black plastic handle fouled with crimson.

Then Jack crumpled up a paper towel and tried rubbing. The paper ripped to shreds. It added a layer of sticky white fiber on the goo, like grass clippings blown onto fresh road tar.

Finally, he tried putting two layers of paper towel around the end of the putty knife. Pushing with the covered end of the blade, he was able to plow up a ridge of gum. Then he could close the paper towel around the glob and pull it off. The threads created by pulling off wads of gum fell onto the workshop floor. The mess kept spreading to a wider and wider area.

Gob after strand after wad, Jack scraped and pulled and rubbed until, twenty minutes later, only a massive smear was left.

Time for the solvent. Jack read the directions on the can and then poured some OFFIT onto a folded paper towel and started to rub. The gum dissolved as if by magic, staining the paper towel crimson but leaving a clean surface behind. Inch by inch, Jack rubbed and rubbed until the job was done.

The desk was no longer sticky, gooey, or smelly, but Jack was another story. There was gum on the front and back of both hands, and bits of paper towel were stuck between his fingers. There were thin strands of gum crisscrossing his shoes and shoelaces. Both knees of his jeans had crimson spots, and there was a glob the size of a pea stuck in the hair of his right eyebrow.

Carefully reading the OFFIT label again, Jack made sure it was safe to use the solvent on himself. In another few minutes he had got most of the gum off his hands and shoes and pants. The can said to keep the liquid away from eyes, so Jack just picked and pulled at the gum in his eyebrow until he'd got most of it out. It still felt funny, but when he looked at his face in the mirror over the utility sink, he could see only a trace of crimson. Good enough for now.

Jack stuffed the sticky paper towels into a trash barrel by the stairs. Then he took the clean desk back to the music room, and had to find Lou to have him open the door. On the way back he stopped at his locker to get his backpack and coat, and finally ran back to the workshop to put the equipment away.

It was 3:25, and today's hour of gum patrol was officially over.

Jack ran up the workshop stairs, streaked down the hallway toward the back door, and just barely got onto the last late bus. Dropping onto a squeaky seat as the bus lurched out of the parking lot, Jack was panting, but relieved.

41

If he had missed this bus, it would have caused other problems. He would have had to hang out for at least another hour and ride home with his dad, something he didn't want to do, not ever—and especially not today.

If he had ridden home with his dad, then the *other* note from Mr. Ackerby would have been delivered to both his parents at once. Jack was pretty sure things would go better if his mom read the note first, all by herself.

At least, that's what he hoped.

Chapter 8

HUNG JURY

Mrs. Rankin got home from work at four fifteen every day, so Jack was cutting it close. He ran the half block from the bus stop, let himself in, and hung up his coat and backpack in the front closet. He could tell by sniffing that his mom wasn't home yet and that dinner hadn't been started.

Jack dashed into the living room and struck a quick deal with his little sister. "Listen, Lois. Don't tell Mom I got home so late today, okay? And don't tell her I forgot to call Mrs. Genarro. It's worth a dollar if you keep your mouth shut, okay?"

If Jack missed the bus, he was supposed to call their neighbor so she could keep a lookout for Lois.

His sister didn't take her eyes off the TV. She asked, "Is it worth a dollar fifty?" Lois was in third grade. She thought her parents made too big a deal about her life after school. But now and then it was useful to have everyone worried about her.

Jack gritted his teeth. "Fine. A dollar fifty." He

43

didn't have time to haggle, and he didn't need another issue, not right now, not just before a trial.

A minute later the station wagon pulled into the driveway, a door slammed at the garage on the alley, and Mom was at the kitchen door, her huge purse over one arm and a bag of groceries in the other. Jack was down the steps in no time, being helpful.

"Thanks, Jackie. Put the ice cream in the freezer right away, would you? And the milk needs to be put away too." His mom came up the stairs behind him, laid her coat over the back of a chair, and immediately pulled out a box of macaroni. "Put some water on to boil, will you, Jack? Use the deep saucepan."

"Mmmm . . . macaroni and cheese tonight?" asked Jack, reaching into the cabinet below the stove for the pan.

His mom nodded. "Yup." Then she added with a smile, "How'd you guess?"

Jack grinned back. "Just a genius."

Things were going well. A little helpfulness, a little humor.

Jack knew all about timing. In a case like this timing was everything. Now was the right moment, because at the first real pause in the flow his mom would ask that dreaded question, "What happened at school today?" He had to tell her before she asked, so it wouldn't look like he had been trying to hold something back. A point for helpfulness, a point for cheerfulness, a point for being honest about bad news. Jack needed all the points he could get.

Mrs. Rankin sat down at the table with her recipe box, looking for her old baked macaroni and cheese recipe. Jack took notice. Sitting down is good, more relaxed.

Jack quickly slipped into the chair next to her and said, "Mom, I got in some trouble at school today. I got caught sticking gum on the bottom of a desk. I know it was wrong, and I'm being punished for it. I've got a note for you and Dad from the vice principal." He handed her the note.

One clean, smooth action. A brief introduction, a complete confession, a dash of sorrow, and a short explanation. Jack hoped his opening remarks would lessen the impact of Mr. Ackerby's note. The man had only taken about a minute to write it—how bad could it be?

Lois had a built-in radar for drama. The show in the kitchen was a lot better than the one on TV. She crept silently to the doorway behind her mom and peered around the corner at Jack. She made a face and shook her finger at him, as if she were saying, *Naughty, naughty, naughty.* Jack glared at her, but Lois stayed put, a smug little smile on her face.

45

Mrs. Rankin broke the seal on the envelope. It was time for Exhibit A, the note.

Jack thought the jury would be sympathetic to his case. He was hoping he would get time off for good behavior.

Jack had underestimated Mr. Ackerby's talents as a writer.

As Mrs. Rankin scanned the note her lips pressed together into a thin line and her eyes narrowed.

Not good.

Then she read Exhibit A aloud:

Dear Mr. and Mrs. Rankin:

I'm sorry to report that your son, Jack, did his best to ruin a desk today. In a deliberate act of vandalism he completely fouled the underside of a folding desk during his music class. The quantity of bubble gum he applied can only be described as enormous. His action required forethought and planning. It seems like an angry gesture to me. Yet when I asked him why he did it, he did not answer me. I will alert our counseling staff to this incident.

In the meantime, Jack will be required to stay after school one hour each day for the next three weeks. He will be helping our custodial staff clean gum off of furniture throughout the school.

Please call if you wish to discuss this matter further.

Sincerely,

Mr. Ronald Ackerby

Vice Principal, Huntington Middle School

Helen Rankin did not explode. It took some doing, but she was too smart to get angry. Not about this. Anger would be the wrong response.

Helen wasn't angry, because she knew something that Mr. Ackerby didn't—at least, not yet. She knew that the "custodial staff" was headed up by Jack's dad, John Rankin.

She also knew her son. She knew this stunt was not about destroying property. She knew Jack hadn't done this just for kicks.

There was something else going on.

Helen Rankin had seen this coming, and here it was.

Jack was trying to get some clues from his mom's face after she'd read the note out loud. It was a tough call. Angry? Not quite. Sad? Yes, there was some sadness. But there was a whole bunch of other stuff going on that Jack couldn't pin down. He couldn't tell what was going to happen.

Helen Rankin spoke quietly, and all she said was, "Jack, I'm going to have to talk to your dad about this. You should go to your room and do homework until I call you for dinner."

Lois vanished from the doorway.

Jack said, "Okay, Mom." He pushed his chair back from the table, stood up, and walked out to the front closet to get his backpack.

It was the old go-wait-in-your-room situation. No decision. A hung jury. He headed up the stairs.

As Jack passed Lois's room she opened her door six inches, smiled sweetly, and stuck out her hand.

Jack thought, *Here I am, waiting on death row, and she wants her stinking dollar fifty!*

But there was something on Lois's palm. She batted her eyelashes, nodded down at her hand, and whispered, "Hey, Jack, want a piece of . . . *gum?*"

Lois got the door shut and locked just in time.

Jack put his face next to the door and hissed, "You are dead meat, funny girl."

Lois giggled and said, "I think I shall need *two* dollars. . . . Yes, two dollars will be enough. For now. But no coins—nice, crisp bills, please."

Jack kicked the bottom of her door and went down the hallway to his cell.

Chapter 9

Boy Territory

Jack's mom had known her husband since they went to Huntington High School together. Helen Parkman had first met John Rankin when he was in eleventh grade and she was in ninth. She had watched him catching touchdown passes for the Huntington Heralds during Friday-night football games. She had seen him at dances with his girl-friend, a cheerleader. She had seen him washing cars on Saturdays at his dad's used-car lot.

Helen Parkman had watched John Rankin from a distance. They knew each other, but they had never really been friends, not back then. John's family had some money, and they lived on the nicer side of town. Helen's family didn't. It was as simple as that. John Rankin was a golden boy, one of those kids "Most Likely to Succeed."

Then one day in the spring of 1967, just two months before his high school graduation, John Rankin disappeared. He had joined the army. It made quite a stir at Huntington High School. A lot of boys were getting drafted into the army because it was the middle of the Vietnam War. But no one was signing up for military service on purpose, not the infantry, and not for a four-year hitch. John had just turned eighteen, he had been accepted at a good college, and he might not have had to go into the service at all. There were savage pictures of the war on the evening news every day. It seemed like you'd have to be crazy to join the army.

It was a mystery back then. Why did he leave? When had he come back? How did he end up as the janitor at the high school?

Now Helen Rankin knew all the hows and whens and whys. Now she understood. And it all made perfect sense in the flow of her husband's life, in the long view.

But how could she help an eleven-year-old understand all that?

And how could she help her husband not feel hurt to learn that Jack was embarrassed—ashamed to have his classmates know his father was the school janitor?

Helen Rankin was a strong person. She had taken courses at the local junior college, and now she worked as a paralegal secretary for the town government. She had the respect of her co-workers and her boss. She took good care of her kids, and she and her husband made a good home for their family.

The only thing that made Helen feel helpless was this—being caught between her husband and her son.

She had a name for the feeling.

Helen Rankin was lost in Boy Territory.

When John Rankin's pickup pulled into the driveway at quarter of six, everybody in the house heard it.

For Jack it meant that the rest of his jury had arrived.

For his sister it meant that there would be more drama, more adventures in spying.

For his mom it meant that a delicate balancing act was about to begin.

Helen Rankin looked through the window over the sink. John didn't get out of the truck right away. When he did, he looked tired. She met him at the back door with a hug and a kiss.

He smiled and held her at arm's length. "So how's my best girl?"

She smiled back and said, "I've been better. I hear from Mr. Ackerby that you've got a new assistant for the next three weeks."

Helen hadn't been planning to bring up the subject so soon, but it seemed the most honest thing to do. No sense pretending they weren't both thinking about it.

Following his wife up the steps to the kitchen, John said, "That's a fact. Jack cleaned the desk he gummed up today. Took him most of an hour, but he did a good job. 'Course, the shop's a wreck, and I hate to think what his clothes are like. I've never seen such a mess."

John pulled out a chair and straddled it, his elbows on the seat back. Helen started peeling carrots at the sink. She asked, "Any idea why he did it?"

John pulled his note from Mr. Ackerby out of his shirt pocket and tapped it on the chair back. "Well, the vice principal says it was just vandalism, but I think there's more to it, don't you? And you know what? I helped Ackerby plan and organize that move all last summer, so you'd think he could put two and two together—I don't think that guy has it figured out that Jack's my son."

Helen kept peeling carrots, but turned and nodded toward the table. "I'm sure he doesn't know yet. That's the note . . . to the parents." Helen went to the refrigerator and got out a head of lettuce, glancing at John's face as he opened the second letter and started to read.

Turning back to the sink, she kept her voice even and asked, "What do you think? Is Mr. Ackerby right? Do you think Jack was angry?"

John Rankin didn't answer right away.

Helen wasn't sure what was coming. This was Boy Territory.

John started slowly. "Here's how I see it. We know Jack had to do it on purpose, and he knew a desk that messy would end up down in my shop. So I'm guessing that Jack's mad at me. It's been like he's wanted nothing to do with me for a long time. He hasn't said a word to me at school so far, not until last Monday."

Then John told Helen about cleaning up the floor and saying hi to Jack in his math class—and about the collision in the hall.

It was the perfect opening. Helen said, "John, I think Jack was very embarrassed by that. I think that solves the mystery."

John spoke slowly. "I know he was embarrassed by that fall in the hallway—but you mean he was embarrassed about *me*, right?"

Helen nodded.

There was an awkward silence. John said, "Makes sense. Smart, good-looking kid, and his old man's the janitor."

Another silence.

Then John said, "And thanks to Ackerby, now Jack's a janitor too. John Junior, the little janitor. He's really going to hate me now."

Helen turned around and said, "It'll all work out. You know Jack could never hate you, John."

John shook his head. "You'd maybe think different if you'd seen what he did to that desk." With some bitterness in his voice he added, "Of course, Jack doesn't stop and remember that he's never gone to bed hungry in his life, and that when he needs a new pair of shoes, there they are, just like magic. He's happy to have the money I make by cleaning up after people, isn't he?"

John stood up stiffly and walked to the side window. After a minute he said, "But there's no use getting mad about it. I just wish I knew what to do."

Helen wished the same thing. She said, "Well, you're going to see a lot more of each other during the next three weeks. It'll work out all right. I'm sure it will."

John Rankin hoped she was right.

Chapter 10

RUMORS

Jack couldn't believe it.

Dinner was a breeze. No yelling. No angry silences. His dad seemed a little quieter than usual, but that was about it. Jack kept quiet too.

There was some chitchat about school assignments and grades. Mom had some news about Aunt Mary and Uncle Bob driving up from Des Moines to visit at Thanksgiving. Ordinary dinner talk, with Mom doing most of the talking.

Lois was disappointed. She had been hoping for fireworks, a major scene with red faces and everybody spitting mad. Just once she wanted to see a big family blowup—with Jack as the target, of course. She stabbed her fork into the last piece of macaroni on her plate, ate it, drained her milk glass, and asked to be excused from the table.

As bedtime approached, Jack took inventory.

He wasn't grounded.

He still had full telephone privileges.

His allowance was intact.

Jack was pretty sure he could even get away without paying Lois her hush money.

It was almost like nothing had happened.

Jack was expecting a long, serious talk at bedtime, but it didn't happen. Mom said she was sure he had learned his lesson, and Jack said he was sure he had. She kissed him on the forehead, tucked the covers around him, said, "Sweet dreams," and shut his door.

Down the hall Jack heard his dad open Lois's door and say, "Good night, sweetheart." And he heard Lois say, "G'night, Daddy."

"Little Miss Perfect," Jack muttered.

Then Jack heard his dad's footsteps come toward his door. He thought, *Oh boy, here it comes.* He braced himself and quickly decided to pretend he was asleep.

The footsteps stopped. Then they began again, but his dad had turned around. Jack listened until his dad started down the stairs.

"That's fine by me," Jack said aloud to himself. "The last thing I need is a little sermon from the Broom King."

So the public part of Jack's long Monday ended.

But Jack's private day wasn't over. He lay awake for almost an hour.

Tuesday was coming. Jack looked at his alarm clock. The bus would arrive at his corner in exactly ten hours and twelve minutes—no, eleven minutes.

On Tuesday he'd have to go back to school.

Back to the scene of the crime.

Tuesday morning came right on schedule. The bus ride was uneventful, which was good. Jack needed to be on time so he could get rid of the letter his mom and dad had signed. He had to get it back to Mr. Ackerby.

Jack didn't go to his locker. He went right to the office, arriving there just as the sixth-grade buses were pulling up at the curb on Main Street. Jack chose that moment on purpose. He knew that Mr. Ackerby always met the morning buses out front.

He walked up to the school secretary's desk and said, "Excuse me. . . . Mr. Ackerby said I had to bring this letter back to him."

Mrs. Carter looked up from her computer screen, and her eyes flickered as she recognized him. "Oh . . . yes. Jack Rankin." Jack blushed a little.

She looked him in the face, trying to connect the story she'd heard with this polite young man standing in front of her desk. He certainly didn't look like a troublemaker to her. *Still,* she thought, *looks can be deceiving.*

Mrs. Carter held out her hand. "Mr. Ackerby's not here right now. Leave it with me, and I'll be sure he gets it."

Jack handed it to her with a polite smile, said, "Thank you," and left.

Easy as pie. Jack had passed the Note Return Test with flying colors.

It wasn't that he was afraid to meet up with Mr. Ackerby again. Jack just didn't see what good it would do. They would meet again, guaranteed. And whenever that was, that would be soon enough for Jack.

A school is like a small town. Even ordinary news travels fast.

But a really juicy story that involves crime and punishment can easily hit speeds of one or two hundred mouths an hour.

By eight forty-five on Tuesday morning the legend of Jack the Gummer was just hitting warp speed.

Jack's best friend was Pete Ramsey. The spelling of their last names had kept them sitting next to each other almost every year since kindergarten. This year they had the same homeroom and their lockers were side by side.

Jack had just pulled open the metal door when he noticed Pete. Pete had recently started wearing cologne, and Jack could always tell when he was in the area. Today Pete was also chewing gum— *Juicy Fruit,* Jack said to himself.

Without looking around, Jack said, "Hi, Pete."

There was no answer. Jack turned, and Pete was there, but he was just staring at him, his mouth open, gum on his tongue.

Pete said, "What are *you* doing here?"

"Uhh . . . standing at my locker?" asked Jack. "Is that the answer? Do I win the big prize?"

Pete was serious. "I thought you got expelled."

"Expelled?" said Jack. "What for?"

"For swearing at Mr. Pike during chorus and then sticking gum all over Mr. Ackerby's desk. Did you call Mr. Pike names—or what?"

Jack said, "Who told you all that?"

"It's everywhere," said Pete. "I heard it waiting in line down at the school store."

"Well, it's not true," said Jack. "All I did was stick a bunch of gum on the bottom of a folding desk—one desk. I got caught, and now I have to stay and clean off gum after school. That's all."

Pete said, "No swearing?"

"None," said Jack.

59

"No big fight with Mr. Ackerby?"

Jack shook his head. "Nope. He yelled at me, and he sent a note home to my folks, but I'm not even grounded."

The facts were pretty boring, and Pete lost interest immediately. As he began to dial his combination he shrugged. Then he said, "Hey, Little League registration is at the new high school gym this Saturday. You going?"

Jack leaned against the lockers and listened to Pete. He said "uh-huh" and nodded at the right moments, but he was thinking about the outrageous rumors.

Then, above Pete's chatter, Jack heard Luke using his best stage voice.

Luke said, "Hey, Kirk, look who's here! It's Gumbo."

Kirk Dorfmann's locker was across the hall. Kirk walked over, and Luke followed along.

Kirk said, "Yeah, you're right. It's Gumbo, son of Scumbo the Janitor. So, how's it going, Gumbo?"

Pete stepped between Jack and Kirk, his shoulders squared and fists clenched. With a sneer he said, "Hey look, Jack. It knows how to talk. I think its name is Tommy Polo Nautica. Run along now, Tommy Polo Nautica. You might get your nice yellow jacket all messed up."

Pete was not kidding, and Kirk knew it.

"Sure," said Kirk, "no problem. We were just leaving anyway—right, Luke? We want to go watch the janitor fold up the tables in the cafeteria."

Luke said, "Yeah, because he's so talented, y'know? See you guys later."

Pete and Jack watched them until they turned the corner at the end of the hallway.

"Dirtbags," said Pete.

"Yeah," said Jack. "Grade-A jerks. Thanks, Pete."

From what Pete had said about the rumors, Jack didn't know what to expect for the rest of the day.

But homeroom was normal, and the morning classes, too. Every once in a while Jack would notice a kid looking at him curiously. But when the rumor says you're expelled and you clearly are *not* expelled, reality wins.

Still, as he headed up the stairs after lunch Jack thought he saw two seventh-grade teachers giving him weird sideways glances. *Figures*, he thought. *Teachers gossip too.*

After school there was a note for Jack taped to the door of the supply closet in the workshop. It was from his dad.

Jack—

Start on the tables and chairs in the library today. Mrs. Stokely is usually there after school, but if she's not, you can find Lou down near the auditorium, and Arnie is sweeping on two and three. I'll be fixing a toilet up on four if you need me.

Dad

Toilets, thought Jack. *Great. My dad's in the toilet repair business.*

Jack pushed the door open and went into the supply closet. First, he got a fresh roll of paper towels. The putty knife, the solvent, and the rubber gloves were right where he had left them. Today he planned to use the rubber gloves.

Then he remembered his dad had said to use a bucket to carry stuff around. *Why not?* Jack thought. *After all, he's the big expert.*

Jack turned around to look on the other set of shelves. There were wet-mop heads and dust-mop heads, mop wringers, handle setups, big cans of liquid wax, two-gallon bottles of ammonia—but no buckets. Jack pulled the door out of the way and found what he needed: two stacks of buckets, metal and plastic.

Glancing up, Jack saw a gray wooden cabinet

hanging on the wall. It had been hidden behind the open door. Shallower than a medicine cabinet, it came out only about two inches from the wall. It was almost three feet wide and had hinges on either side so the doors could open out from the center. A hasp and a padlock held the cabinet doors shut.

It was an unusual padlock, the old kind—round, and made of solid brass, with rivets and a little flap on the side to cover the keyhole. Jack pushed the door of the closet out of the way to let the light shine on the lock.

As he took half a step forward to get a closer look Jack discovered something interesting.

The old brass lock was not snapped shut.

Chapter 11

Open Sesame

An open lock is a temptation for some people. For Jack it was more like an invitation. It wasn't like he was cracking a safe or robbing a bank. He was only interested in the lock—at first.

He pulled on it, and the curved shackle swung open on its pivot. Sliding the shackle out of the loop of the hasp, he turned toward the light to get a better look at the thing.

Cool and heavy in his hand, it was like a work of art. Jack flipped it over and read the words engraved on the back—THE CHAMPION LOCK COMPANY. And below the name was the patent date—1898! It was the kind of lock that stirs the imagination.

Turning back to the cabinet, Jack was all set to put the lock back just as he'd found it. But almost as an afterthought he flipped the latch off the doors and pulled on both at once.

There was a soft jingling, and as the doors opened wide so did Jack's eyes and mouth.

Keys.

They ran from the top left of the left-hand door to the bottom right of the right-hand door.

Row after row after row of keys.

Jack had found the key safe. Almost every big building has one. The cabinet held long rows of nails spaced far enough apart so keys could hang side by side and top to bottom without bumping. Each nail was tilted slightly upward so the keys would not fall off as the doors were opened and closed.

Each nail held at least one key, and some held as many as ten or twelve in little brass-and-silver stacks. On top of each pile there was a small, round identification tag.

Jack's eyes roamed over the stacks of keys, reading the tags. RM. 227, RM. 228, and so on; BOYS LCKR. RM.; ART SUPPL. CLOSET; CAFT. FREEZER; MAIN OFFICE.

Every classroom, every closet, every washroom, every office, every desk and cabinet and cupboard in the old high school had a lock, and every lock had a key, and every key was right there, staring Jack Rankin in the face.

His mind was reeling, and it's a credit to Jack's character that he didn't immediately begin to imagine some real crimes. It would have been so simple.

Jack sensed this. It made him uneasy.

He was about to close the doors, but then he thought,

Hey, wait a second—I'm like a janitor now, right? And the janitor can have any keys he wants. I'll just consider this a little present from Ackerby and dear old Dad.

Stepping in closer, Jack looked over the key tags again. Down near the lower right-hand corner he saw two stacks of keys, side by side. One was labeled BELL TOWER. The other was labeled STEAM TUNNEL.

For Jack these labels didn't suggest the chance to steal something, the chance to look up answers in a teacher's textbook, the chance to mess with the principal's computer or goof up the clock and bell system.

The attraction of these particular keys was much more powerful.

These keys suggested adventure.

BELL TOWER. No secret there. The tower on the high school ruled Huntington's tiny skyline. And finding it would be easy—just keep going up.

But STEAM TUNNEL? That was different. That was a mystery.

Jack thought, *What the heck is a steam tunnel anyway? And where would I look for one? And if I found it, where would it go?*

Carefully, suddenly alert to each small sound, Jack hooked the padlock onto the belt loop of his jeans. Then he used both hands to lift the stack of tower keys off its nail. There were seven keys in all, each one stamped with the number 501. Jack took the key from the bottom of the stack and then put the other six back on the board. He quickly repeated the process for the tunnel keys, taking the fifth one and replacing the remaining four. The tunnel keys were stamped with the number 73.

Stepping back with the two keys in his hand, Jack scanned the rows in the cabinet. No one would be able to tell that two little keys were missing, not just by looking. It was like borrowing two pebbles from a beach. *Borrowing,* Jack said to himself, *not stealing.*

Footsteps.

On the metal stairs.

Coming down into the shop.

Jamming the keys into the front pocket of his jeans, Jack closed the cabinet quickly, trying not to make anything jangle. He pulled the padlock from his belt loop and set it back in place, almost shut, just like it had been.

Grabbing a plastic bucket from the stack, he bumped into the metal pails on purpose. He tossed the can of OFFIT and the putty knife noisily into his bucket, grabbed the towels and gloves, and went out through the supply closet door just as Arnie reached the bottom of the stairs.

"Hi, Arnie," he said, smiling. His heart was pounding.

"Hey, Jack. Heard that I'd be seeing you around.

67

Got *stuck* with a little project, right?"

Arnie was a big joker, and he found himself very easy to amuse. He was a heavyset guy, and going up or down stairs made Arnie's face match his red hair and freckles. Laughing turned him a shade or two deeper. That much red made a striking contrast to the green collar of his work shirt.

Jack laughed too, mostly from relief. He was glad it hadn't been his dad coming to the shop. His dad might have noticed his uneasiness. Jack was not a good liar, and he felt like he was telling a lie by trying to act normal as he headed toward the stairs.

"That's a good one, Arnie. Yeah, I'm stuck all right. Well, got to get to work—see ya."

As Jack took the steps two at a time Arnie said, "Yup, time to *double your pleasure*—eh, Jackie?" But Jack was up the stairs and into the hallway, and Arnie was left laughing all by himself.

Jack headed for the library, up on the second floor, but gum was the last thing on his mind.

Swinging the bucket of supplies in his left hand, he reached into his pocket with the other one. Key number 501, key number 73.

He wasn't Jack the Gummer.

He wasn't Jack the janitor's son.

He was Jack the explorer.

Today, the tower; tomorrow—who knows?

Chapter 12

CHEWOLOGY

Jack's hour in the library was educational. When he knocked on her door at 2:35, Mrs. Stokely was bustling about behind the glass walls of her office. Smiling, she opened her door, looked him in the face, and immediately said, "You must be John's boy—and you must hear that a lot."

Jack nodded. "Yes, ma'am, I hear that pretty often. My name is Jack. . . . I . . . I'm supposed to start cleaning the gum off the bottoms of the chairs and tables."

The librarian's face darkened. Shaking her head, she said, "It burns me up, the way kids leave that stuff around." Then, smiling at Jack again, she said, "Well, it's sure nice of you to lend your dad a hand. If it weren't for his help, I'd have never got this place ready for the opening of school. And I've still got plenty to do, believe you me!"

Jack didn't correct Mrs. Stokely's misunderstanding about why he was working. Instead he nodded and said, "Well . . . better get busy."

The high school library was a big room. Fourteen large wooden tables ran in two rows down the center of the space. The old card catalog stood on massive cast-iron legs to the left of the circulation desk. There were three computer terminals on top of it now, their screens dark except for blinking cursors.

Working first on the pair of tables nearest the circulation desk, Jack was tricked. He thought, *This is going to be a breeze.* There were only six or seven wads of gum per table, and most of them were not sticky at all. He didn't even have to tip the tables on their sides, but was simply able to lean over and reach up with the putty knife. He only had to use the OFFIT two or three times.

But as Jack worked his way toward the back of the deep room the volume of gum increased. Dramatically.

Distance from the librarian = safer chewing = more gum.

By the time he reached the seventh and eighth tables, Jack was digging and chipping his way through gum that was sometimes more than half an inch thick. He felt like an archaeologist performing an excavation, examining clues left by a vanished civilization—Minnesota Jack and the Temple of Goo.

70

He began to count gum layers, like counting growth rings on a tree stump. He noticed the subtle difference in color between peppermint and spearmint gum, the sharp contrast in scent and texture between chewing gum and bubble gum.

Examining the deposits from recent years, Jack found an extraordinary range of colors. There were blues of every shade and at least fifteen different pinks. There were deep reds, bright turquoises, and soft aquamarines. Brilliant oranges, glaring yellows, and muted greens of a dozen different hues rounded out the spectrum.

Occasionally a group of gum wads would suggest an image to Jack's wandering mind, like cloud formations on a summer afternoon. He saw a shape that reminded him of his grandfather's face. He saw cars and houses, birds, and an elephant.

Mrs. Stokely interrupted. She had her coat and hat on. Looking into the bucket where Jack had been dropping the scrapings, she said, "My goodness, I had no idea there could be that much gum in here, and you're only a little more than half done!" Jack groaned inwardly at that. "Well, good night, and be sure to pull the door shut when you go, Jack."

Jack looked up at the clock. He had another fifteen minutes.

Back on task and thinking scientifically now,

71

Jack noticed how the gum formed two crude, over-lapping semicircles on the bottom of the table above each chair. Four chairs, eight semicircles. Simple—one semicircle for the right-handed gum stickers, the other for lefties.

The radius of each semicircle was about the length of a kid's arm from the elbow to the finger-tips. He observed that, overall, kids using fingers to jam gum onto the table outnumbered those using thumbs. Jack also noticed that kids using their left hand to off-load gum were twice as likely to use their thumb as the kids using their right hand.

The fluorescent lights were not quite bright enough to create clear contrast, but on some of the wads he could see perfect fingerprints pressed into the gum. Jack thought, *I wonder if Ackerby knows about this.*

By the end of his hour in the library Jack was ready to give a long and scholarly lecture:

"A Very Sticky Decade"
by Professor Jack Rankin
Chairman, Department of Chewology

Hurrying back to the empty shop, Jack put his stuff away in the supply closet. Then he had a thought.

He got another plastic bucket from the stack and knocked the day's gum scrapings into it. He estimated that it was about a half gallon of chewed gum of every color imaginable. Grinning, he set the bucket in the corner. Maybe a gallon or two of dead gum could be used for something. At the very least, it was . . . interesting—in a creepy, disgusting sort of way.

Then Jack moved fast, hoping to be gone before anyone came. He pulled a piece of paper out of his backpack and wrote a hurried note.

Dear Dad—
  I didn't take the bus, so can I ride home with you? I'm going to find a quiet place and do homework. I'll meet you back here at five, OK?
                                                    Jack

He left the note on his dad's desk, weighed it down with a stapler, and turned on the lamp. His dad would be sure to see it.

Then he grabbed his coat and backpack and headed for the stairs. He had almost an hour and a half.

The tower was waiting.

Chapter 13

ALtitude

An empty school can be spooky. In a building that's seventy-five years old it's a feeling that's hard to shake.

Jack walked quietly up the east stairwell, every sense on alert. At the second-floor landing he stopped. He could hear Arnie shaking his dust mop just around the corner. Jack waited, holding his breath. When the heavy footsteps headed away, he rounded the corner and kept climbing.

The thick slate treads on the stairs were worn smooth from countless thousands of trudging feet, but Jack's shoes barely touched down as he headed up and up.

The fourth floor was the end of the line. It was also where his dad had been fixing a toilet, and maybe he still was.

Jack had been up on four only once or twice, and not at all this year. All of the fifth-grade classrooms were on the second floor, except for gym and music.

The tower rose from the middle of the building, so Jack went to his right. He edged his way down the corridor. He passed a hallway that ran south toward the back of the school.

He reached the exact center of the building, just where he thought there would have to be a door, but there was nothing. Frustrated, Jack stopped to think.

Then it dawned on him. The door to the tower could be along either of the two hallways that ran back from the long front corridor. The question was, if his dad was still working up here, which of the two north-south halls was he in? A loud *clank* from his right answered that question. Jack headed back the way he had come, and when he got to the hallway he'd passed a minute before, turned right.

There were classrooms and lockers on the left side of the hall. Jack was focused on the right. Lockers, three classrooms, a girls bathroom, and then . . . a door.

There was no number on the door, no lettering.

Digging into his front pocket, Jack pulled out a key.

Number 73. Wrong one.

Digging again, he pulled out key 501 and slid it into the lock. Holding his breath, he applied pressure and the key turned.

He was in.

The hinges creaked and Jack stopped. He tried inching the door open, but that made the creaking worse. Hoping that the distance would hide the sound from his dad, he gave the door a bold shove, got himself inside, pulled the key out of the lock, and shut the door behind him, holding the knob so the latch wouldn't click.

Darkness.

It smelled musty, closed in.

He groped around on the wall and found a light switch. He flipped it, and instead of bright fluorescence there was the shadowy glow of a single bare bulb.

He was in a narrow passage, made narrower by things piled along the right-hand wall. Stacks of old books. A heap of broken chairs. A discolored state flag in an iron floor stand. There was a pile of torn roller maps and five or six dusty globes. Bookcases with jumbled shelves were stacked three high.

It was an educational graveyard.

Jack picked his way, careful not to let his backpack bump anything. Just past the bookcases there was another door. Its doorknob had no place for a key.

With his heart racing, Jack turned the knob and pushed. Pale daylight filtered down from above, and ten feet in front of him lay the first flight of tower stairs. Walking in and peering up, he saw that there were five more flights, maybe six.

At the first landing there was a narrow window, but the glass was so grimy Jack could hardly see through it. The window at the second landing was even worse.

But at the third landing Jack sucked in a quick breath. This window was on the front of the tower, the side facing north toward the front lawn. The window was much cleaner, and a partial view of Huntington lay spread out before him.

Someone had hauled one of the old wooden chairs up to the landing. Its broken rungs had been artfully spliced and then held in place with a few turns of twisted wire. Jack dragged the chair over to the window and stood on the seat to get a clearer view from the top panes.

Craning his neck to look northwest, he could see where Randall Street crossed the railroad tracks. He counted six blocks north of the tracks— that was his street, Greenwood. The leafless trees didn't hide much, and by counting off the brick bungalows from the corner, he thought he could see the roof of his own home.

The bright October air was frosty and clear, and the flat land of the upper Midwest stretched on and on, dotted here and there with ponds and lakes.

Northward on the distant horizon he thought he could see Minneapolis, just the hint of a skyline.

Jack kept going up. The fourth and fifth landings each had windows, but Jack wanted to get to the top. He wanted to reach the summit.

At the sixth landing Jack had to crouch. The concrete ceiling above it was only about four feet tall. And there was a metal hatch.

He shrugged off his backpack and set it on the floor. Then Jack reached up, turned the handle on the hatch, put his shoulder against the steel, and straightened up.

Forty or fifty pigeons took flight with such a sudden noise that Jack dropped back into the opening, terrified. Then, realizing what had made the sound, he quickly stood up again, his head and shoulders above the level of the bell platform.

The fresh air was chilly, and the brightness made his eyes smart. He reached down for his backpack and swung it up, then pulled himself onto the platform. It was a square about twelve feet wide. Each side had two arches with a round limestone pillar that went to the floor between them. Chicken wire had been fastened across all the openings to keep the pigeons out, and for the most part, it had worked.

In the middle of the space a pair of I beams about six feet tall were set into the concrete floor, and a third one was bolted between them. Three bronze bells hung from the cross beam. Each bell had a clapper in the center, along with some kind of black metal box that almost touched the outer rim, probably some kind of electric bell ringer.

The largest bell was about two feet across, and the smallest was only about a foot. Jack had the urge to grab the clapper of the biggest bell and start swinging. He resisted.

Jack kept low to the floor under the bells in the center, partly to keep from being seen by anyone who might glance up, but mostly to keep from feeling like he was going to plunge to his death. The view was dizzying, spectacular, a true panorama. Westward toward the town center he could see the green copper roof of the public library, and a little farther on, the gold eagle on the town hall weather vane, up above the treetops.

Turning in a slow circle, Jack picked out all the places he knew. It was like looking at a picture book of his life. The park near his house, the one with the tall swing set. His elementary school. The Good Shepherd Lutheran Church. Grampa Parkman's house. Capitol Bank, where he had his savings account—almost three hundred dollars. Half a mile to the south he could see the metal framing and some brick walls of the new junior high. And off to the west the red roof of the gymnasium at the new high school caught the afternoon sun.

It was all there—his past, his present, his future.

And that made Jack feel good.

Until he saw Grampa's house again. Then he thought, *Mom has lived here all her life—and so has Dad. It's his town too. He grew up here. What if I'm growing up to be just like him?*

Out loud Jack said, "But I am *not* like him!" The fierceness in his own voice startled him, and another cloud of pigeons took off from the roof of the tower.

Grabbing a pen, he flipped his notebook open to a blank page and wrote at the top,

Ways I Am NOT Like My Dad

I like to keep <u>my</u> room messy.
I am not going to live in Huntington
when I grow up.
I do <u>not</u> like to clean things.
I read more books.
I am going to go to college.
I am great at using computers.
I like loud music.

The list filled most of the page, and toward the end Jack even wrote, "I hate tomatoes."

Scanning the list made Jack feel better, and when he glanced down at the town, Huntington looked good again, safer. Jack closed his binder and then got out his math book, a spiral notebook, and a pencil. He zipped his jacket and pulled up the hood. He leaned against one of the bell supports and angled himself to catch the best light.

He'd found a quiet place, and now he was doing his homework, just like he'd said in the note to his dad.

Math went fast—it was always easy for Jack. Then he opened up the book he was reading in English, *The Indian in the Cupboard.* He had read it before, but that didn't matter. He always read the books he liked again and again. He was supposed to stop after chapter four, but the action swept him along. He knew exactly how Omri felt, and Little Bear, too.

Looking up some time later, Jack saw it was getting dark. He shivered, and his back ached from leaning against the steel post. He hadn't noticed while he was reading.

Leaning forward near the pillar at the front of the tower, Jack could just read the time and temperature sign at his bank down on Main Street.

Four fifty-three. Only seven minutes to get back to the shop in time to meet his dad. Jack said he'd be there at five, and he would be. He hadn't been late for anything in years—not school, not a rehearsal, not a single assignment.

It was downhill all the way to the shop, and Jack made it with a minute to spare.

Chapter 14

Homeward

John Rankin's Chevy pickup was getting to be an antique. It was a '72, but if it hadn't been for the changes in styling, no one would have guessed. The original green paint was still in great shape, and underneath the denim seat covers the vinyl seats weren't worn at all.

The old green Chevy didn't look like some trophy truck, the kind you see at a truck rally at the Holiday Inn on a Sunday afternoon. This was a real truck, a working truck. It was a tool, and John Rankin took good care of his tools.

Climbing up onto the seat next to his dad, Jack knew the routine by heart. Pump the gas pedal four times. Pull the choke lever out two clicks. Count to fifteen, turn the key, and *vooOOOm*, the engine jumps to life. Worked every time, heart of summer or dead of winter.

Jack was glad it was so late, and almost dark, too. He didn't want any kids to see him riding with his dad. Jack thought, *And that's another thing that's different. I'd never want a truck, and my dad has had this one forever.*

Easing out of the back lot onto Summer Street, his dad asked, "So how was the library?"

Jack said, "Not so bad."

"Hmmm."

They waited for the light to change, and John Rankin sat stiffly, both hands on the steering wheel, his index fingers tapping along with the clicking turn signal.

Jack wanted to know what his dad thought about him messing up that desk—and why he hadn't even yelled at him. Now would be the perfect time to talk . . . maybe even say he was sorry.

The light seemed to stay red forever. The silence felt uncomfortable, but Jack couldn't think of what to say. Then he remembered his talk with the librarian. "Mrs. Stokely said it was hard to get the library moved last summer." His voice sounded too loud.

His dad nodded and said, "Yup." He put the truck into first gear and pulled forward.

Jack saw they weren't heading toward home. Instead of turning north onto Randall Street, they kept going west on Main Street and turned onto South Grand Boulevard. Jack pictured where they were, remembering how the town had looked from the top of the tower.

Waiting at the next traffic light, John Rankin cleared his throat. Trying to sound casual, he said, "You get teased much about your dad being a janitor?"

The question caught Jack by surprise, but he didn't show it. "Nah. One or two kids have said stuff, but they're jerks. I don't pay any attention to it."

"That's good. Hate to think you're getting razzed on my account." His dad fell silent again.

Jack could have opened up and said a lot more, but he stopped himself. Thinking about having a talk was easier than actually doing it.

The light changed, and the traffic eased ahead. Jack looked out at the store windows and the new-car dealerships, and his dad kept focused on his driving. It was rush hour in Huntington. There were no real slowdowns, but the major streets were pretty full for twenty or thirty minutes every afternoon.

After a mile or so, his dad pulled the truck up next to the curb in front of a big used-car lot and shut off the engine. "I know I've told you that my dad was in the car business." Pointing to the right, out the window by Jack, he said, "My dad used to own that lot back in the fifties—Honest Phil Rankin. He ran it right up to the day he died. That man could sell anything to anybody, and he made a good bit of money—it's his money that's going to put you and your sister through college before too long."

He paused, both hands back on the steering wheel.

Jack looked over at his dad's face, lit up by the string of bulbs that ran above the first row of cars. His eyes were open, but he wasn't really looking at anything.

"I worked for my dad every Saturday morning from the time I was twelve until I left home to join the army. Hated it. I washed cars, all year-round, every Saturday, sometimes after school, too. Hardly got paid at all.

"He used to bring a customer over to where I was washing. He'd come near on purpose and do his sales pitch, and when the deal was closed, he'd come find me. He waves a check or a stack of fifty-dollar bills at me. 'Did you hear how I did that?' he says. 'See how I cut off every possible escape? I hope you listen good, Johnny boy, because some-day this is going to be your place. You learn how to do this right, and it's like finding money on the sidewalk.' I nodded and just kept on washing. I didn't like to think about that."

85

John Rankin paused, reaching for words. Jack could tell he was forcing himself to talk. His dad had never said this much to him at one time before, not even when they used to go fishing and sit together all day in the old red canoe.

"And you know what really drove me crazy?"

Jack shook his head but immediately felt silly. His dad wasn't waiting for a response from him. He was years and years away.

"I never had a car—no car, all during high school. Here it would have been so easy for my dad to set me up with any old car, just something to call my own, just a little independence. But that wasn't his way.

"Then one Saturday night when I was a senior in high school, I swiped his office keys, went down to the lot, and drove off in a red Corvette. I was borrowing it, just for the night."

Jack hardly breathed. Almost without meaning to, he slipped a hand into his right pocket and felt the two keys he had "borrowed."

As he described the Corvette, a little smile played at the corners of his dad's mouth. "That was quite a rig, let me tell you. First gear would run out to fifty miles an hour. Way too much car for me. And wouldn't you know, I whacked that thing into a phone pole about a mile and a half from here. That fiberglass body just broke up into a million pieces."

Jack gasped. "You mean you *totaled* a Corvette? Did you get hurt?"

"I was shaken up, and I had a cut on my chin, but I was mostly okay. The car was another story. That thing wasn't even good for parts. Bent the frame, cracked the engine block. Blue-book price was sixty-five hundred dollars—that's still a lot of money, but back then that was a *whole* lot of money."

Jack asked, "What did your dad say?"

"He came right over to the hospital, of course, but he didn't even ask if I was all right. First thing he says is, 'You got a big debt to pay off, mister. And you're going to pay it too. This summer you're coming to work for me—full-time. You got college plans, but till you dig out of this hole, you can forget all about 'em.'

"Well, I was never going to be some used-car salesman, not even for a summer. And I told him so. 'You're just a loud-mouthed junk dealer in a cheap sport coat.' That's what I said to him. And I said I'd rather join the army than work for him. And come next morning that's what I did, just to spite him. And I don't know what hurt him worse—calling him a junk dealer or me running off to the army."

The flow of the story seemed to stop, but Jack felt there was more coming. He waited, and his dad began speaking again, his voice a little quieter.

"You were about two years old when your grandpa died. At the wake a man came up to me and said, 'Your daddy gave me a car one afternoon, and he made me promise I'd never tell a soul. That car got me to and from my first job for three years. Your dad was quite a guy.' I thought the man was nuts. He had to be thinking of someone else.

"But then the next day at the funeral three other people came up and said almost the same thing.

"Well, your mom and me, we went through all my dad's papers, and sure enough, every year he gave away one or two cars—about thirty in all over the years. That's a lot of money. I mean, these weren't fancy cars, and old Honest Phil figured out how to take some tax deductions, but still. And we found a box of letters from the people he'd helped out. It was like a whole part of himself he never let me see. And I thought, 'If he could give all these cars away to strangers, why couldn't he give just one to me?' Took me a long time to figure that one out."

Jack asked, "Was he just being stingy?"

John Rankin shook his head. "If he was stingy, then he wouldn't have given all those cars away. No, I think he just wanted me to learn that I had to make my own way. He loved me, and he didn't want me to be spoiled."

Jack had been watching his dad's face as he told the story. He had that same feeling he got from one of those trick puzzles—the kind where you stare and stare, and a picture suddenly appears. He was just beginning to see a new image.

Jack and his dad sat quietly. The traffic kept whizzing by, and two or three couples were walking around the lot, looking at the used cars. The salespeople circled like eagles.

Then the traffic slowed to a crawl, and a guy driving a big blue Oldsmobile leaned on his horn right next to the pickup. Both Jack and John jumped in their seats, and then laughed nervously.

John put the truck in neutral and reached for the ignition. As he started the engine he turned to look at Jack. "Just so you know it for good and sure, I don't expect you'll ever be a janitor, Jackie. My life is my life, and yours is yours. I'm just glad that we get to run side by side for a few years, that's all."

Checking the rearview mirror, he said, "Now,

we'd better shoot on home, or your mom'll start calling the hospitals."

The green pickup bucked a little in first gear as John Rankin edged out into the stream of traffic on South Grand Boulevard.

At the next corner he swung a right turn onto Oak Street and headed north.

During that short drive home Jack realized two things.

He didn't know much about his dad—hardly anything.

And he definitely wanted to know more.

Chapter 15

DISCOVERIES

As he hauled his gum-busting equipment around the high school, it began to dawn on Jack just how huge the place was. It was like four of his old elementary schools stacked up, one on top of the other. Four times more floor space, four times as many classrooms and wastebaskets and pencil sharpeners, four times as many lights and light switches and radiators, four times as many restrooms and sinks, not to mention the gyms and the locker rooms and the industrial arts shops and all the rest of it.

And it all worked. It was more than seventy-five years old, and everything worked every day. Jack tried to imagine what it would be like to be responsible for keeping the whole place going, and quickly gave up. It was almost too much to think about.

It took Jack two more scraping sessions to get the library free of gum.

The last four tables were the worst, and by the time he was done with all the chairs, the three-gallon bucket tucked behind the door in the supply closet was nearly full of gum. The loaded bucket weighed about twenty pounds, and it gave off a sickening combination of odd, gummy smells. Jack kept his gum bucket covered with a cloth to keep the odor from filling the supply closet.

Looking at his pail of trophies, Jack thought, *I wonder if I've invented a new category for* The Guinness Book of World Records?—*Greatest Quantity of Gum Ever Removed from School Property during Four Hours!*

Both Wednesday and Thursday Jack had wanted to stay late like he had on Tuesday. He discovered he was actually looking forward to another ride home with his dad. It seemed like there was never time to talk to him at home. Dad was always tired, or spending time with Mom—and then there was Lois, the world's biggest pest. Another ride home would be good.

Jack thought a lot about what his dad had told him on Tuesday, and now he wanted to ask him a million questions. Especially about the Vietnam War, about being in the army. Jack also wanted to know more about his grandfather, Honest Phil. And about how Dad and Mom met and got married. Tons of questions.

Jack had also wanted to stay late so he could use the time after gum patrol to search for the door that matched key number 73. He'd been on the lookout. He watched for doors in odd places, but Jack was pretty sure he would not find the steam tunnel door without a serious hunting expedition.

Still, as much as he wanted to stay, on Wednesday and Thursday he went right home because he had too much work. He had to do a big social studies project about the thirteen original colonies, and he had to prepare an oral report on *The Indian in the Cupboard.* The project and the book report were both due on Monday—another conspiracy hatched by evil teachers to overwork him.

Jack sometimes wished he could put things off to the last minute, but he just wasn't glued together that way. He had to start an assignment the moment it was given and work steadily until it was out of the way. It was like he couldn't help it. He had to get things done on time, had to be places on time.

So Jack had ridden the late bus home on both Wednesday and Thursday, right after gum patrol.

Friday morning there was a light dusting of snow over Huntington. Jack listened to the morning newscast, and a woman reported that there had been a full three inches in Minneapolis overnight, and that it looked like it was going to be a snowy fall and winter. As if that were news in Minnesota.

Jack loved snow, and the more the better.

But, walking into the old high school, Jack noticed what the snow and salt and sand were doing to the floors.

Instantly Jack thought of his dad.

He realized that his dad probably hated to see the first snow. The long, cold Minnesota winter must mean a lot of extra work for him.

Mrs. Lambert wasn't in the room when the bell rang at the start of Friday's math class, and Jack wished she were. Kirk Dorfmann had not taken any more cheap shots at him, but that was just because he hadn't had the opportunity. In the halls Kirk and Luke laid off because they were afraid of what Pete might do. Math class was the only other time Jack saw them, and Mrs. Lambert had kept a sharp lookout for trouble.

Kirk had been moved two rows away from Jack, and the distance helped. The problem was that Luke Karnes sat between them.

Making sure that Kirk was watching, Luke pulled a piece of pink gum out of his mouth and made a big show of sticking it to the underside of his desk. Then he said, "Hey, Kirk, do you think I should get old John to clean this off? . . . Or should we ask Ackerby to have young Jackie do it?"

Kirk gave a little sneer and said, "What's the difference? If you've seen one janitor, you've seen 'em all."

Jack ignored both of them. They were idiots, completely clueless—pathetic. Jack found it remarkable, but he wasn't even tempted to trade words with them, much less trade punches. It was like he had moved into a whole different world, and they were still stuck somewhere else, trying to reach him.

But Luke wasn't done. He felt like he needed to impress Kirk today, and he thought Jack was ignoring him out of fear.

Big mistake.

Luke reached across the aisle and flicked Jack's ear. "What's the matter, Jackie? Didn't your hear me, or are you just acting *stuck up*?"

Jack didn't lose his temper, but he did respond. Glancing quickly back toward the door to be sure Mrs. Lambert was still absent, he swung left to face Luke, his legs out in the aisle. Before Luke could even flinch, Jack stuck his right foot under Luke's long leg, just behind the knee, and lifted the leg straight up—no violence, just a little muscle.

Luke pulled his leg away, and Jack didn't try to

stop him. Jack had accomplished his mission. Because as Luke jerked his leg away he banged it against the bottom of his desk and jammed it right into his own gob of fresh, sticky gum.

As Jack swung around to face front again Mrs. Lambert walked in the classroom door. Striding to the front of the room, she said, "Quiet down, everyone. I know how you all hate to miss even a little bit of your precious math class, so please get your homework out."

Then Mrs. Lambert noticed Luke trying to deal with the pink blob that was smeared onto the right leg of his new Abercrombie corduroys. Turning around, she pulled a tissue from the box on her desk. "Here, Luke, just cover it up for now so it doesn't get stuck anywhere else. I've told you never to bring gum into my classroom, haven't I? *That* is one of the reasons why."

With a perfectly straight face Jack said, "Hey, Luke, there's this stuff that'll take that mess right out. Stop down in the janitor's shop sometime, and I'll show you what to do."

Mrs. Lambert smiled and said, "That's nice of you, Jack."

And Jack said, "Oh, it's nothing—all in a day's work."

Chapter 16

Behind the Curtain

After school Jack was surprised to find Mr. Ackerby waiting for him in the workshop. His first thought was that Luke Karnes had ratted, and now he would have a whole bunch of new trouble.

Mr. Ackerby said, "Hello, Jack. I wanted you to know that I've been checking up on you. I got a good report from Mrs. Stokely. She says you're a hard worker, and I'm glad to hear it."

Jack nodded and tried to look pleasant. Mr. Ackerby's compliment was sort of like having the jailer praise you for being a wonderful little prisoner.

Mr. Ackerby went on. "I also came down here to find John. I feel pretty stupid not realizing right away that you were his son. I worked with him on our move all summer long. We'd come up against a problem, and he'd figure out a way to solve it, every time. He certainly has this building in great shape. A big place this old doesn't keep working all by itself, that's for sure."

Jack didn't know what to say, so he just nodded and said, "Yeah."

Mr. Ackerby was used to having kids feel uncomfortable when he talked to them—it was usually what he wanted. But he'd snooped around, and he had learned that Jack Rankin was a pretty good kid. Good student, honest, and rarely in trouble. Every teacher Mr. Ackerby had approached seemed quite surprised about the incident in music class.

So Mr. Ackerby was trying to give their relationship a friendlier tone. He asked, "Where are you working today?"

Jack said, "I have to start in the auditorium," and to himself Jack added, —*thanks to you and your slave labor program.*

Mr. Ackerby nodded, his eyebrows lifting. "Another big job. Well, I won't keep you. I'm going to wait here another few minutes to see if I can catch your dad. And, Jack . . . what with the three-day weekend coming up and all, if you want to cut out at three today instead of three thirty, that'll be okay."

"Um . . . yeah. Thanks." Pretty chintzy gift, but it was better than nothing.

Jack left the workshop with a new impression of Mr. Ackerby.

The guy seemed almost human.

Mr. Ackerby was the second person who had said that cleaning gum in the auditorium would be a big job. When Jack told Lou where he would be working, Lou whistled and then said, "Well, nobody's going to accuse your daddy of giving you special treatment, that's for sure."

So it would be a big job. So what? The bigger the better. He was Jack, the Fearless One, the Climber of Towers, the Keeper of the Keys.

Ready to do battle, Jack pulled open the center door at the back of the auditorium.

His heart sank.

He stood there, one medium-size boy armed with a red bucket and a putty knife.

Eight hundred seventy-five folding seats stared at him in silent defiance.

The place was vast. The floor sloped sharply downward toward a wide stage. The dusty gold curtain was two-thirds open, and the area backstage was completely dark.

The pale green walls needed fresh paint. High windows along the east wall let in the gloomy afternoon light. It looked to Jack like more snow was on the way.

The theater-style seats swung in a graceful arc,

with an aisle on the east and west, and one up the center. The backs and seat bottoms were covered with fake brown leather fastened on by brass upholstery tacks. And the wooden underside of almost every seat was pockmarked with wads of gum.

With a deep sigh Jack set down his bucket and began removing gum from the bottom of seat number 1 in row W. The scraping and rubbing sounds that had seemed so loud in the library were lost in the huge room, as if they floated off into outer space.

Jack got into the rhythm of the work. Seat by seat he moved across the wide back row, turned the corner, and headed back. He would work on a seat until it was done, straighten up, push the bucket forward with his foot, then bend down and start the next one. He scraped carefully, trying not to scratch the dark plywood, and he wasn't satisfied until a seat bottom was completely clean.

By the time he had cleaned two rows, it was getting so dark that sometimes Jack couldn't tell if he had got all the gum off by scraping, or if he should use the OFFIT to finish the job. He put his putty knife in the bucket, went to the center aisle, and walked downhill toward the stage. Time to turn on some lights.

Vaulting easily up onto the front of the stage, Jack walked behind the curtain toward the right, his footsteps hollow on the wooden floor. He had worked on the lighting crew for a play at his old school, and he knew what to look for. Somewhere there had to be a switch labeled HOUSE LIGHTS. He headed for the right-hand wall.

Backstage was a mess. Music stands and folding chairs were scattered about, and a set of dented kettledrums was half covered by large cardboard panels. They were pieces of scenery that had been painted to look like big blocks of stone along the top of a castle wall. A rack that used to hold costumes had tipped over, and wire coat hangers lay in a tangled heap.

Jack's eyes adjusted to the darkness of the stage, and he could see there was no light panel near the right-hand door. He did an about-face and headed left, walking along the back wall of the stage area.

Near the middle of the stage Jack tripped on something and went sprawling onto the floor. Rubbing his elbow, he stood up and looked back to see what had caused the fall. It was the silver blade of a long sword, half hidden by a black curtain covering the rear wall of the stage. He bent over, pulled the whole thing out from behind the

101

curtain, and straightened up to get a good look at it.

It was just a stage prop, made of wood. But it had been well made and carefully painted. It was a knight's broadsword, with a wide hilt and a long handle, made to be swung using both hands. It was almost four feet long.

Jack swung it, and it made a pleasant whirring sound as he carved the air. It felt good in his hands. Holding it out in front of him at eye level, he lunged toward the curtain, pretending to jab the Evil Knight.

A *clank* came from behind the curtain—maybe armor or something. There was a break in the curtain about six feet to his left, so Jack walked over, grabbed it, and held on as he stepped about ten paces back toward the right.

Just as Jack suspected, more stuff lay hidden behind the curtain. He saw a long jousting lance made from a bamboo pole, and a shield that had once been a metal trash can lid. It had been spray-painted white and then decorated with a red lion wearing a gold crown.

But that wasn't the best thing. The best thing had nothing to do with knights and armor and swordplay. The best thing was very simple.

It was a door.

On the door there was just one word.

ACCESS.

Jack put down his wooden sword and reached into his pocket. He pulled out a key. The light was too dim to see the number, but he could feel there were only two numerals stamped on it. It had to be key 73.

He pushed the key into the jagged keyhole, held his breath, and turned.

Bingo.

The door hinged on the left, and Jack pulled it open wide. Peering into the shadows, he saw a short landing just inside the door, and a set of metal stairs—nine steps down, maybe more. It was very dark in there.

There was a light switch on the wall to the right of the landing, but when Jack flipped it, nothing happened.

Suddenly aware of how his heart was pounding, Jack let himself off the hook. There was no hurry.

Now that the door was found, he could take his time, gather some equipment, do a proper exploration. No need to go rushing down into . . . into that place.

So he started to shut the door.

And when he had the door almost shut, Jack noticed something strange.

When a door is almost shut, there's usually a flow of air—either in or out. The flow of air hitting Jack in the face was coming out of the tunnel.

Nothing strange about that.

It wasn't the air itself that was odd. It was what the air was carrying.

The air was carrying a smell.

It was faint, so faint that Jack thought he must be imagining it—but it was a smell Jack knew very well. . . . Too well.

It was the smell of watermelon bubble gum.

Chapter 17

One-Way Ticket

Jack sniffed the air coming out of the steam tunnel again, carefully. Nothing now. But there really had been the barest hint before, in that first rush of upward air. Watermelon bubble gum. Jack was sure. Well, he was pretty sure.

Gently, Jack closed the door. He pulled the black curtain to cover it again, tucking the wooden sword out of sight.

Abandoning his search for the auditorium lights, he hurried across the stage, jumped down to the floor, and trotted up to where he had left his bucket. Jack looked up at the clock and saw it was already three forty-five. He had missed out on Mr. Ackerby's offer to quit early. Maybe the offer would carry over to Tuesday?

He ran silently through the halls. When he reached the door at the top of the workshop stairs, Jack paused to listen. If possible, he wanted to get in, borrow a few important items, and then get

105

back to the auditorium without meeting anyone.

He didn't hear anything, so he opened the door and scooted down the stairs. He put his supplies away and then went over to his dad's desk. He was betting there would be a flashlight in it somewhere, and he was right. In the top right drawer there was a small black Mag-Lite with the name of a plumbing supply company printed on its side in gold letters. Jack twisted the end and the light came on, bright and steady. Perfect.

He tucked the light in his back pocket and went over to the workbench, trying to imagine what else he might need. He couldn't really think of anything else, not for a quick first look. But when he saw a spool of nylon string, his mind flashed to the story in *Huckleberry Finn,* the part where Huck and Tom get lost in the caves. Jack grabbed the spool and stuffed it into the outer pocket of his backpack. Then he pulled out his old white Minnesota Vikings cap and put it on.

He was all set to leave, was actually on the stairs, and then stopped. He needed to leave a note for his dad. It was Friday, and Jack was sure his dad would want to leave right at five.

Rushing back to the desk, he scribbled the message and dashed back up to the landing, where he almost collided with Lou.

Lou flattened up against the wall, exaggerating his close call. "Whoa, there. Where you off to in such a big hurry? Late bus already left. You about ran me down."

Jack said, "Sorry, Lou. I'm going to go and study for a while, maybe walk over to the library or something. Then I'm going to ride home with my dad. I left him a note."

Lou hurried down the stairs and grabbed the gray toolbox off the cluttered bench. "Your dad sent me to get the toolbox, and he said if you were still here, would you mind cleaning up the bench for him while you're waiting? We've got a busted door he wants to get fixed before quittin' time." Lou was already back at the landing. "So I'll just tell him I gave you the message, okay? If I don't see you again, you have a good weekend, Jackie."

Jack stood on the landing. Looking down, he could see that the workbench was a wreck after a busy week. He used to love putting it all back in order when he came to visit his dad at work. *Yeah,* Jack thought, *back when I was about six. First I've got to scrape junk off of ten thousand seats, and then I have to clean up his messes, too? No way.*

Jack stomped back down the steps, crumpled the first note he'd left, and tossed it into the trash. On a new piece of paper he scrawled,

Dad—

    Couldn't clean up the bench.
    I have some other stuff I've got to do.
    See you at five.

Jack

Jack made sure that no one saw him go back into the auditorium.

Walking directly to the back of the stage, he left the wall curtain in place. No sense advertising that someone was here. He took out the spool of string, set his backpack and jacket on the floor beside the door, and turned on the flashlight. Pulling both keys from his pocket, he chose the right one and opened the door, just a crack.

He wanted to check himself. Had he just imagined that watermelon smell?

Jack sniffed the airflow. He shook his head and sniffed again.

Nothing, at least nothing he could recognize. Mostly it smelled like his basement at home, but not as damp.

Stepping inside the doorway onto the metal landing, Jack shone the light down the steps. Five steps ran down to a short corridor maybe fifteen feet long and only about three feet wide. The floor of the corridor was concrete, and the walls were terra-cotta building bricks, the hollow kind. The ceiling was also concrete, a little less than six feet high. At the end of the corridor there was an opening, no door, just an opening, rectangular and dark.

Jack wanted to leave the access door open, but it swung outward too far on its own. He tried putting his backpack against it, but then his backpack made a bulge in the velvet curtain that hid the door. Shining the flashlight around to see if there was something else to prop it with, he saw the wooden sword. He bent down and picked it up. Smiling, he decided to take it with him. After all, most of the really great explorers had swords, didn't they?

Sword in hand, he stepped back inside onto the landing and bravely pulled the door shut behind him.

Instantly he wished he hadn't, and he reached for the knob on the inside of the door. It wouldn't turn. Shining the light, Jack saw why. It was a double-keyed door. It needed a key to open it from the inside, too.

Reaching into his pocket, Jack froze. He only had one key. He didn't even bother getting it out to shine the light on it. He knew it was the wrong one, the tower key.

He needed the other key.

It was close, only about six inches away.

But Jack couldn't reach it.

Key number 73 was sticking from the lock on the outside of the door.

Chapter 18

UNDERGROUND

Jack had known panic before.

When he was four, he had wandered away from his mom at a big department store in Minneapolis, lost for half an hour.

That was panic.

There was the time just last summer in the deep end of the municipal swimming pool. He had come up for a big gulp of air and got water instead.

That was panic too.

But this, this was different.

It was as if Jack had discovered a new land.

Off in the distance there were sheer mountains of panic poking into a dark and twisted sky. Frantic waterfalls and desperate rivers of liquid panic swept toward him with a churning noise that blotted out all thought. Standing there on the landing, flashlight in one hand, wooden sword in the other, Jack saw before him an entire unexplored continent of pure, numbing terror.

His heart pounded.

His hands shook.

And his mind raced.

It was Friday afternoon before a three-day weekend.

The school was emptying fast.

He was trapped.

He was cold.

And no one knew where he was. But Jack could change that. He could kick on the door. He could scream and pound and yell for help.

And Jack did, for two full minutes.

Then he stopped, his ears ringing, his hands hurting, breathing hard.

And he listened. Nothing.

The sound had been muffled by soft velvet curtains. And the little noise that made it across the stage had been swallowed whole by the yawning auditorium.

Jack felt completely alone—but only for about twenty seconds.

Small scritching sounds came from the darkness behind him.

Wheeling around, the beam of his flashlight caught the flick of a long pink tail as it disappeared through the low doorway.

Rats.

An involuntary shiver shook him. All of a sudden the wooden sword Jack gripped in his hand didn't seem silly at all.

Did the beam of light flicker? Hard to say how long the flashlight had been lying in his dad's desk. Batteries don't last forever.

Then Jack remembered.

Maybe there was someone else in the tunnels, someone other than him and the rats. Someone who liked watermelon gum.

And that someone must know how to get in and out.

Maybe there would even be a way to get out without being caught, without having to deal with Mr. Ackerby again.

Jack's Vikings cap had fallen off while he was pounding on the door. He picked it up, put it on. Then he walked down the steps, along the short corridor, and ducked through the opening into the main tunnel.

The tunnel was about five feet wide, its ceiling as high as the one in the access corridor. It ran off in both directions farther than his light would shine. A large pipe ran along the roof near the right-hand wall, suspended by steel rods embedded in the ceiling. It looked like cantaloupes could have rolled through the iron cylinder with ease.

Every twenty feet or so there was a joint, like a round steel collar, studded with six large nuts and bolts.

An electrical line ran along the center of the ceiling, with lightbulb sockets at intervals. Some were broken, some were missing, but others looked fine. Scanning the area, Jack saw no switch.

There were some other bundles of wire running the length of the tunnel on the side opposite the pipeline. Some looked like electrical wires, some looked like telephone cables.

The floor of the tunnel was level and smooth, and to Jack's relief there were no rats in sight. An old paper cup and a dusty soda can lay on the floor near the opening, evidence of some workman's lunch or coffee break. A thick layer of dust coated the floor. There were footprints—rats' and humans'. But with no weather to disturb them, the human footprints could have been decades old.

Decision time: Walk right or left?

Jack sniffed, and smelled nothing. There was no airflow, which made sense—no open door. Then he crouched down and leaned over so his nose was only about six inches from the floor. The air was cooler close to the floor, and there seemed to be a flow coming from the right.

Jack's instinct was to walk toward where the air was coming from. But what if there were a lot of little flows? So Jack ran a test.

Turning to his left, Jack walked fifty paces, stopped, stooped, and got his face down near the floor again. The flow of air was weaker, but it was still coming from the same direction. Turning back to his right, he walked the fifty paces back to the access opening. By going to the right, Jack was pretty sure he would be walking in a westerly direction, basically parallel with Main Street, headed toward the public library, the police station, and downtown Huntington. At least that's the way it seemed. Jack decided to go right.

With a direction established, Jack did not hesitate. He walked.

As he walked Jack's mind ran ahead into the darkness. He thought, *Let's say I find somebody. How do I know this person's going to want to help me? . . . What kind of a person would be hanging out down here, anyway?*

That thought stopped Jack in his tracks. He thought, *What if it's some weirdo? Even a murderer . . . or some* Phantom of the Opera-*type creep, completely crazy . . . limping around with a knife . . . or an ax?*

Standing still, listening to his heart pound in the silence, Jack decided he had no choice. The light from the flashlight was definitely dimmer. He did *not* want to be down here in the dark. He had to find a way out.

Taking a fresh grip on his wooden sword, Jack went forward. He kept up a strong pace, stooping every three or four minutes to test the air current and make sure he was still on course. After about ten minutes at a brisk walk he came to a junction, a crossroads.

Stranger and stranger.

As Jack stood in the center of the junction his nose picked up a familiar scent. And he knew he wasn't imagining. It wasn't the smell of watermelon gum. Now there was the faint but unmistakable scent of peanut butter.

But the junction posed a problem. He could either walk straight or go down one of three other tunnels—one to his right, or two to his left. He tried to imagine where he was. Had he walked as far as the library—about four blocks? Or was he farther along, say, at the town hall or the small shopping area? It was impossible to know. And did he really want to try pounding on a door that might be in the basement of the town hall? Or the police station?

Jack decided to go with his nose again, but when he sniffed at the opening of each tunnel, the peanut scent seemed to be everywhere.

So starting with the tunnel on his left, and then each tunnel in order, he did the fifty-paces-stoop-and-sniff test. After about fifteen minutes of walking back and forth Jack reached a verdict. The only tunnel that had any scent at all was the one he would have taken just by going straight when he first came to the junction.

Jack sat down to rest for a few minutes. He was winded, sweating. But sitting was no good. For one thing, he started to get cold quickly, and for another, it was too quiet, too much like a tomb. Jack didn't like the thoughts that crowded into that silence. And Jack didn't like sitting on the same floor the rats scurried around on. So he got up and continued moving.

After another ten minutes Jack didn't need to stoop to smell the peanut butter. It wasn't a strong smell, but compared to how faint it had been, it seemed to Jack like he was eating a sandwich. He kept walking, careful not to let his wooden sword tap on the floor of the tunnel. After another hundred steps Jack stopped to listen. Was that a distant car horn? Was he under a street? He heard nothing but the occasional scurry of little feet. He decided to keep still for another few minutes, and he turned off his flashlight to save the batteries.

The darkness of underground places is different. Underground darkness is complete. No streetlights, no stars, no moon, no light reflected from clouds. Jack knew this. He had seen pictures of animals living in caves. Some of them gradually evolved to have no eyes at all.

With zero light the pupil of the human eye opens up so wide that the colored iris almost disappears. The eye strains to see, and without the essential ingredient—light—it sees absolutely nothing.

Jack shut his eyes, leaning against the wall opposite the big pipe. He wanted his eyes to forget the brightness of the flashlight. He wanted to experience that utter darkness, that cave darkness.

When he opened his eyes, Jack had to blink to be sure they were really open. He held up his hand, touched his nose, and then waved his hand around, just inches from his face. Nothing. He opened his eyes until he imagined they must be as big as oranges. Nothing.

Pushing away from the wall, standing in the center of the tunnel, Jack put his arms out and turned in a slow circle, eyes open wide. And an odd thing happened. As he turned it was as if there was a small, dark rectangle hanging in midair—dark, but not so dark as everything else—

118

and it seemed to sweep past as he turned.

Jack rotated until the dark rectangle was directly in front of his eyes, and when he stood still, so did the rectangle.

It could be only one thing. It was light. The small rectangle was the shape of the tunnel, farther on in the direction he had been walking. Somewhere up ahead there was light. And peanut butter. And what else?

Jack turned on his flashlight and walked ahead quickly—and quietly.

Chapter 19

WALK into the Light

As Jack walked silently forward, every hundred steps or so he turned off his flashlight. The light ahead of him grew brighter.

Abruptly, he came to a T in the tunnel. And at that moment he learned why it was called the steam tunnel.

Heat radiated from the large iron pipe, and there was a faint hissing sound. Where the pipe he had been walking beside met the pipe in the new tunnel, there was a valve with a large, round handle. A steady drip of hot water had made a puddle on the floor at the junction.

There was no guesswork now. The light was coming from the left. There was enough of a glow bouncing from the walls of the tunnel that Jack turned off his flashlight to let his eyes adjust to the dimness.

The light grew stronger with every twenty paces, and coming around a 45-degree bend to the left, Jack stopped in his tracks.

It was a place where two tunnels crossed, and the junction was like a tic-tac-toe frame—four corridors meeting at a center square. In the corridor to Jack's right an old refrigerator stood against the wall below the steam pipe. Some coat hooks had been fastened to the wall beside the refrigerator, and a navy blue wool coat, a gray scarf, and a green backpack were hung up.

On the left wall of the corridor straight ahead Jack saw a folding army cot with an olive green blanket folded neatly at one end, a pillow on top of the blanket. On the tunnel wall opposite the cot there was a low wooden bookcase. A large black-and-white cat sat on the bookcase and looked at Jack with wide green eyes, a statue with a twitching tail.

In the center square a card table and one folding metal chair sat on a piece of dark green carpet. On the table lay a pencil and a newspaper turned to a half-finished crossword puzzle. There was a paper plate and a plastic knife—and an open jar of crunchy peanut butter.

In the corridor to Jack's left a tall floor lamp with a fringed shade stood beside a worn-out easy chair. The lamp was on, and in the chair sat a young man wearing black jeans and a tie-dyed T-shirt. A book lay open on his lap. Pushing a strand of long blond hair out of his eyes, he looked up as if seeing Jack appear was the most natural thing in the world. He looked curiously at Jack's sword.

"Nice sword. I've been listening to you coming for about half an hour now. Sound travels a long way down here. Was that you did all the yelling?"

Jack nodded. "Locked myself in . . . I got scared." Pointing at the peanut butter, Jack said, "Then I followed my nose." Taking a closer look, Jack guessed the boy was seventeen or eighteen. "Do you *live* here?"

The boy shook his head. "Nah, I'm just hanging out for a while."

Jack looked around. "Where did all this stuff come from? Did you bring it here?"

"Nope. I guess it's been here a long time. There's a guest list on the wall by the fridge, and it goes way back. Pretty strange."

Jack was still trying to take it all in. "But . . . I mean, like the refrigerator, and the electricity, and . . . everything. It's like a little apartment."

The kid grinned, and said with friendly sarcasm, "That's what it is. It is, in fact, like a little apartment. I think you have now understood. You have now said about all that can be said about it."

Jack didn't pick up on the sarcasm. "And . . . what about the rats?"

The kid jerked his head toward the cat. "That's Caesar's job. He comes with the place."

"So, like . . . you're *allowed* to be here?" Jack asked.

The boy shrugged. "Allowed? I don't know. And I don't care. All I know is that until my dad calms down or gets some serious help, I'm spending my nights right here. I mean, it's a little spooky, and I don't have my stereo, but it's a whole lot safer than my house is right now. And John said I could use the place, so, yeah—I guess I'm allowed."

Jack knew. Right away he knew.

But he asked to make sure. "*John* said you could use the place? John who?"

"John the janitor. Works at the old high school. He knows my dad, and last year he said if I ever needed help I should tell him. So about a week ago I needed help, and I told him, and here I am."

"You talked to John last year?"

The kid nodded. "Some of my friends said he was a good guy, so I checked him out, you know, just started shootin' the breeze with him one afternoon when I was in detention. He was working on something in the room, light switch or something. He was just easy to talk to. Like, first I just asked what he was doing, and he didn't brush me off. Really told me stuff, showed me how the circuits

123

worked, the whole deal. I'm interested in stuff like that, and he could tell, so he just kept showing. Then he asks me my name, and I say, 'I'm Eddie Wahlson.' And that's when he tells me if I ever need help, look him up. Turns out he knows my dad from the VFW."

Jack shook his head, not understanding. "The VFW?"

Eddie said, "That little white house near the diner downtown? Has the sign? Veterans of Foreign Wars?—VFW. It's like a club for guys that were in the service, fought in wars and stuff. Guys can help each other, talk about problems and stuff. War messes a lot of guys up. Messed up my dad. He was in the National Guard, and his unit got called up for Desert Storm—the Gulf War?"

Jack nodded.

"Anyway, that's how come John knew my dad, and that's how come I'm here." Eddie was done being sociable. Standing up, he said, "You want to get out of here, right?"

Jack nodded. "Yeah. Where are we, anyway?"

Eddie said, "About a block away from the fire station. How'd you get into the tunnels? Find an open door?"

Jack said, "Sort of. At my school."

"That where you found the sword?"

124

Jack nodded.

Eddie nodded back and said, "Cool."

Jack pointed at the wall near the corner by the refrigerator. He took two steps closer and bent down to read. "Did you sign the guest list?"

"You bet," said Eddie. "I'm part of Huntington history now."

Jack scanned the list. He turned on his flashlight so he could read the names. They had been written on a smooth patch of white concrete with pencils and markers, even a crayon or two. Dozens of names, going all the way back to the 1970s. Then Jack did a double take: The first name on the wall was LOU CARSWELL, 1973.

Jack wanted to look at every name. But Eddie had run out of patience. "The best place to get out is where I do. John knows this guy at the fire station, and he gave me a key to the door that comes out in the basement hallway there. That's where the steam comes from—there's a big boiler at the fire station. Still heats the library and the town hall. Keeps me toasty too. So let's go."

Jack almost had to trot to keep up with Eddie's longer strides. There were no lights once they left the living area, but Eddie didn't slow down and he didn't use a flashlight. Jack thought, *Maybe Eddie is evolving. Maybe one day Eddie will have no eyes at all.*

In five minutes they came to an opening in the wall, and Eddie said, "This is it." He ducked into the opening and flipped a switch by the door. A dim bulb lit the short corridor.

Eddie listened by the door. There were voices on the other side. They got louder and then began to get fainter. Eddie pulled out a key and put it into the lock, but held up his hand. He whispered, "Wait a minute or so. Anybody sees you out there, just tell 'em you came in the back door to use the bathroom. It's right down the hall to the left."

After half a minute of silence Eddie asked, "What grade you in?"

Jack said, "Fifth."

"So you're at the old high school this year, right?"

Jack nodded.

"When you see John, tell him Eddie says hi, okay?"

Jack said, "I'll tell him."

"And listen, John's a good guy to know, like if you ever get in trouble—I mean, like, real trouble. You ought to get to know him."

Jack said, "Yeah. I'm gonna do that."

It was quiet in the hallway, so Eddie opened the door a crack.

Jack said, "Eddie, I think you should keep this

sword, okay? I don't think I better try to carry it through downtown."

Eddie took the sword and hefted it appreciatively. He nodded. "Cool."

Jack said, "Hey . . . do you have any gum, Eddie?"

Eddie reached into his pocket. "Yeah."

"What flavor?" asked Jack.

Eddie pulled out an opened pack. "Watermelon—want a piece?"

Jack smiled and said, "No, thanks."

Eddie opened the door and said, "See you, little buddy."

Jack stepped out. "So long, Eddie—thanks."

And Eddie closed the door.

Chapter 20

TWO PLUS TWO

Outside the steam tunnel door Jack blinked in the bright bluish light. The corridor in the basement of the firehouse was empty, so he headed for the Exit sign and the stairs to his right.

Thirty seconds later Jack was standing in steadily falling snow at the corner of Maple and Williams. And then it hit him. Jack realized he must be late. He'd said he would be back at the shop at five. Looking in the window of a convenience store, Jack saw the time. It was five forty-five.

Instinctively he started running north on Williams toward Main Street. A quick fall on the snowy sidewalk and Jack realized running was not a good idea. Unhurt, he dusted himself off and then walked as quickly as he could.

Jack knew his dad would be worried. He might have even left. The school might be locked. Should he go into a store and try to call the school, or call home? He hoped his dad wouldn't be too angry, or even worse, disappointed in him again. Jack tried to pick up his pace as he continued slipping along toward the high school.

When he got to Main Street and turned east, he had to walk against the wind. It wasn't really cold, not by Minnesota standards, but the wind cut through his sweatshirt. By bending his head down, the brim of his Vikings cap kept the snow out of his face, and he only had to look up to check for cross traffic when he reached a curb.

When Jack passed the library, he picked up his pace. The sidewalk in the heart of downtown had already been sanded, so there was less danger of falling. He only had about four blocks to go.

Lifting his head to look out from under the brim of his cap, Jack saw something through the snow. At the next street, Randall Street.

A car with its lights on was parked behind the stop sign.

But it wasn't a car. It was a pickup. A green pickup.

John Rankin flashed his headlights, and Jack waved at him. Jack wanted to slow down. Thirty more steps and he would be there. *Think fast, think, think!* What could he say? No coat, no backpack, walking alone downtown in the snow.

Jack thought, *I can say I left my stuff at the*

*library, got involved in a book, saw the time, ran out-
side.* Jack felt the lie strangling him, and deep
down he knew it wouldn't work, knew he didn't
want to try to make it work.

Jack could see the truck's wipers ticking back
and forth. Jack stood at the crosswalk, waited for a
salt truck to rumble past, and then crossed the
street.

John Rankin rolled his window down halfway.

Jack smiled as best he could. "Hi, Dad. I—"

His dad cut him off, a sharp edge to his voice.
"Come get in out of the snow, Jack."

Jack said, "But my coat and my backpack are—"

"Just get in the truck, Jack. I've got 'em."

Jack didn't understand. "My coat? . . . And my
backpack?"

"Just get in." It was that angry-and-relieved
voice, the kind parents only use when they've
finally located a missing child.

Jack walked around the back of the truck and
got in on the passenger side. As he shut the door
his dad reached over and flicked the fan switch to
high. In the light from one of the old downtown
lampposts Jack saw his coat and backpack on the
seat. He said, "You . . . you found them."

His dad said, "Yup—no thanks to you. You had
me and everybody else worried sick."

John Rankin paused, getting control of himself. "I've been waiting here for about twenty minutes. About five fifteen I called home just to be sure you didn't snag a ride with a friend. Lois said you weren't there, so I started putting two and two together."

Very meekly Jack said, "Two and two?"

His dad nodded. "I checked the supply closet and saw you'd put your stuff away. Then I smelled something funny. Over behind the door. That's quite a load of gum in that pail."

Jack said, "But how—"

His dad held up his hand and said, "If you'll just hold your horses, I'll tell you. I found you because I look up from your bucket full of gum in the closet there and I see the lock on the key safe isn't latched. That's when it clicked."

John Rankin paused a few seconds, then said, "How'd you like that view from the bell tower?"

Jack gulped.

His dad went on. "That was you up there, right? On Tuesday? I thought I heard something. A school gets real quiet once the kids leave." Another pause. "So, did you like the view?"

Jack nodded. He could tell his dad wasn't really mad now, so he said, "I just wanted to see it. I never saw the whole town before."

John Rankin allowed himself to smile a little. "What gets me is that from all those keys you pick my two favorites. I've been up that tower. . . . I don't know how many times. I go up there to sit and think sometimes." Jack remembered the chair on the third landing.

"And the other key?" asked Jack. "How did you find out I had that one?"

His dad said, "Now, that was more like a lucky guess. I mean, I could have figured it out, but I would have had to get out the master key log and start counting until I found another stack that was one key short—but that would have taken me all night. It was because the tunnel key was right there near the bottom next to the tower key. I guessed that if I were you, I'd go and take one of each. And of course, I knew you were working in the auditorium. So, two plus two equals four."

"I'm sorry I made you worry, Dad."

John Rankin cleared his throat. "Well, I could see just what happened, you leaving the key in the door, and all. I went down in the tunnel with a light and I saw your footprints. I almost started yelling, and you probably could have heard me too. But I knew you wouldn't come to any harm. If I needed to find you, I knew I could. And sometimes you just have to step back and let things play out."

His dad fell silent and flipped the heater switch back to low. As the fan got quieter the rhythmic sound of the windshield wipers seemed louder.

Jack felt funny, like he was different. He wanted to tell his dad everything, and he wanted to know more. Jack said, "I met Eddie, Dad—Eddie Wahlson. I saw the place in the tunnel. And Eddie let me out the door at the fire station."

John Rankin leaned forward and released the parking brake. He pushed in the clutch, dropped the shift lever into first, and eased out onto Main Street.

And all he said was, "We'd better head home now."

Chapter 21
Something Permanent

It was slow-going on Main Street. The road crews were out, but the temperature was dropping quickly and the snow was coming faster than the salt could melt it.

The pickup crawled along past the library, and Jack stared out at the snow. It came rushing at the windshield. Jack loved looking up at streetlights during a snowstorm. Those millions of swirling flakes had always reminded him of a wild, happy dance.

But not now. Now they looked frantic, confused. The flakes crashed and tumbled in the air, fierce and chaotic.

Had he said something wrong? His dad was three feet away, but he seemed like he was in a distant room. Jack felt like a door had slammed in his face.

"Dad, I didn't mean to . . . I mean, about the tunnel . . . I won't tell anybody."

John Rankin looked across at him and smiled. Jack had never seen a smile like that before. His dad said, "Jackie, I know that. I know you wouldn't tell anyone. It's just that that place is . . . well, it's a whole other story. . . . And I think it's a story you're old enough to know about. . . . And when I try to think about how to tell it to you, it brings back a lot of memories." His dad looked close to tears.

Jack said, "I saw Lou's name on the wall. It said 'Lou Carswell, 1973.' Did Lou really stay there?"

John Rankin laughed and looked out his side window for a moment. "You sure do get right to the heart of things, Jackie. Yes, Lou did spend some time living down there, and that's a pretty good place to start the story. . . . But really I have to go back a few years before."

Jack knew what that meant. A few years before 1973 was when his dad had been in the army.

John Rankin said, "That time I spent in the army—that was a hard time for me. I mean, going into the service is never an easy thing, and thank God there are men and women who still take on that job. I had two tours of duty, with the infantry, down on the ground. I went through some awful times, and I lived through things I pray you or nobody else ever has to live through."

In the moving light and shadows Jack could see

135

his dad's jaw clenched tight. Then he took a deep breath and let it out slowly. "When I got back to Huntington after Vietnam, I was in a bad way. I was scared a lot of the time. I got sick real easy. I lived at home for a while, but my dad didn't know how to help and Mom wasn't well enough herself. I was the last thing she needed right then.

"I wasn't doing well at all, and for about a year I went and stayed at the veterans hospital this side of Minneapolis. I was just barely holding on.

"Then once, when I came down for the day to see Mom and Dad, I got it in my head to go say hello to my senior English teacher at the high school. I went to her room after school, and she wasn't there. Janitor said she'd moved to St. Paul. Well, he and I got to talking, and turns out he'd been in the same field division as me, but during the Korean War. And right out of the blue he asks me if I can work nights cleaning up at the high school. Said he really needed the help. I didn't learn till about three years later that he gave up his overtime hours to let me get back to feeling useful.

"Those nights at the school were good for me. I was in a familiar place, a place full of good memories. It was just what I needed. Tom Baldridge. That's his name. He retired about twelve years ago. I'm not just talking when I tell you that the day Tom put a broom in my hands, he saved my life."

Jack said, "Is that Lou in the picture on your dresser? And that big knife in your top drawer? Was that your knife in the army?"

John Rankin laughed out loud. "You ought to go into detective work, get paid for all your snooping. That sure is my knife, and you keep clear of it, Mister Nosyman. And yes, that's Lou in the picture. I met Lou on my second tour, and we teamed up, looked out for each other. You do a dozen or so patrols with the same person and you get to be close, like family. I carried a letter to his parents and his girlfriend, and he carried a letter to my folks, just in case. We used to joke that we kept each other alive because we neither of us wanted to have to deliver those letters. But when I got out at the end of my hitch, Lou still had another twelve months to go.

"Lou was from Chicago, and after he'd been home awhile, he came up to visit me. He needed work, and he needed a place to stay where he wouldn't be a bother to anyone. So that's when I rigged up that place in the tunnel. Friend of mine at the fire station helped me and Lou get the place fitted out, and I helped Lou get a job working nights cleaning up at the town hall. Once he had steady work, he moved into a rented room, but we left all the stuff in the tunnel. A few years later there was an opening at the high school. So that's the story of Lou Carswell."

They were only about three blocks from Greenwood Street, and Jack still had so many questions. "What about all the other names?" he asked. "It's a long list. Are all the others your friends too?"

His dad nodded. "My friends, Lou's friends, sometimes it's a kid like Eddie, caught in a hard spot, needs a safe place for a few days. A lot of people know that place is there, and when there's a need, someone gets in touch."

"A lot of people know?" asked Jack. "What if someone told the principal or the school committee—or the police? Don't you think it's probably against the law?"

John Rankin smiled. It felt odd to have his son worried about him for a change. "Well, I've looked into that, and as far as I can tell, the only thing I might be guilty of is using some town electricity. I put in an electric meter right at the get-go, and every month since October of 1973 I've been paying the going rate in a cash donation to the annual Veterans Day parade fund, and I keep careful records. Anyone wants to take me to court, I'm all set. I think I can pull together a pretty good group of witnesses." Then with a wink he said, "Now, you on the other hand—*you* just might have to go to jail for having a pocket full of keys. But don't you think we could get Mr. Ackerby to testify that you're a genuine temporary janitor?"

"And a darn good one, too," said Jack with a grin, "just like you."

Jack and his dad were still laughing as the truck turned into the snowy driveway at 920 Greenwood Street. Above the basketball backboard on the garage the floodlights were lit. As the pickup came to a stop Jack looked through the windshield, up into the light, and he saw millions of flakes swirling in a wild, happy dance.

Helen Rankin pulled aside the curtain above the sink and looked out the back window. She saw two boys get out of the truck. Or was it two men?

As they came toward the house John Rankin carried Jack's backpack in one hand, and his other hand was on his son's shoulder to steady himself.

They were trying to catch snowflakes on their tongues, laughing, almost falling down.

Helen was struck with the image. Her first baby, her little Jack, didn't seem so little. Somehow he was older, stronger.

And her husband, her best friend, her own

John—he seemed younger, less burdened.

Helen knew what she was looking at.

This wasn't an illusion. It wasn't a fleeting sensation. It wasn't something exclusive happening across the border in Boy Territory.

Helen was completely familiar with what she was seeing.

It was something good, something permanent.

It was love.

With a full heart Helen let the curtain fall back into place.

Walking to the front of the house, she called up the stairs, "Lois—they're home. Come for dinner now."

Then she went back to the kitchen to open the door for Jack and his dad.

**Here's a look at the next terrific
school story from ANDREW CLEMENTS**

CHAPTER 1

ZIPPED

Dave Packer was in the middle of his fourth hour of not talking. He was also in the middle of his social studies class on a Monday morning in the middle of November. And Laketon Elementary School was in the middle of a medium-size town in the middle of New Jersey.

There was a reason Dave was in the middle of his fourth hour of not talking, but this isn't the time to tell about that. This is the time to tell what he figured out in the middle of his social studies class.

Dave figured out that not talking is *extra* hard at school. And the reason? Teachers. Because at

11:35 Mrs. Overby clapped her hands and said, "Class—class! Quiet down!" Then she looked at her list and said, "Dave and Lynsey, you're next."

So Dave nodded at Lynsey and stood up. It was time to present their report about India.

But giving this report would ruin his experiment. Because Dave was trying to keep his mouth shut all day. He wanted to keep his lips zipped right up to the very end of the day, to not say one single word until the last bell rang at ten after three. And the reason Dave had decided to clam up . . . but it still isn't the time to tell about that. This is the time to tell what he did about the report.

Dave and Lynsey walked to the front of the room. Dave was supposed to begin the presentation by telling about the history of India. He looked down at his index cards, looked up at Mrs. Overby, looked out at the class, and he opened his mouth.

But he didn't talk.

He coughed. Dave coughed for about ten seconds. Then he wiped his mouth, looked at his index cards again, looked at Mrs. Overby again,

looked at the class again, opened his mouth again, and . . . coughed some more. He coughed and coughed and coughed until his face was bright red and he was all bent over.

Lynsey stood there, feeling helpless. Dave hadn't told her about his experiment, so all she could do was watch—and listen to his horrible coughing. Lynsey's opinion of Dave had never been high, and it sank lower by the second.

Mrs. Overby thought she knew what was happening with Dave. She had seen this before—kids who got so nervous that they made themselves sick rather than talk in front of the class. It surprised her, because Dave wasn't shy at all. Ever. In fact, *none* of this year's fifth graders were the least bit shy or nervous about talking. Ever.

But the teacher took pity, and she said, "You'd better go get some water. You two can give your report later."

Lynsey gave Dave a disgusted look and went back to her desk.

Dave nodded at Mrs. Overby, coughed a few more times for good measure, and hurried out of the room.

And with Dave out in the hall getting a drink, it's the perfect time to tell why he was in the middle of his fourth hour of not talking, and why he had decided to keep quiet in the first place.

CHAPTER 2

GANDHI

When something happens, there's usually a simple explanation. But that simple explanation is almost never the full story.

Here's the simple explanation anyway: Dave had decided to stop talking for a whole day because of something he'd read in a book.

See? Very simple, very clear. But it's not the whole story.

So here's a little more.

Dave and a partner had to prepare a report on India—not a long one, just some basic facts. Something about the history, something about the government, something about the land and the

industry, something about the Indian people and their culture. Five minutes or less.

Dave's report partner was Lynsey Burgess, and neither one of them was happy about that—there were some boy-girl problems at Laketon Elementary School. But this isn't the time to tell about that.

Even though Dave and Lynsey had to *give* their report together, they both agreed that they did *not* want to *prepare* it together. So they divided the topics in half, and each worked alone.

Dave was a good student, and he had found two books about India, and he had checked them out of the library. He hadn't read both books, not completely—he wasn't *that* good a student. But he had read parts of both books.

Dave thought the most interesting section in each book was the part about how India became independent, how the country broke away from England to become a free nation—sort of like the United States did.

And Dave thought the most interesting person in the story of India's independence was Mahatma Gandhi.

Dave was amazed by Gandhi. This one skinny little man practically pushed the whole British army out of India all by himself. But he didn't use weapons or violence. He fought with words and ideas. It was an incredible story, all of it true.

And in one of the books, Dave read this about Gandhi:

> For many years, one day each week
> Gandhi did not speak at all.
> Gandhi believed this was a way to
> bring order to his mind.

Dave read that bit of information on Thursday afternoon, and he read it again on Sunday night as he prepared for his oral report. And it made him wonder what that would be like—to go a whole day without saying a single word. And Dave began to wonder if not talking would bring order to *his* mind too.

In fact, Dave wondered what that meant, "to bring order to his mind." Could something as simple as not talking change the way your mind worked? Seemed like it must have been good for

Gandhi. But what would it do for a regular kid in New Jersey?

Would not talking make him . . . smarter? Would he finally understand fractions? If he had more order in his mind, would he be able to look at a sentence and *see* which word was an adverb—instead of just guessing? And how about sports? Would someone with a more orderly mind be a better baseball player?

Powerful questions.

So Dave decided to zip his lip and give it a try.

Was it hard for him to keep quiet? You bet, especially at first, like when he got to the bus stop, where his friends were arguing about why the Jets had lost to the Patriots. But Dave had learned quickly that by nodding and smiling, by frowning and shrugging, by shaking his head, by giving a thumbs-up or a high five, or even by just putting his hands in his coat pockets and turning away, not talking was possible. And by the time he'd ridden the bus to school, Dave had gotten pretty good at fitting in without speaking up.

There. That explains what's going on a little

better. And it's probably enough, at least for the moment. But there's more. There's *always* more.

And now we're back in class on Monday with Dave, who got through the rest of social studies without saying a word. And when the bell rang at the end of the period, it was time for fifth-grade lunch.

More than a hundred and twenty-five kids began hurrying toward the cafeteria. And by the time they got there, the fifth graders were already talking like crazy—all except one.

Reading Group Guide

Discussion Topics

• Jack makes a careful plan to deface a music room desk. Explain Jack's plan. Do you think most kids put gum under desks or do other damage to school property in similar ways, or for similar reasons? What does Jack hope to achieve with his gum plan?

• In chapter two, Andrew Clements writes: "...laughter from kids is more powerful than words from teachers." What does this mean? In what ways is this statement correct? In what ways is this statement incorrect?

• What do Luke and Kirk do to Jack after his dad cleans up their classroom in chapter three? What other encounters does Jack have with Luke and Kirk? How does he handle them? Do you think Jack uses a good strategy to handle these boys? Explain your answer. Have you ever teased another kid about something he or she could not change? Why did you do this? How did you feel about it afterwards?

• Chapter six begins with a discussion of ways in which Jack is like his dad. Are you ever told you are like your father, mother, or another family member? How does this comparison make you feel? How does the comparison make Jack feel? What is the real reason he feels this way?

• Describe Jack's mother and sister. Do you think Jack has a good home life? How might this story have been different had Jack explained his feelings to one of his parents? Do you think he understood his feelings well enough to explain them?

• How does Jack's father react to Jack's bad behavior and punishment? What does Jack think about this reaction?

• What is the thing that Helen calls "Boy Territory"? Do you think there is a comparable place that could be called "Girl Territory"? What is the author really describing when he speaks of "Boy Territory"?

• What does Jack learn about gum from his three-week punishment? What does he learn about the old school building? What does he learn about his father's job?

• What happens when Jack discovers that one of the mystery keys leads him to the tower? Late in the story, another character admits to spending time up in the tower. Who admits this? Did this admission surprise you? What does the tower section of the story show readers about this character? What does it teach readers about Jack?

• What does Jack's father tell him about his grandfather? Why do you think he tells him this story? Do you think Jack's grandfather was a good person? Was he a good father? In what ways is Jack's dad similar to or different from Jack's grandfather? Do you think Jack's dad would have reacted the same way to the totaled car? Explain your answer.

• Explain what John means when he says, "My life is my life, and yours is yours. I'm just glad that we get to run side by side for a few years, that's all."

• Can you think of a moment in time when you felt you really understood a parent's point of view? Describe this moment and how it affected your relationship with this adult.

THE
LANDRY NEWS

Andrew Clements

Illustrated by Brian Selznick

ATHENEUM BOOKS FOR YOUNG READERS

New York London Toronto Sydney

For my brother Denney—
a good writer, a good journalist,
a good man

First paperback edition September 2000
Text copyright © 1999 by Andrew Clements
Illustrations copyright © 2000 by Brian Selznick

Atheneum Books for Young Readers
An imprint of Simon & Schuster Children's Publishing Division
1230 Avenue of the Americas, New York, New York 10020

Designed by Anahid Hamparian
The text for this book was set in 13-point Clearface.
Manufactured in the United States of America
0119 OFF
46 48 50 49 47

The Library of Congress has cataloged the hardcover edition as follows:
Clements, Andrew, 1949-
The Landry News / by Andrew Clements.—1st ed.
p.   cm.
Summary: A fifth-grader starts a newspaper with an editorial that
prompts her burnt-out classroom teacher to really begin teaching again,
but he is later threatened with disciplinary action as a result.
ISBN 978-0-689-81817-2 (hc)
[1. Newspapers—Fiction. 2. Teachers—Fiction. 3. Schools—Fiction.
4. Divorce—Fiction.] I. Title.   PZ7.C59118Lan 1999   [Fic]—dc21   98-34376
ISBN 978-0-689-82868-3 (pbk)

The First Amendment to the Constitution of the United States

✳✳✳✳✳✳✳✳✳✳✳✳✳✳✳✳✳✳✳✳✳✳✳✳✳✳✳✳✳✳✳✳

AMENDMENT I

Congress shall make no law respecting an establishment of religion, or prohibiting the free exercise thereof; or abridging the freedom of speech, or of the press; or the right of the people peaceably to assemble, and to petition the Government for a redress of grievances.

Cara Landry, editor in chief of *The Landry News*, and star of this story.

CHAPTER 1

NEW KID GETS OLD TEACHER

"CARA LOUISE, I am *talking* to you!"

Cara Landry didn't answer her mom. She was busy.

She sat at the gray folding table in the kitchenette, a heap of torn paper scraps in front of her. Using a roll of clear tape, Cara was putting the pieces back together. Little by little, they fell into place on a fresh sheet of paper about eighteen inches wide. The top part was already taking shape—a row of neat block letters, carefully drawn to look like newspaper type.

"Cara, honey, you *promised* you wouldn't start that again. Didn't you learn one little thing from the last time?"

Cara's mom was talking about what had happened at the school Cara had attended for most of fourth grade, just after her dad had left. There had been some problems.

"Don't worry, Mom," Cara said absentmindedly, absorbed in her task.

Cara Landry had only lived in Carlton for six months. From the day she moved to town, during April of fourth grade, everyone had completely ignored her. She had been easy for the other kids to ignore. Just another brainy, quiet girl, the kind who always turns in assignments on time, always aces tests. She dressed in a brown plaid skirt and a clean white blouse every day, dependable as the tile pattern on the classroom floor. Average height, skinny arms and legs, white socks, black shoes. Her light brown hair was always pulled back into a thin ponytail, and her pale blue eyes hardly ever connected with anyone else's. As far as the other kids were concerned, Cara was there, but just barely.

All that changed in one afternoon soon after Cara started fifth grade.

It was like any other Friday for Cara at Denton Elementary School. Math first thing in the morning, then science and gym, lunch and health, and finally, reading, language arts, and social studies in Mr. Larson's room.

Mr. Larson was the kind of teacher parents write letters to the principal about, letters like:

Dear Dr. Barnes:
We know our child is only in second grade this

year, but please be *sure* that he [or she] is NOT put into Mr. Larson's class for fifth grade.

Our lawyer tells us that we have the right to make our educational choices known to the principal and that you are not allowed to tell anyone we have written you this letter.

So in closing, we again urge you to take steps to see that our son [or daughter] is *not* put into Mr. Larson's classroom.

Sincerely yours,

Mr. and Mrs. Everybody-who-lives-in-Carlton

Still, *someone* had to be in Mr. Larson's class; and if your mom was always too tired to join the PTA or a volunteer group, and if you mostly hung out at the library by yourself or sat around your apartment reading and doing homework, it was possible to live in Carlton for half a year and not know that Mr. Larson was a lousy teacher. And if your mom didn't know enough to write a letter to the principal, you were pretty much guaranteed to get Mr. Larson.

Mr. Larson said he believed in the open classroom. At parents' night every September, Mr. Larson explained that children learn best when they learn things on their own.

This was not a new idea. This idea about learning was being used successfully by practically every teacher in America.

But Mr. Larson used it in his own special way. Almost every day, he would get the class started on a story or a worksheet or a word list or some reading and then go to his desk, pour some coffee from his big red thermos, open up his newspaper, and sit.

Over the years, Mr. Larson had taught himself how to ignore the chaos that erupted in his classroom every day. Unless there was the sound of breaking glass, screams, or splintering furniture, Mr. Larson didn't even look up. If other teachers or the principal complained about the noise, he would ask a student to shut the door, and then go back to reading his newspaper.

Even though Mr. Larson had not done much day-to-day teaching for a number of years, quite a bit of learning happened in room 145 anyway. The room itself had a lot to do with that. Room 145 was like a giant educational glacier, with layer upon layer of accumulated materials. Mr. Larson read constantly, and every magazine he had subscribed to or purchased during the past twenty years had ended up in his classroom. *Time, Good Housekeeping, U.S. News & World Report, Smithsonian, Cricket, Rolling Stone, National Geographic, Boys' Life, Organic Gardening, The New Yorker, Life, Highlights, Fine Woodworking, Reader's Digest, Popular Mechanics*, and dozens of others. Heaps of them filled the shelves and cluttered the corners. Newspapers, too, were stacked in front of the windows;

recent ones were piled next to Mr. Larson's chair. This stack was almost level with his desktop, and it made a convenient place to rest his coffee cup.

Each square inch of wall space and a good portion of the ceiling were covered with maps, old report covers, newspaper clippings, diagrammed sentences, cartoons, Halloween decorations, a cursive handwriting chart, quotations from the Gettysburg Address and the Declaration of Independence, and the complete Bill of Rights—a dizzying assortment of historical, grammatical, and literary information.

The bulletin boards were like huge paper time warps—shaggy, colorful collages. Whenever Mr. Larson happened to find an article or a poster or an illustration that looked interesting, he would staple it up, and he always invited the kids to do the same. But for the past eight or ten years, Mr. Larson had not bothered to take down the old papers—he just wallpapered over them with the new ones. Every few months—especially when it was hot and humid—the weight of the built-up paper would become too much for the staples, and a slow avalanche of clippings would lean forward and whisper to the floor. When that happened, a student repair committee would grab some staplers from the supply cabinet, and the room would shake as they pounded flat pieces of history back onto the wall.

Freestanding racks of books were scattered all

around room 145. There were racks loaded with mysteries, Newbery winners, historical fiction, biographies, and short stories. There were racks of almanacs, nature books, world records books, old encyclopedias, and dictionaries. There was even a rack of well-worn picture books for those days when fifth-graders felt like looking back at the books they grew up on.

The reading corner was jammed with pillows and was sheltered by half of an old cardboard geodesic dome. The dome had won first prize at a school fair about fifteen years ago. Each triangle of the dome had been painted blue or yellow or green and was designed by kids to teach something—like the flags of African nations or the presidents of the United States or the last ten Indianapolis-500 winners—dozens and dozens of different minilessons. The dome was missing half its top and looked a little like an igloo after a week of warm weather. Still, every class period there would be a scramble to see which small group of friends would take possession of the dome.

The principal didn't approve of Mr. Larson's room one bit. It gave him the creeps. Dr. Barnes liked things to be spotless and orderly, like his own office—a place for everything, and everything in its place. Occasionally he threatened to make Mr. Larson change rooms—but there was really no other room he could move to. Besides, room 145 was on the lower level of the school in the back corner. It was the room that was the farthest away from the office, and Dr. Barnes couldn't bear the thought of Mr. Larson being one inch closer to him.

Even though it was chaotic and cluttered, Mr. Larson's class suited Cara Landry just fine. She was able to tune out the noise, and she liked being left alone for the last two hours of every day. She would always get to class early and pull a desk and chair over to the back corner by some low bookcases. Then she would pull the large map tripod up behind her chair. She would spread out her books and papers on the bookshelf to her right, and she would tack her plastic pencil case on the bulletin board to her left. It was a small private space, like her own little office, where Cara could just sit and read, think, and write.

Then, on the first Friday afternoon in October, Cara took what she'd been working on and without saying anything to anybody, she used four thumbtacks and stuck it onto the overloaded bulletin board at the back of Mr. Larson's room. It was Denton Elementary School's first edition of *The Landry News*.

CHAPTER 2

ROOF BLOWS OFF SCHOOLROOM

AFTER THE COMICS and the crossword puzzle, the sports section was Mr. Larson's favorite part of the newspaper. He always saved the sports for the last hour of the day, as a reward for himself. On this particular Friday afternoon in October, Mr. Larson was reading an important article about the baseball pennant races. He was trying hard to give the article his full attention, but he couldn't.

Something was wrong.

There were no shattering windows, no toppling chairs, no screaming or yelling. It was worse than that. It was too quiet.

Mr. Larson looked up from his paper and saw all twenty-three kids gathered around the bulletin board. Some girls were giggling, there were some gasps and pokes and whispers, and some of the bigger boys were elbowing to get in closer. Over the top of his reading glasses, the scene came into focus for Mr. Larson, and he could see what they were staring at: a large sheet of paper laid out in columns, with a banner at the top, *The Landry News*.

Mr. Larson smiled. It was a pleased, self-satisfied smile. "There—you see," he said to himself, as if he were talking to the principal, *"that* is my open classroom at work! Here's living proof. I have not been involved one bit, and that quiet new girl—Laura . . . or Tara? Or . . . well . . . that little Landry girl—she has gone right ahead and made her own newspaper! And look! Just look! All the other kids are getting involved in the learning!" Mr. Larson kept talking to himself, now imagining that he was defending himself in front of the whole school board. "Go right ahead. You're the principal, Dr. Barnes. You can put all the letters you want into my file, Dr. Barnes. But here's proof, right here! I *do* know what I'm doing, and *I'm* the teacher in my classroom, not you!"

Mr. Larson carefully folded up his newspaper and put it onto the large stack beside his desk. He would have to finish that World Series article on Monday.

He carefully straightened his long legs under his desk, then tensed his back and stretched his arms, tilting his head slowly from side to side. He was getting ready to stand up. This was the perfect time for some meaningful interaction with the class. Also, it was only five minutes before the end of the day, and he'd have to stand up then anyway because he had bus duty this week.

Moving carefully among the jumble of desks and

chairs, Mr. Larson got close enough to the bulletin board to read *The Landry News*. He nodded at the headline of the lead story: SECOND-GRADER GAGS ON OVERCOOKED JELL-O. Mr. Larson remembered. That little problem had required a call to 911.

A sports column caught his eye, and squinting, he could read the neatly printed description of a noon-recess touch football game. The game had ended with a fist fight and one-day suspensions for three fifth-grade boys. Mr. Larson read slowly, smiling in approval. The writing was clear, no spelling mistakes, no wasted words. This girl had talent. He was just about to turn and compliment . . . Sara? . . . no—well, the Landry girl, when something caught his eye.

It was in the editorial section. There, in the lower right-hand corner of the paper, Mr. Larson saw his own name. He started reading.

From the Editor's Desk
A Question of Fairness

There has been no teaching so far this year in Mr. Larson's classroom. There has been learning, but there has been no teaching. There is a teacher in the classroom, but he does not teach.

In his handout from parents' night, Mr. Larson says that in his classroom "the students must learn how to learn by themselves, and they must learn to learn from each other, too."

So here is the question: If the students teach themselves, and they also teach each other, why is Mr. Larson the one who gets paid for being a teacher?

In the public records at the Carlton Memorial Library it shows that Mr. Larson got paid $39,324 last year. If that money was paid to the real teachers in Mr. Larson's classroom, then each student would get $9.50 every day during the whole school year. I don't know about you, but that would definitely help my attitude toward school.

And that's the view this week from the News desk.

Cara Landry, Editor in Chief

The kids watched Mr. Larson's face as he stood there reading. His jaw slowly clenched—tighter and tighter. His face reddened, and his short blond hair seemed to bristle all over his head. Instinctively, the kids backed away, clearing a path between Mr. Larson and the bulletin board. With one long stride he was there, and the four thumbtacks shot off and skittered across the floor as he tore the paper down.

Mr. Larson was tall—six feet, two inches. Now he seemed twice that size to the kids. He turned slowly from left to right, looking down at their faces. Without raising his voice he said, "There is a kind of writing that is appropriate in school, and there is a kind that is INappropriate." Turning back to look directly at Cara, he held up the sheet and shook it. "THIS," he shouted, "is INappropriate!"

Folding the paper in half, he walked quickly to his desk, ripping the sheet into smaller and smaller bits as he went. It was deathly still. Mr. Larson turned to look at Cara, still standing beside the bulletin board. Her face was as pale as his was red, and she was biting her lower lip, but she didn't flinch. No one dared to breathe. The silence was shattered by the bell, and as Mr. Larson dropped the shredded paper into the trash basket, he barked, "Class dismissed!"

The room emptied in record time, and Cara was swept along toward the lockers and the waiting buses. Mr. Larson was right behind, on his way to bus duty. He hurried out to the curb, still angry but back under control. The hubbub and confusion of the scene was a welcome distraction, and during the next ten minutes buses one, two, and three filled up and pulled away with their noisy loads.

The last person to get on to bus 4 was Cara Landry. She was running, dragging her jacket, her gray backpack heavy on her thin shoulders.

Mr. Larson did not smile, but he did manage to say, "Good-bye, Cara." He knew her name now.

As she climbed aboard, he turned quickly and went

Karl Larson, a teacher at Denton Elementary School, holding *The Landry News*. He has called it "INappropriate."

back into the school. Bus 4 pulled away.

Mr. Larson went to the teachers' room, got his empty lunch bag off the shelf, and went straight from there out the back door of the school to the staff parking lot. He did not return to room 145 to get his red thermos of coffee. He did not want to go back there until he had to, until Monday.

And it's a good thing he didn't go get his thermos. Because if he had gone into the room and up to his desk, he probably would have glanced down into the wastebasket. And he would have seen that every scrap of *The Landry News* was gone.

Someone had returned to the empty room to pick up all the pieces.

CHAPTER 3

ANCIENT HISTORY, MODERN MYSTERY

THERE WERE SIXTEEN fifth-graders on Cara's bus, and seven of them had been in Mr. Larson's class. Cara usually sat by herself on the bus, but today LeeAnn Ennis slipped into the seat beside her.

As the bus pulled away LeeAnn looked over her shoulder to watch Mr. Larson stomp back into the school. "He was so mad! I've never even heard of him getting mad before. But he was mad today, real mad. I can't believe you wrote that, Cara! Oh . . . you know, I don't think we ever met, but I'm in Mr. Larson's class with you."

"I know who you are," said Cara. "You're LeeAnn Ennis. Ellen Hatcher is your best friend, you like Deke Deopolis, your sister is a cheerleader at the high school, and your mom is secretary of the Denton School PTA. Math is your favorite subject, you love cats, and you went to the big sleepover party at Betsy

Lowenstein's house last weekend."

LeeAnn's mouth dropped open. "What, are you a spy or something? How do you know all that?"

Feeling embarrassed, Cara smiled, something LeeAnn had never seen her do before. "No, I'm not a spy. I'm a journalist. People who make newspapers need to know what's going on, that's all. When things happen, or when people say things, I just pay attention."

Ed Thomson and Joey DeLucca were in the seat right behind LeeAnn and Cara, and they were listening. They were in Mr. Larson's class, too.

Joey leaned forward over the seat and looked at Cara. "You mean you know stuff like that about *everybody*?"

"No, not everybody. Some people are newsmakers and some aren't." Cara blushed. She thought Joey was cute. He had never said a word to her until now. Somehow, she made herself talk naturally. "It's not like I memorize all this stuff or anything. But if something happens that might be news, then I ask questions and pay attention so I can report on it. News has got to be accurate. Like that kid who choked on the rubber Jell-O? That was Alan Cortez. He's in second grade in Mrs. Atkins's class. The lady in the kitchen who cooked the Jell-O that day is Alice Rentsler. The principal made her write a letter of apology to Alan's parents. Alice also had to have a special Jell-O-making session with the kitchen supervisor to make sure she cooks it right from now on.

I thought that was all pretty interesting, so I looked around and I got the facts."

Ed piped up. "But all that stuff about LeeAnn? What's that about? Is she such a big newsmaker?" LeeAnn narrowed her eyes at Ed and pretended like she was going to whack him with her backpack.

Cara smiled and said, "No, that's just stuff I've noticed—or heard kids talk about. LeeAnn has cat stickers all over her notebook and her locker, her mom's name is on the PTA newsletter we got in the mail at my house this summer, her big sister drops LeeAnn off at school sometimes when she's wearing her cheerleader outfit, and everybody knows that LeeAnn likes Deke."

Ed was impressed. "Okay, okay . . . all that makes sense. But tell me why you wrote that thing about Mr. Larson. Are you mad at him or something?"

Cara didn't answer right away. "No, I'm not mad at him," she said thoughtfully. "I just don't think it's right that he doesn't teach us anything." Cara was quiet while about ten kids got up and pushed and shuffled and yelled their way off the bus. Her stop was next.

As the bus lurched forward again, Cara lowered her voice and said, "Can you guys keep a secret?" Joey and LeeAnn and Ed nodded. "Promise?" All three kids nodded again, leaning closer. Looking from face to face, Cara said, "Have you ever looked in those glass cases in the front hall by the office?"

"You mean all the sports trophies?" asked Joey. "Yeah, I've seen them."

Cara said, "Well, you're right, it's mostly sports, but there's some other stuff there, too—Writer of the Month awards, and Math Club honors—all sorts of things. And there's one plaque for Teacher of the Year."

LeeAnn said, "Oh, yeah . . . I've seen that. Mrs. Palmer—my teacher in third grade—well, she won it last year."

Cara shook her head. "No, that's the new plaque. I'm talking about the *old* one, way back in the corner of the case. The teachers and the PTA have been giving that award for over twenty-five years. And about fifteen years ago, guess whose name got carved on that plaque?"

"Him?" asked LeeAnn. The bus was stopping at Edgewater Village. LeeAnn got up to let Cara into the aisle.

Cara nodded. "Yup. Mr. Karl Larson—Teacher of the Year, *three years in a row*." Cara heaved her backpack up onto one shoulder. As she headed for the door she looked back at the three kids staring after her, and she said, "Now *that's* what I call *news*."

CHAPTER 4

MISSING TEACHER FOUND IN NEARBY SUBURB

IT WAS A LONG drive home for Mr. Larson that Friday afternoon.

He was angry. Angry at that Landry girl. Angry at life in general, but most of all, angry at himself.

He'd been a teacher for almost twenty years now, and he couldn't remember the last time he had gotten mad in front of a class. All his talk about respect for one another, respect for different opinions, respect for honesty and real learning. Talk, talk, talk. All his words flew back into his face as he drove south on Interstate 55. Above the half-harvested cornfields on either side of the road, the flat gray sky was a good mirror for his thoughts.

Well . . . what about that little girl's respect for *him*? Mr. Larson tried to build a case for himself, tried to find a way to let himself off the hook for losing control. But he had to face facts. He knew Cara Landry had only been telling the truth. That was the hardest thing for him to admit.

By the time he drove into Williston, then down Ash Street and into his driveway, he was feeling a little better.

But when he opened the kitchen door and stepped into the empty house, the self-pity kicked in again. He opened the refrigerator and poured himself a tall glass of cider. He walked into the living room and slumped into the big armchair.

"What do those kids know about me, anyway?" he thought. "What gives that Landry girl the right to judge me?"

Mr. Larson remembered his own fifth-grade teacher, Mrs. Spellman. She had been perfect. Her clothes and hair and lipstick were always just so. Her classroom was always quiet and orderly. She never raised her voice—she never had to. She wrote in that flawless cursive, and a little gold star on a paper from Mrs. Spellman was like a treasure, even for the toughest boys.

Then young Karl Larson saw Mrs. Spellman at the beach on Memorial Day with her family. She was sitting under an umbrella, and she wore a black swimsuit that did not hide any of her midriff bulges or the purple veins on her legs. Her hair was all straggly from swimming, and without any makeup or lipstick she looked washed out, tired. She had two kids, a girl and a boy, and she yelled at them as they wrestled and got sand all over the beach towels. Her husband lay flat on his back in the sun, a large man with lots of hair on his stomach, and it wasn't a small stomach. As Karl stood there staring, Mrs. Spellman's husband lifted his head off the sand, turned toward his wife, pointed at the cooler, and said, "Hey Mabel, hand me another cold one, would you?"

Karl was thunderstruck, and he turned and stumbled back to where his own family had set up their picnic on the beach. This big, hairy guy looked at *his* Mrs. Spellman and said, "Hey Mabel." At that moment, Karl Larson realized that the Mrs. Spellman he knew at school was mostly a fictional character, partly created by him, and partly created by Mrs. Spellman herself. The students and . . . and *Mabel* created Mrs. Spellman together, in order to do the job—the job of schooling.

As Karl Larson sat there sipping cider, he considered the Mr. Larson that Cara Landry and the rest of the class knew. They had no idea who Karl Larson was. They didn't know that he was the first person in his family who had ever gone to college. They didn't know about the sacrifices he and his parents had made so he could get an education, and how proud he had been to get his first job teaching school in Carlton over nineteen years ago.

They probably didn't know that his wife was a teacher too—eighth grade English at a school on Chicago's South Side. The kids had no idea how much Karl Larson had hated seeing his wife's job get harder and harder over the years. Barbara Larson worried day and night about whether she could ever make a real difference in the lives of those kids she loved so much. Her school had always been a pretty rough place, but now . . . now there were metal detectors at the doors, and an armed guard escorted teachers to a padlocked parking lot at the end of each school day.

These kids didn't know that he and his wife had two daughters, a sophomore and a senior at the University of Illinois. Both girls were happy there, good students, doing well. But each of them had been accepted at top-notch colleges in Connecticut and Ohio and California, and each had chosen to go to the state school because that was the college their parents could afford. And Karl Larson couldn't forgive himself.

How could fifth-graders understand how hard it had been for him and his wife to take care of their aging parents over the past eight years—first hers and now his? The kids didn't know, they couldn't know.

So here he was. It was a Friday afternoon, and he was sitting alone in a dark house, waiting for his wife to fight her way home through the rush-hour traffic. After about fifteen minutes he finally gathered enough energy to get up and go to the kitchen and start cooking supper.

Later, after dinner, Mr. Larson told his wife about the editorial. He was expecting some sympathy, but he should have known better. His wife was much too honest for that. It was one of the things he loved best about her. Barbara Larson leaned across the kitchen table and squeezed his arm and said, "Sounds like this little girl is looking for a teacher, Karl—that's all. She's just looking for a teacher."

Mr. Larson tried to remember when he had stopped being a good teacher. But it wasn't like there was one particular moment you could point to. Teachers don't burn out all at once. It happens a little at a time, like the weariness that can overtake a person walking up a steep hill—you begin to get tired and you slow down, and then you feel like you just have to stop and sit and rest.

And that's how Karl Larson felt—overburdened and depressed. Some mornings he could barely get out of bed, and now this . . . this *editorial*. It didn't seem fair to be judged this way.

But still, could he blame anyone but himself? Were those kids *supposed* to know anything about him? Should anything outside of the classroom even matter to them? Should it have mattered to young Karl Larson that Mrs. Spellman was also this lady named Mabel who had a beer-drinking husband with a large hairy stomach? No. At school, Mabel was Mrs. Spellman, and she was a good teacher.

Karl Larson could see it clearly. The only reason

that he and those kids were together was to do the job—the job of schooling. The kids didn't need Karl Larson's life story. They needed *Mr. Larson*, the teacher.

So, over the weekend Karl Larson gradually faced the facts. *The Landry News* had told the truth. Mr. Larson the teacher was guilty as charged.

And Karl Larson knew he had to do something about it.

CHAPTER 5

HOMEWORK: HARD BUT IMPORTANT

WHEN CARA FINISHED taping it back together late Friday afternoon, she left the first edition of *The Landry News* on the kitchen table and went to her bedroom. She wanted to find the stack of newspapers she had made during fourth grade. When she came back with the small pile of earlier editions, her mother was standing at the table, reading the editorial about Mr. Larson.

Looking up, her mother said, "Let me guess: The teacher tore this up after he read it, right?"

Cara nodded.

"Cara, honey, you have done it this time." Her mother scanned the patchwork newspaper and heaved a long, tired sigh. "Well, at least this is the only copy and Mr. Larson didn't run it down the hall to the principal—like some other teachers have done."

Mrs. Landry dropped heavily onto one of the chairs beside the table. She looked at her daughter standing there. "Now tell me, Cara: Are you angry at me? Is that why you do this? Because if you are trying to hurt me, I just want to tell you that it's working. It's working just great."

Tears welled up in her mother's eyes, and Cara looked at her, unblinking. "No, Mother, I am not trying to hurt you. And you shouldn't be upset. This is just a newspaper. These are just facts, Mother."

"Facts? Just look right here, young lady." Joanna Landry stabbed a red fingernail at the editorial. "This is not just *facts*. You have unloosed your acid little tongue on this man and said mean and hurtful things here."

Cara flinched at the accusation, but she jumped to defend herself. "It's an *editorial*, Mother, so it's *allowed* to have opinions in it. And all the opinions are based on facts. I didn't make any of that up. I never have made anything up. I just report the facts. *You* are the one who taught me to always tell the truth, remember? Well, I'm just telling the truth here."

Mrs. Landry was outgunned, and she knew it. It had been years since she had won an argument with Cara, and she wasn't going to win this one. But having to admit that her daughter was only telling the truth did not make things any easier. Here they were only one month into a new school year in a new town, and Cara was already stirring the pot, stewing up trouble. Joanna Landry could feel her hair getting grayer by the minute.

She took a deep breath. "You may *call* it just telling the truth, but ever since your father left, you have gone out of your way to tell the truth in the most *hateful* way you know how. And it just makes me sad, Cara. It's not fair to me, and it's bad for you, and it just makes me *sad*." And with that, Mrs. Landry stood up and went to her room and closed the door.

Cara's thin shoulders hunched together as she sat on the dinette chair, looking at the paper, waiting for the sobs to begin in her mother's bedroom. *She's wrong*, thought Cara. *This time, she's wrong*.

But last year, it was like her mother said. Cara *had* been hateful—to everyone. When her dad left, Cara was sure it was because of her. Her mom and dad had always argued about money and about saving for Cara's college and about buying Cara better clothes, about taking Cara on a nice vacation. When her father left and filed for divorce, she thought it was because he didn't want to feel responsible for a family—for her.

It was just bad timing that turned Cara into an outlaw journalist. The week her father moved out, Cara's fourth-grade teacher had begun a unit on newspapers, and Cara seized hold of the idea with murder in her heart. She became a ferocious reporter—aloof, remote, detached. She turned a cold, hard eye on her classmates and teachers, saw their weaknesses and silliness, and used her strong language skills to lash out. She stuck close to the truth, but the truth wasn't always pretty.

When she learned that a rather large teacher kept a desk drawer filled with candy bars and fatty treats, Cara wrote an editorial with the title, "Let's Chat about Fat." The story got some laughs, but it was too mean, almost cruel. It did not win Cara any new friends, and it sent all her old friends ducking for cover.

When she noticed that the cafeteria staff would sometimes carry home leftovers at the end of the day, Cara blew the whistle in a banner headline: FOOD WORKERS PERFORM DISAPPEARING ACT. But she hadn't done enough research. What they were doing was all legal and approved. The practice actually saved the school money by decreasing the garbage-disposal expenses. The principal made Cara go and apologize to the cafeteria workers. After that she thought it best to bring bag lunches to school.

Every week, somewhere in the school, Cara would put up the newest edition of The Landry News, and then wait for the consequences. After the story about the cafeteria workers, her research got more careful, and she was always sure of her facts. But the way she told her news stories was always designed to create a stir and get a reaction, and she was never disappointed. There were conferences with her mother and the principal, conferences with the principal and the school psychologist, and conferences with her mother and every one of her teachers. And every conference would then become the subject of a sarcastic editorial, published in the very next edition of *The Landry News*.

The only person who never showed up at a conference was the only person Cara really wanted to see: her dad.

Now as Cara sat at the kitchen table looking through the sheaf of fourth-grade editions, she had trouble imagining herself writing all this. So much anger. But this newest paper wasn't like the ones she had made last year. She was still sad, but she wasn't angry anymore. Things were better now.

Over the summer, she had started getting letters from her dad. He worked in Indianapolis now, and he had promised Cara that she could come and visit him there—maybe at Thanksgiving or Christmas. And he would be coming to Chicago pretty often, too. He had called to tell her he was sorry about the way things had worked out. He explained why he and her mom had split up. And it didn't have anything to do with her. Cara could see that now, and she could believe it was true, even if all the rest of it still didn't make any sense to her.

Cara tiptoed to her mother's door and listened. It was quiet. She knocked softly and her mom said, "Come on in, honey."

Her mom was on the bed, sitting with her back against the headboard. Her old leather-bound Bible lay open on her lap. There were some wadded tissues on the bedspread, and Joanna Landry swept them aside and patted the bed. Cara sat on the edge and took her mother's hand.

"Mom, I'm not writing the news because I'm angry. Honest. I'm really not mad anymore. I was. I was real mad last year, and I know I hurt a lot of people's feelings, and I'm sorry about that now. And I guess I should have stopped to think before I wrote this new editorial . . . and I'll tell Mr. Larson I'm sorry—I will. But I still think it's okay to tell the truth, and to publish it, too. I *like* being a reporter. It's something I'm *good* at, Mom."

Her mother reached for a fresh tissue with her free hand and dabbed at her eyes. "Cara honey, you know I just want the best for you, that's all. I just don't want you to make things hard for yourself. I feel so bad already—about me and your dad, I mean. I know that's been tough on you, and you took it so hard. But it wasn't anything to do with you. Can you see that?"

Cara nodded. "I know. It just felt that way, that's all. And I'm sorry I gave you so much more to worry about, Mom. But . . . but don't you think it'll be all right to keep on making my newspaper—if I'm careful, and if I only report the truth?"

Her mom smiled. "Listen to this, Cara. It's from the book of Psalms."

Joanna Landry and her daughter, Cara, discussing truth and mercy in their home in Carlton, Illinois.

MERCY AND TRUTH ARE MET TOGETHER;
RIGHTEOUSNESS AND PEACE HAVE KISSED
EACH OTHER.
TRUTH SHALL SPRING OUT OF THE EARTH;
AND RIGHTEOUSNESS SHALL LOOK DOWN
FROM HEAVEN.

Her mother smiled at her and said, "Truth is good, and it's all right to let the truth be known. But when you are publishing all that truth, just be sure there's some mercy, too. Then you'll be okay."

At that quiet moment, safe at home, it all sounded so simple to Cara Landry. But the test would come on Monday.

CHAPTER 6

TOP STRESS CAUSE FOR KIDS? ONE WORD: *FEAR*

AS CARA SAT in health class on Monday afternoon, she was sweating. She never sweated, not even during gym. But this wasn't a hot sweat. It was a dry, sticky-mouthed sweat. A scared sweat.

It was also a mad-at-herself sweat. Cara hated feeling like a coward. She fumed at herself. "But that's what I am: a big, fat coward."

Her mom had dropped her off at school early that morning. Cara had wanted to be there before the other kids arrived. She wanted to give a note to Mr. Larson.

Cara had spent most of Sunday night working on the note. She had ripped up about twenty pieces of paper trying to get it right. She practically knew it by heart:

Dear Mr. Larson:

I want to say I'm sorry for the part of *The Landry News* that was about you. Maybe I should not have surprised you by just sticking it up on the wall like that for everyone else to read. It's just that I like making newspapers. I try to print only what's true, but I guess sometimes I don't think enough about how that can make people feel.

I mean, I still think that what I said was pretty true, but I didn't mean to make you mad like that. So, I'm sorry.

Sincerely yours,
Cara L. Landry

At seven-thirty that morning Cara had been on her way through the halls, her shoes squeaking on the newly waxed floors. Cara had the note in her hand. She turned the corner, and there he was, coming out of room 145. As he turned to go the other way, toward the teachers' room, Cara wanted to call out, "Hey, Mr. Larson!" and then run right over, smile a little, and hand him the note. Instead she turned to stone, and her tongue stuck to the roof of her mouth. She flattened up against the lockers, then backed around the corner, making sure her rubber soles didn't squeak. She jammed the note into the pocket of her dress and ran out the nearest door to the playground.

All day long she had skulked around, making sure that wherever she was, Mr. Larson wasn't. LeeAnn had come with Betsy Lowenstein and three other girls to sit with her at lunch, and Cara had hardly said three words, she was so mad at herself. She just sat there like an idiot, chewing on her lower lip, and nodding and smiling once in a while as LeeAnn went on and on about how mad Mr. Larson had been on Friday.

But in ten minutes, there would be no escape. Unless . . . no. If she went to the nurse, the nurse would call her mom at her office, so that wouldn't work. And if she didn't go to class, then Mr. Larson would know she was a coward, and Joey DeLucca and LeeAnn Ennis would know she was a coward. And worst of all, Cara thought, "*I* would know that I am the biggest, fattest, weakest, lamest, chickenest *coward* who ever lived."

So when the bell rang, Cara Landry, the secret coward with the cold sweats, put on her bravest face and walked like a robot down the hall and into room 145.

CHAPTER 7

FANS BRACE FOR GRUDGE MATCH

AS THE BELL rang someone else was sweating. The tall man in the rumpled sport coat hunched lower in his chair, holding his newspaper a little higher than usual. He was staring at the batting averages, but he saw nothing except the image of a little girl in a brown plaid skirt, scared out of her wits, biting her lower lip. This was the same image he had seen all weekend long. And now that little girl would be in his classroom again, the room where he was supposed to be the teacher. Mr. Larson reached for his thermos for the tenth time that day and remembered for the tenth time that it contained nothing but last Friday's coffee, as cold as the palms of his hands and as bitter as his churning stomach.

The kids came in and immediately began pulling the jumbled desks into rows. A room somehow feels safer with the desks all lined up. Everyone sat down. There was no goofing off, no loud talking like there had been at the start of class on Friday. It was the same teacher reading his newspaper, same kids, same room. But everything was different, and everyone knew it. And Cara Landry knew it best.

Cara sat as close as she could to the door at the back of the room. She wasn't really thinking about it, but somewhere on the edge of her mind she wanted to be ready for a quick getaway. She stared at her library book, reading the same paragraph over and over and over. When the bell rang, she jumped at the sound and quickly looked around to see if anyone had seen her jump. Joey DeLucca had been watching her, and he smiled and gave her a thumbs up. Cara tried to smile back but shivered instead, and forced her eyes back to the safety of the open book on her desk. Her note to Mr. Larson was tucked inside the front of the book. She gripped the cover tightly, as if trying to keep her apology trapped there, afraid it might leap out and throw itself into Mr. Larson's hands.

Mr. Larson cleared his throat, noisily folded his paper, and stood up, still holding the rumpled sheets. Right away he wished he hadn't stood up. He felt so tall, towering alone up at the front of the classroom. Some of the kids looked at him, but just as many kept their eyes elsewhere, and the little girl in the brown plaid skirt and the white-collared shirt stared at her book, her knuckles white. Mr. Larson noticed she was reading *Incident at Hawk Hill*, and his mind tried to recall the plot, searching for some hidden meaning in Cara's choice of that particular book. He shook that thought away, like a pitcher shaking off a bad signal from a catcher.

Clearing his throat again, he said, "How many of you looked at a Sunday paper this weekend?" Timidly, almost all the kids raised their hands.

Without taking her eyes off her book, Cara raised her hand, too. She always read the Sunday *Chicago Tribune*, and the Sunday *Sun Times*. And if she could get her mom to pay for it at the newsstand on the way home from church, she read *The New York Times*, too. The Sunday papers were Cara's favorite part of the weekend.

Mr. Larson said, "How many of you looked at the *Chicago Tribune*?"

Over half of the same hands went up again.

"Fine—hands down. Now, how many of you read a part of the *Tribune other* than the comics?"

That question thinned out the crowd. Only four kids kept their hands up: Cara and Joey and two other boys. Cara looked up from her book, just for a second, glancing at Mr. Larson. He wasn't looking at her, but she could tell he had just looked away. And in that instant, Cara knew where these questions were heading.

Mr. Larson continued, "Now. How many of you read something other than the comics and the sports section in the *Tribune*?" Joey and the two other guys lowered their hands, and now only Cara had her hand up. Her face was pale, and her lips were pressed into a thin line, but she kept her hand up.

"You can put your hand down, Cara," said Mr. Larson. "But tell me, can you remember any particular story you read in the *Tribune*?"

To the rest of the class, it seemed like an accident that Mr. Larson was talking to Cara now, having a normal student-to-teacher, question-and-answer session. But it wasn't an accident at all. Mr. Larson knew that, and he knew from the expression on Cara's face that she knew it, too.

Cara looked right at Mr. Larson now, and looking at him made her feel better. He wasn't mad at her, Cara could tell. Mr. Larson wasn't angry, and he was just as uncomfortable as she was, as scared as everyone in the class. It was as if the whole class had taken a deep breath and held it. And now they were starting to exhale, Cara first.

Lowering her hand, Cara spoke carefully, at first with a little tremor in her voice. "I remember all the stories I read in the *Tribune*. The lead story on page one was about the meeting on the Middle East crisis, the second lead story was about the murder rate in Chicago compared to New York City, and then there were about three other smaller stories, including one about the oldest horse on the Chicago police force."

Mr. Larson raised his eyebrows, wrinkling his forehead. "You say you remember *all* the stories you read? Did you read the whole first section of the paper?"

Cara nodded.

"How about the Arts and Living section?"

Another nod.

"Finance? . . . Travel?"

Cara nodded, then nodded again.

"So what you're saying," said Mr. Larson, "is that basically, you read the entire *Chicago Tribune* this Sunday?"

The kids in the class had been following this exchange like a crowd watching a tennis match, their eyes going from one player to the other. All eyes were on Cara. In a steady, clear voice she said, "Well, maybe not every word in the whole paper—but yes, I read the whole thing."

With his eyes locked on hers, Mr. Larson said, "How about . . . the *editorials*?"

The whole class stopped breathing again. But Cara didn't miss a beat. If Mr. Larson wanted to play twenty questions about the newspaper, she wasn't going to back down and freeze up. "Editorials?" Cara said. "I always read the editorials. It's the part of the paper I like the best, so I save it for last. Some people like to save . . . the *sports* section for last. But I like the editorials."

As Cara said "the sports section," Mr. Larson almost flinched. *Phew—this one doesn't miss a thing!* he thought to himself. Out loud he said, "And why do *you* like the editorials so much, Cara?"

Cara was all set to say, "Because an editor can speak right up and tell the world if someone is being *lazy* or *stupid* or *crooked* or *mean*." Those biting words were already forming in her mouth. But then she remembered what her mom had said on Friday night—about always telling the truth but adding some mercy.

And in that heartbeat of a moment between the thought and the spoken word, it struck Cara that Mr. Larson didn't have to be doing or saying any of this. He could have just walked into class, poured himself a cup of coffee, and hidden behind his newspaper all afternoon. Why was he asking her all these questions? And then Cara saw it. Mr. Larson was being a teacher. He was telling her that her editorial had been correct—truthful. And now Mr. Larson was giving Cara a chance to add a little mercy, if she wanted to.

Mr. Larson prompted her, "You like the editorials because . . . why?"

Cara took another few seconds, choosing her words with great care. "Because it's where the newspaper can say the things that are hard to say, and it's where the newspaper apologizes if it makes a mistake. It's where you get to see the heart of the newspaper."

Mr. Larson smiled, and his pale eyebrows went up as he said, "The *heart* of the newspaper? I didn't know newspapers had hearts."

Cara couldn't help smiling a little herself, and she

said, "Only the *good* newspapers have hearts."

"Hmmm." That's all Mr. Larson said. Just, "Hmmm," and their conversation was over.

Mr. Larson took three steps back, and bending over a little, he patted the stack of newspapers beside his desk. "These old papers aren't good for much, so I want each of you to take one or two of them, and find the editorials. Clip them out, read them, pass them around, compare them. And then see what kind of . . . what kind of a heart you think the *Sun Times* or the *Tribune* has. Write down what you think, and then maybe the class can talk about it in a couple of days."

And with that, Mr. Larson sat down in his chair and opened up his paper. With his eyes on the sports page, he reached for his thermos, and poured some of Friday's cold coffee into a cup. He wasn't planning on drinking any of it, but he wanted things to look and feel normal again.

A line formed as some of the kids came up to get old newspapers. The tension in the classroom was gone, and the familiar hum of noise returned, increasing rapidly. Cara immediately stood up, dragged a desk into her back corner, and pulled the map tripod over behind her. She sat down in her makeshift office, her heart racing.

And she smiled. Mr. Larson wasn't mad at her, and she had gotten to apologize to him, sort of. She also smiled because the whole class had an assignment, the first real assignment Mr. Larson had given since school started.

But it was more than that. Cara smiled because she had just gotten an idea, a new idea for her editorial in the next edition of *The Landry News*.

CHAPTER 8

VOLUNTEERS LINE UP FOR DANGER

IF THE PRINCIPAL had walked past Mr. Larson's doorway on that Monday, he would have thought it was just another out-of-control afternoon in Larsonland. But in fact, the room was filled with focused activity. It looked like chaos, but the kids were doing an assignment. Sprawled on the floor, standing around in small groups, or sitting on desktops, they were leafing through old newspapers, looking for the editorial pages. And as they flipped through the wide sheets of newsprint, kids kept finding all the other odds and ends that fill up a big city newspaper.

LeeAnn called out, "Hey Sharon, I just found a story about a lady in Cicero who died and left her house to her Siamese cat—I'm not kidding—to her *cat*. Look . . . there's a picture. This cat owns a house!"

Steven had been reading an article about some new animals being added to the Brookfield Zoo, and now he was arguing with Alan about which was more dangerous: a lion or a black rhinoceros.

Phil was reading the obituaries, and every few minutes he discovered a person who had the same last name as a kid in the class. Then he'd call out things like, "Hey, Tommy. Did you have a relative named Kasimir who owned a bakery in Glen Ellyn? The guy died in a car crash on Saturday."

Some kids had actually found the editorial pages and were now hunting around the classroom, searching for scissors and tape and glue and construction paper.

Cara wasn't doing the assignment. She was going to, of course, just not right now. She was working on something more important: the second edition of *The Landry News*. A spiral notebook was open on the desk in front of her, and she was making a list of possible lead stories.

Joey tapped at the bulletin board behind Cara as if it were the door to a room. "Knock, knock," he said. "Anybody here?"

The sound startled Cara. She swung around in her chair, annoyed at the interruption, but when she saw it was Joey, her mind went almost blank for a moment. Then Cara smiled and said, "Sure, I'm here."

Joey grinned and leaned one shoulder up against the wall. "So what do you think?" he asked, his voice lowered. "What's up with Larson? Is he crazy or what? I thought he would still be mad."

Cara nodded. "So did I, but he really wasn't. It's kind of weird, because now he knows that we're all thinking about what kind of a teacher he is. I think he's just trying to figure out what to do next. And did you notice that we all have an *assignment*—a real assignment?"

Joey rolled his eyes and wrinkled his nose. "Yeah, I noticed—everybody noticed. Thanks a lot, little miss newspaper girl." Then with a devilish grin Joey said, "And Mr. Larson didn't say a thing about *The Landry News*—like 'You'd better not say anything else about me,' or 'You can just forget about making another newspaper.' So are you going to?"

Cara looked at Joey like he was crazy. "Make another one? Did you think I *wasn't* going to? Of course I'm going to make another edition!"

Joey pushed off the wall and held up his hands as if Cara had jumped toward his throat. "Hey, hey—just asking, that's all. I figured you would. Everyone's gonna be watching for it, and not just the kids in this class, either. You know Ted Barrett on the red team? Well, I told him about what happened on Friday, and he said for me to be sure to tell him when your next paper comes out."

Cara was flattered, but her smile turned to a frown. She said, "But I only make one copy of the newspaper, and I'm going to put it up on the wall in here, and we're on the blue team—so how's Ted even going to see it?"

"Duh—," said Joey. "Ever hear of something called a

computer?" He pointed to the two computer workstations on the other side of the classroom. Ellen Rogers was using the encyclopedia on one of them, and David Fox sat at the other, headphones clamped on his head, playing some sort of geography game. Joey said, "You make your newspaper on a computer, and then you can print up as many copies as you want. Simple."

"I . . . I don't really know how to use a computer," stammered Cara, blushing. "At least not well enough for something like this. We . . . I don't have one at home, and the school where I used to live only had a couple of computers, and no one ever let me get near them. I think I had a . . . a bad reputation there."

"A bad reputation?" Joey grinned. "You? Hmmm. Let me guess . . . could that have had something to do with making newspapers?" Then he went on seriously, "But really, it's not hard to use a computer. I talked with Ed, and we want to be on your staff, you know, like work for the newspaper. You can do your writing right here in the classroom, or anywhere. Ed and me, we're really good with the computers down in the resource center—those are the newest ones in the school. And as long as a teacher says it's okay, Ms. Steinert will let us use the whole setup—printers, paper, everything. What do you think?"

Cara hesitated. She wasn't expecting this. *The Landry News* was *her* newspaper, something she did all by herself.

Still, this offer was something to think about. If she kept on making just one copy by hand, yes, she could keep total control of it. But with only one copy, not many kids would ever get to read the *News*. And as Mr. Larson had proved, making only one copy means that it only takes one angry reader to shut off the whole circulation instantly.

Cara thought about what she had said to her mom. It was true. She wasn't making *The Landry News* now because she was angry. She was making it because she was good at it, because she liked being a reporter and a newswriter. She was determined to be a good journalist, and every good journalist knows that circulation is important.

And besides all that, it was Joey DeLucca standing here smiling at her, offering to help. So Cara made a decision.

She smiled at Joey and stood up. She said, "Sounds good. Let's ask Mr. Larson if we can go and talk to Ms. Steinert right now."

A minute later Mr. Larson looked at Joey and Cara over the top of his newspaper. "The library?" he said. "You want to go to the library?"

Joey nodded. "We need your permission to use the computers there for a . . . a project."

Mr. Larson looked from Joey's face to Cara's. Without showing any approval or disapproval, he lay

Karl Larson listens closely as Cara and Joey DeLucca ask permission to work on a "project."

down his paper, pulled open the top drawer of his desk, and found a memo pad with his name on the top. He picked up a pen and said, "What's the date?"

Cara said, "October eighth."

As Joey and Cara watched, Mr. Larson started writing, saying the words out loud as he did. "Dear Ms. Steinert—Joey DeLucca and Cara Landry have my permission to use the resource-center computers for a . . ."

Mr. Larson lifted his pen off the paper and looked up at Cara, and then at Joey. Then he wrote the last word, and said, "For a . . . project." He added his initials below the sentence, tore the memo from the pad, and folded it in half.

Handing the note to Cara, Mr. Larson said, "Hope this project is a good one."

Cara nodded and said, "Oh, it is. It's a good one."

"Well," said Mr. Larson, "you'll have to tell me all about it one of these days." As he dropped the memo pad into his drawer and opened up his newspaper again, Mr. Larson said, "Please be sure you're both back here five minutes before the last bell."

Looking over the top of his reading glasses, Mr. Larson watched Cara and Joey walk quickly out the classroom door.

And sitting there behind his newspaper, Mr. Larson grinned.

CHAPTER 9

K-9 UNIT SNIFFS SUSPICIOUS ACTIVITIES

LATE IN THE DAY on that same Monday afternoon, all the kids were gone, and the school was quiet. Mr. Larson had picked up his briefcase, his red thermos, and his raincoat, and he was headed toward the back door of the school. As usual, he walked past the window wall in front of the resource center. Through the glass he saw Ms. Steinert pushing a cart of books.

She looked up as he was going past, and Mr. Larson nodded and gave a friendly smile. But when Ms. Steinert saw him, she stopped in her tracks and waved excitedly, motioning him to come inside. She trotted over and met him at the door.

"Karl, I'm so glad I caught you! This journalism project you are doing with your afternoon group?— it sounds sooo *in*teresting—but I just wanted to give you a heads-up about the possible extra expenses."

Mr. Larson thought, *Journalism project? What journalism project?!* He was surprised, but he didn't let it show. He just asked, "Expenses? Expenses for what?"

Ms. Steinert said, "Now before you get all worried, just let me say that Joey DeLucca is a *very* trustworthy young man, and I *know* that he will not be wasting *any* materials. But the children *have* asked to use the big printer and the eleven-by-seventeen paper, and *that's* an extra expense. However, I really agree with them that if it's going to feel like a *real* newspaper, it needs to be on a large sheet, don't you think so, too? Now, the little Landry girl said that eventually they will want to be printing on *both* sides of the paper, and that can be pretty hard on the toner cartridges and the imaging rollers—so *that's* another possible expense."

Katherine Steinert had always reminded Mr. Larson of a schnauzer—the kind of small dog that runs around and around in circles, yipping and jumping up and chasing its tail. Her close-cropped, gray-and-white curly hair added to this impression. Ms. Steinert talked so fast that she often seemed to be panting. Mr. Larson admired her energy and enthusiasm, but talking with her always made him feel tired. He wanted to ask her what Cara and Joey had said about this newspaper they wanted to print, but before he could get a sentence started, she was talking again.

"Now, as you *know* from the memo that Mr.—I mean *Dr.* Barnes sent around at the start of the school year, the office is now tracking expenses for supplies and materials. You'll recall that the principal said they are tracking the expenses by grade, by team, and also by teacher. Each teacher and each team is allotted so much credit for each semester, and then, if you haven't used up your credits before . . ."

Mr. Larson nodded and smiled, but he was lost. The details of school administration were not one of his strong points, and Ms. Steinert was talking too fast anyway. But he waited patiently for her to be done, because he wanted more information.

"So if you'll just step over to my desk," Ms. Steinert continued, "I have the requisition forms all ready for you to sign, and then your students can come in anytime and have what they need. It's *such* a good idea, and they are *sooo excited* about it."

Before she could take another breath, Mr. Larson blurted out, "Did they say when they wanted to have something ready to print?"

"Oh my, yes!" said Ms. Steinert. "Cara was convinced that they would have a paper all finished by *this* Friday—*imagine*—this *Fri*day! Of course, I expect it will be more like three weeks from now—but they were *sooo eager* to get going that I didn't have the heart to tell them that they are looking at an *awful* lot of work here. You know, kids underestimate things like this all the time. Why, just last week . . ."

Mr. Larson signed the expense forms. As Ms. Steinert went on talking about a South America project that a group of second-graders had just finished, Mr. Larson smiled and nodded and began backing toward the door. She walked right along with him, held the door open for him, and when he was all the way out in the hallway, Ms. Steinert finished up by saying, "And, Karl, I really do think this is a *won*derful idea you've had, and like I was saying, the kids should finish up a great little newspaper project in about three weeks or so—I'll be watching! Now, you have a safe drive home tonight, Karl."

Mr. Larson smiled, turned, and walked. He took several deep breaths. Finishing a conversation with Ms. Steinert always made him feel like he had just escaped from drowning.

As he walked along the familiar corridor, he thought over what Ms. Steinert had told him. It shouldn't have surprised him. When Cara and Joey left the room earlier to go use the computer, hadn't he known that their "project" would have something to do with Cara's newspaper? Of course he had. And hadn't he expected Cara to keep on publishing her newspaper? Absolutely.

There was only one thing Ms. Steinert had told him that Mr. Larson knew wasn't true. There was no way it would take three weeks to produce the next *Landry News*. If Cara Landry said she would be ready to print by Friday, then Friday it would be.

CHAPTER 10

NEW TEAM PICKS UP STEAM

JOEY HADN'T BEEN bragging. He really did know what he was doing with that new computer. The first time he and Cara went to the resource center on Monday afternoon, it took him only twenty minutes to set up the basic framework of the newspaper. Cara watched as the newspaper took shape in front of her eyes on the computer monitor. Joey selected the eleven-by-seventeen-inch paper size, and then across the top he typed THE LANDRY NEWS in ninety-point type. Seeing the name like that, large and crisp and clear, gave Cara a thrill. The finished paper would not be quite as large as the newspapers she had made by hand, but it would look much more real, more important. It was like a new beginning.

Joey showed Cara how she could choose different styles of type, and after trying five or six, she decided that the one called Palatino looked best for the name of the newspaper—clear and readable without being show-offy.

"Now we can draw some boxes where the columns will go," Joey explained. "The paper is eleven inches wide . . . and there needs to be about a quarter-inch margin on both sides . . . so we have ten and a half inches to work with. How about five columns that are each two inches wide? That will leave an eighth of an inch between them." Almost as quickly as Joey said it, the columns appeared on the screen. He pointed at the lines around each column and said, "On the real paper, these lines won't be there, but we can leave them for now so you can see how much space there is to fill."

Cara gulped and said, "There's a *lot* of space to fill, isn't there."

"Well . . . yeah," Joey said, "but remember, there can be headlines and drawings and pictures and dingbats— they all take up space, too."

"Pictures?" asked Cara. "I can put *pictures* in the paper?"

"Yup," said Joey. "Pictures, drawings, cartoons— whatever you want." He pointed at a little machine on the table beside the monitor. "That thing is called a scanner. You can put a sheet into that slot, the scanner will make a copy of whatever's on it, then you can add it to the newspaper on the screen and print it out—bingo!"

Cara was feeling a little overwhelmed by all the choices. "So . . . so do I have to type up all my news stories on a computer now?" she asked.

"Well, someone does," said Joey. "But it doesn't really have to be you. If you like, write things down the way you want them, then me or Ed could type it up—or even someone else. Alan's real good at keyboarding, and so is Sarah. I bet they'd help out if you ask."

Joey turned back to the computer screen. "Now I'm going to print out a copy. Then you can use a pencil to sketch in where headlines should go . . . what pictures you want—whatever. I'll print out two copies. They'll be good for your planning."

A minute later, Joey handed Cara the sheets, still warm from the printer. Holding the actual pieces of paper, seeing the name large and clear across the top, Cara stopped worrying. She didn't understand all the computer stuff—not yet—but she understood paper. In the end it was just going to be a piece of paper—paper and ink and ideas.

With a big smile Cara looked up and said, "This is great, Joey."

And four days later, there it was—paper and ink and ideas. Joey DeLucca and Ed Thomson were standing at the doorway of room 145, handing out crisp, clean copies of *The Landry News*. It had not been easy, but they had made the Friday deadline.

The lead story was the results of a survey that Cara and LeeAnn had taken on Tuesday and Wednesday. They had asked seventy-five fifth-graders to name their favorite teacher at Denton Elementary School, and to explain their choice. The headline was: MRS. PALMER CHOSEN FAVORITE TEACHER.

There was a "Top-Ten List of the Least-Favorite Cafeteria Foods." The list ended with:

> And the number one least-favorite cafeteria food at
> Denton Elementary School—two words: creamed corn.

There was sports news about the recreation department basketball season, with the total wins and losses so far for each of the fifth-grade teams.

In the center of the page there was a picture of the boys' locker-room door. Ed had brought his dad's instant camera to take the picture, and Joey had scanned it in. The headline below the picture said HOLD YOUR NOSE! and the article was about why the locker rooms—boys' and girls'—smell so bad.

And of course there was an editorial.

As Ed and Joey handed out papers, Cara took a copy from the four or five papers she was keeping for herself and walked up to Mr. Larson's desk. He saw Cara coming out of the corner of his eye but kept reading the sports page until she said, "Mr. Larson?"

He said, "Yes? Oh—hi, Cara. What can I do for you?"

Cara was nervous. She held the copy of *The Landry*

News behind her back and, trying to smile, she said, "You know that project Joey and I wanted to go to the library for? Well, it's done, and I wanted to show it to you . . . here." And Cara handed him the newspaper.

Mr. Larson leaned forward across his desk to take it, acting surprised. "Project? Oh, yes . . . the project in the library." Looking over the newspaper quickly and then back up at Cara's face, he said, "Yes, I remember—I asked you if it was going to be a good project . . . What do you think? Are . . . are you happy with the way it turned out?"

Cara gulped and nodded. "Uh-huh. We had to work kind of quickly, and there's not all that much in it, but . . . but we like the paper, and I . . . and we just wanted you to have a copy."

"Well . . . thank you, Cara," said Mr. Larson, a little haltingly. "I'll enjoy reading this."

Cara nodded, smiled awkwardly, and said, "You're welcome," and backed away from Mr. Larson's desk. She turned and headed for her space in the back corner of the room.

Mr. Larson leaned back in his chair and held up *The Landry News* to get a better look at it. He really didn't know what to expect. As he scanned the page, his eye fell to the lower right-hand corner of the paper—to the editorial.

From the Editor's Desk
New Looks

The Landry News has a new look this week. A lot of people helped to make the improvements. Without Mr. Larson, Ms. Steinert, Joey DeLucca, Ed Thomson, LeeAnn Ennis, Sharon Gifford, and Alan Rogers, the changes and also some of this week's stories would not have been possible.

This paper has taken another new look this week, a look at what a newspaper is for. Above all, a newspaper has to tell the truth. Telling the truth can sometimes make people angry. Does that mean that a newspaper should try to stay away from a story that might bother someone? It all depends on the thought behind the newspaper—the newspaper's heart.

A mean-hearted newspaper tries to find out things that are bad, and then tries to tell the truth in a way that will hurt others. Newspapers can get famous that way, but they don't do much good—for anybody.

A good-hearted newspaper tries to tell the truth in a way that helps people understand things better. A good-hearted newspaper can tell the same story as a mean-hearted paper, but it tells the story in a different way because it's for a different reason.

As a reminder that *The Landry News* is trying to be a good-hearted newspaper, starting with the next edition, below the name of the paper, there will be a new motto: Truth and Mercy.

And that's the view this week from the *News* desk.

Cara Landry, Editor in Chief

Mr. Larson had started slowly swiveling his chair around toward the chalkboard when he was about halfway through the editorial. He could feel his eyes misting up, and he was pretty sure someone would be watching him while he read the paper. When Mr. Larson finished it, he smiled as he blinked hard, and he reached for his coffee to help gulp away the lump in his throat. He hadn't felt this good about being a teacher for a long, long time.

After a minute, Mr. Larson got up and walked back toward Cara's mini-office. Now it was Cara's turn to pretend she didn't see someone coming.

Looking down on her over the top of the tripod map, Mr. Larson said, "Excuse me, Cara . . . would you happen to have an extra copy of this newspaper? My wife's a teacher, too, and I just know she'd love to read this editorial. It's really a good piece of writing."

Beaming with pleasure, Cara said, "Sure . . . sure, Mr. Larson. Here's another copy."

The second edition of *The Landry News* was a big hit. All seventy-five copies had been distributed in less than six minutes.

And late Friday afternoon, one copy of *The Landry News* ended up on the desk of Dr. Philip K. Barnes, Principal.

CHAPTER 11

TREMORS POINT TO MAJOR QUAKE

A COPY OF the second edition found its way to the office because the principal's secretary, Mrs. Cormier, had found one on the floor in the hallway. She thought Dr. Barnes would enjoy reading the article about the best teachers.

Dr. Barnes sat down at his desk and read every word of the newspaper carefully, nodding and smiling now and then. This was good, clean fun—excellent writing, a fine learning experience. The bit about the top-ten least-favorite foods was cleverly done, and the story about favorite teachers was written in a very positive way. The writers didn't take any cheap shots. There was no foul language. There was no criticism of the school, the school administration, or school policies. There was nothing even a little bit controversial about the second edition of *The Landry News*.

But when Dr. Barnes read the editorial, his eyes

narrowed, and his heartbeat quickened. A scowl formed on his broad, fleshy face, and his nostrils flared and quivered. He reached for a red pen, took off the cap, and starting over, he read through the entire paper again, looking for a problem, any problem. But when he was done, he had only circled one item on the whole page. It was in the editorial. He had drawn a heavy red circle around one name: Mr. Larson.

Dr. Phillip Barnes, principal of Denton Elementary School.

Dr. Barnes had strong opinions about Mr. Larson. For the seven years Dr. Barnes had been the principal of Denton Elementary School, Mr. Larson had been a constant problem.

Dr. Barnes didn't *hate* Mr. Larson. That would be too strong a word—too emotional. This had nothing to do with feelings, he told himself. This was a matter of professionalism. Dr. Barnes *disapproved* of Mr. Larson because Mr. Larson did not behave *professionally*. For Dr. Barnes, education was serious business, and Mr.

Larson took his educational responsibilities too lightly.

Dr. Barnes opened his desk drawer and took out the key to the file cabinet where he kept the records about each teacher at Denton Elementary School. Swiveling around in his chair, he unlocked and opened the wide file drawer. It wasn't hard to find Mr. Larson's file. It was three times fatter than any other file in the drawer.

Every year Dr. Barnes got letters about Mr. Larson from worried parents. Parents asked if it was normal to have no homework in social studies, no homework in reading, and no homework in English—no homework *at all* for the *whole year*! Parents wrote to ask if their children could be transferred to the red team, and the real reason was always the same: getting out of Mr. Larson's class.

At the end of every school year each teacher was required to have a meeting with the principal. It was called a performance review. Dr. Barnes flipped through the stack of performance review sheets he had filled out for Mr. Larson—one for each of the last seven years. Poor. Poor. Unacceptable. Poor. Unacceptable. Unacceptable, and—Unacceptable.

At the bottom of each review form, there was room for a brief statement from the teacher. Over the past seven years, every statement from Mr. Larson had been pretty much the same. Turning to last year's review sheet, Dr. Barnes gritted his teeth and read what Mr. Larson had written:

It is clear that Phil and I have very different philosophies of education. I sadly acknowledge that he objects to some of my methods and practices.

Sincerely,

Karl A. Larson, Teacher

Many parents thought that Mr. Larson should not be a teacher. Several school board members thought that Mr. Larson should be fired, and several other board members thought it would be nice if Mr. Larson retired—early.

But as every principal and every school board knows, getting rid of a teacher is not an easy thing to do. There has to be something serious, something provable, something that violates school policies, or something that violates the law.

Dr. Barnes closed up Mr. Larson's fat file folder, put it back in the drawer, shut the cabinet, locked it, and dropped the key back into its place.

He set his copy of *The Landry News* in the center of his desk blotter. Then he laced his fingers behind his head and leaned back in his chair. He smiled. He had a good feeling about this little newspaper. This situation had possibilities. This could turn out to be just what a lot of people had been hoping for.

Sitting up suddenly, Dr. Barnes reached for his

phone. He punched Mrs. Cormier's extension. He could hear her bustling around behind him out in the main office area, no doubt getting ready to leave. He could have swiveled his chair around and talked to her, but he enjoyed using the phone. It seemed more official.

The phone on Mrs. Cormier's desk rang one, two, three, four times. She finally answered. "Yes, Dr. Barnes?" There was an edge to Mrs. Cormier's voice. It was four-fifteen on a Friday, and she was in no mood for secretary games. Standing at her desk with her coat and hat on, Mrs. Cormier could see Dr. Barnes sitting there, fifteen feet away, drumming on the desk with his fingers. Really—how hard could it be for him to just swing around, smile, and *talk*?

"Uh, yes . . . Mrs. Cormier, um . . . please put a note into Mr. Larson's box for me. I want to meet with him Monday, right after school—*right* after school. It's a matter of some importance."

Mrs. Cormier hung up her phone and called through the open door, "Monday is Columbus Day, Dr. Barnes. But I'll leave him a note about a meeting on Tuesday, and then I'll be going. Have a good long weekend, now."

Mrs. Cormier scrawled a hasty note onto a sheet of Dr. Barnes's stationery, stuffed it into Mr. Larson's mail slot, and was out the door in thirty seconds.

CHAPTER 12

GROWTH SPURT DOESN'T HURT

ON TUESDAY AFTERNOON Mr. Larson called the class to order. He wrote three words on the chalkboard, from left to right: Positive, Neutral, Negative.

Mr. Larson said, "An editorial writer has only got a little bit of space, so every word has to be chosen for power." Tapping the board as he said the key words, Mr. Larson continued, "The words a writer chooses can be positive, negative, or neutral. Is the writer building something up? That's positive writing. Tearing something apart? That calls for negative punches. And if the writer is just exploring, just looking all around an issue, that's a neutral treatment."

Cara raised her hand. Mr. Larson said, "Question, Cara?"

"But if an editor is taking a negative position on something like war or drugs, wouldn't that really be positive?"

Mr. Larson said, "Yes, and no. Yes, the *effect* might be

positive. But the *treatment*—the words themselves and the images they communicate—they would be negative. Now, everyone, look over the editorials you clipped. Let's get some lists going up here, positive, neutral, and negative."

For ten minutes the kids peppered Mr. Larson with words and phrases, and he wrote them down as quickly as he could.

The negative column filled up fastest with words like *stupid, disgraceful, foolish, laughable, wasteful, outraged, idiotic, scandalous, uninformed, half-baked, shamefully.*

Positive words and phrases included *generously, public-spirited, wise, beneficial, commendable, carefully researched, useful, honorable, good.*

Neutral words or phrases were a lot harder to find. In fact, the kids only found five: *apparently, clearly, not certain, understandably, presumably.* Then Mr. Larson led a rousing class discussion, more like a shouting match, about which kind of editorial treatment was best. Everyone finally agreed that there were times and places for all three kinds.

Reaching over to his desk, Mr. Larson grabbed a sheet of paper and taped it up onto the chalkboard. The class hushed. It was a copy of *The Landry News.*

"I know you've all seen this new and improved edition of *The Landry News*," he said. "And I know from the condition of the room and my shrinking newspaper stacks that you've all been looking at a lot of *other* newspapers, too." Mr. Larson smiled. "So give me some opinions. How is *The Landry News* different from the other papers you've been looking at—and how is it the same?"

No one said anything. "Come on, now, *we're* not being negative here, we're being neutral. In fact, we have every reason to be very positive." Pointing at the newspaper, he said, "This is quite a big change to happen in one week. I'm not asking for comments about the paper, just tell me—how is it *similar* to the other ones you've been reading, and how is it different . . . " Mr. Larson paused. "Who's got an idea? Ed? You must have an idea. Tell me a difference."

Ed gulped. Glancing at Cara and Joey before he spoke, he said, "Size? Our paper—I mean *The Landry News*—like, it doesn't have as many words?"

"Size! Excellent, Ed. Size." Mr. Larson wrote the word on the board. "Now someone else," said Mr. Larson, "another difference . . . LeeAnn?"

LeeAnn was ready. "Those other newspapers have hundreds of reporters and printers and stuff," she blurted out, "and this newspaper has only a few."

That broke things open. In just a few minutes, there was a long list of differences—things like advertisements, a purchase price, color pictures, comics, gossip columns, advice columns, world news.

Then came the list of similarities. It covered all the basics: *The Landry News* had local news stories, it had reporters, it had writers, it had a black-and-white picture, it had an editorial, it had readers, and it was interesting, just like the other papers.

Looking back and forth from list to list, Sharon raised her hand. Mr. Larson nodded at her. "Sharon?"

She said, "Well, why couldn't *The Landry News* have more of those other things in it, too, like columns and comics and stuff?"

"That's a fair question," said Mr. Larson, "but *I* can't answer it. You all missed another similarity that *The Landry News* has to those other papers. *The Landry News* also has an editor in chief, and if you've got a question about changing *The Landry News*, you'd have to ask her."

All eyes turned to Cara. She was sitting on a desk, one foot on the chair, the other leg crossed, her sharp little chin propped on her fist, with her elbow on her knee. She looked like that famous statue, *The Thinker*, but thin, with her brown plaid skirt covering her skinny knees and her ponytail flopped to one side.

She could feel the color rising in her cheeks. Mr. Larson was asking her to make the decision—Cara Landry, the editor in chief. The first thought that flashed through her mind was how much fun it would be to tell her mom about all this at supper tonight.

A lot had happened to Cara in the last ten days. Less than two weeks ago, Cara Landry had been the invisible girl. Now, every kid and every teacher in the school knew her name and her face. *The Landry News* used to be something Cara did completely on her own, something with a single voice and a single vision, an extension of her own thinking and her own two hands.

To make the newspaper that Mr. Larson had taped up there on the chalkboard, Cara had needed the hands and eyes and ears of others. She had made new friends, and they had all worked and laughed, then argued and thought, and then laughed again. She had seen how good it made all of them feel to make the newspaper together.

Cara didn't feel famous. What she felt was . . . useful. She felt needed. And she liked it.

And if just having four or five kids help with the paper could make it that much better and that much more fun, could it hurt to have the group get bigger?

Cara straightened up and looked around. Then she smiled—a warm, inclusive smile that made her whole face shine. And the editor in chief said, "If it's going to have more features, it's going to need more writers and reporters, more typists, more of everything. And it's not all that easy or fun—just ask LeeAnn or Joey! So whoever wants to help, come back to my desk. The deadline for the next edition is this Friday—and it's a short week!"

The whole class followed Cara back to her desk in the corner, and soon Joey and Ed and LeeAnn were helping Cara figure out how to divide up the work.

Left alone up at the front of the room, Mr. Larson turned around and slowly pulled his copy of *The Landry News* off the chalkboard. Sitting at his desk, he carefully peeled off the piece of tape. Then he pulled open the deep drawer on the bottom left, and took out a new file folder. With a green marker he wrote THE LANDRY NEWS on the tab in neat block letters. He folded the newspaper sheet exactly in half, put it into the file folder, and tucked it into the drawer.

By this time the noise in room 145 had reached a level that would have stunned, or possibly paralyzed, any other teacher at Denton Elementary School. But Mr. Larson heaved a satisfied sigh, poured himself a cup of hot coffee from his big red thermos, smiled, leaned back in his chair, and opened up his *other* newspaper to the sports section.

CHAPTER 13

STRONG WINDS IN FORECAST

MR. LARSON WAS on his way out of the building on Tuesday afternoon, briefcase in one hand, red thermos in the other, when he heard the unmistakable sound of Dr. Barnes's voice.

"Mr. Larson! Mr. Larson!" Dr. Barnes was trotting down the hall toward him, puffing, his face red.

Turning around, Mr. Larson managed to put a neutral expression on his face. He said, "Hi, Phil. How's it going?"

Dr. Barnes winced. He preferred to be called Dr. Barnes, or Principal Barnes. Mr. Larson always called him Phil.

"What are you doing?" Dr. Barnes asked incredulously.

"It's three-thirty—thought I'd go home for the night," said Mr. Larson.

Patting his forehead with a handkerchief, Dr. Barnes said, "Didn't you get my memo? We have a meeting today, right now, and you're fifteen minutes late."

"Hmmm," said Mr. Larson. "Guess I didn't get your note."

"But how could you have missed it? Mrs. Cormier put it in your mailbox on Friday afternoon. Didn't you get your mail this morning?"

Mr. Larson smiled and shrugged. "Guess not."

Dr. Barnes turned and motioned, and Mr. Larson began following him down the hall toward the office. Dr. Barnes said, "I'm glad I caught you. You're *supposed* to get your mail every morning, you know. Your mailbox is an important channel of faculty communication."

With a straight face, Mr. Larson said, "You know, I've heard that, Phil. But it's remarkable how many days I get by just fine without going to the office at all."

Dr. Barnes ignored this comment and opened the door that went directly into his office from the hallway. He held the door, letting Mr. Larson squeeze past him to go in first.

Shutting the door, Dr. Barnes motioned to the chair in front of his desk. Mr. Larson put his thermos and briefcase on the floor beside the chair, sat down, and crossed his long legs. It was not a comfortable chair. Mr. Larson wondered how many other squirming people had sat across from Principal Barnes this way. On the principal's desk was a prism of wood, engraved, PHILIP K. BARNES, B.A., M.ED., M.B.A., ED.D. On the paneled wall behind his chair, framed diplomas and certificates competed for space with photographs of Dr. Barnes shaking hands with important people, some of whom Mr. Larson could actually recognize. Ambition oozed from every photograph.

Dr. Barnes unfolded his copy of *The Landry News*, and slid it across the desk toward Mr. Larson. Mr. Larson saw his name there, circled in red ink. The principal said, "Tell me, Mr. Larson, what exactly is your involvement with this newspaper?"

Mr. Larson put on his reading glasses, looked down at the paper, and then up at Dr. Barnes. "I'm teaching a unit on journalism," said Mr. Larson, "and some of the kids in the class have started a newspaper—sort of as a project. It's good writing, don't you think?"

"Yes," said Dr. Barnes. "The writing is fine. That's not the problem."

"Problem?" said Mr. Larson. "I didn't know there was any sort of a problem. What problem are you talking about, Phil?"

Dr. Barnes leaned back in his chair and began gently swiveling from side to side, with his eyes staying steady on Mr. Larson's face. "Are you familiar with a Supreme Court decision known as the *Hazelwood* case?"

Mr. Larson immediately replied, "*Hazelwood?* Of course. In 1988 the United States Supreme Court ruled that school principals have the legal right to say what does or does not get printed in school newspapers. It was not a unanimous decision, but five justices agreed that a school principal has this authority. Some people think the Court's decision is a violation of the Constitution's guarantee of free speech. Others say that if the school is the publisher, the school gets to make the final decisions, just like the owner of a newspaper would."

Dr. Barnes was impressed. He had underestimated just how well read and well informed Mr. Larson was. Nodding, he said, "You have a clear grasp of the case, I see. And tell me, Mr. Larson, do you *agree* with the Court's decision?"

Mr. Larson smiled and said, "That's kind of like asking if I agree with the law of gravity. Whether I agree with it or not, it's still the law."

Dr. Barnes chuckled. "True, quite true. The law is the law, and since it is, then I assume you will not mind if I review each new edition of this paper before it is distributed, correct?"

Mr. Larson kept smiling, but there was no smile in his voice. He said, "If it was a *school* newspaper, I wouldn't mind that at all. But you see, Phil, it's not. *The Landry News* is a *classroom* newspaper. It's made by my students in room 145, and I have every confidence in their ability to decide what ought to be in it."

Leaning forward so that his stomach pressed against the desk, Dr. Barnes pointed at the newspaper. He said, "If this is a *classroom* newspaper, all the copies should have stayed in your classroom, Mr. Larson. Mrs. Cormier found this copy on the floor all the way over in the third-grade hallway."

"You know, it's a funny thing about paper," said Mr. Larson. "My wife and I once flew to New York City for a long weekend, and after we flew back to Chicago on Sunday night, we walked to our car, drove home, went inside, and then I sat down and put my feet up. And you know what? There was a piece of paper—an advertisement for a New York restaurant—stuck right onto the bottom of my shoe. Paper has a way of getting around."

Dr. Barnes did not appreciate the humor in Mr. Larson's story. Frowning, he patted the paper on his desk. "Do you know how many copies of this newspaper were printed?"

Mr. Larson shook his head, "No, I can honestly say I do not know how many copies the kids made. I left that up to them. They are proud of their work—and they have a right to be. I'm sure they've shared some copies with their friends, probably carried them home to show their folks, too."

"Seventy-five copies," said Dr. Barnes. "According to Ms. Steinert, your students made *seventy-five* copies of this newspaper. You have twenty-three students in your afternoon class, so unless you are trying to tell me that each child kept three or more copies, then this is a *school* newspaper. This newspaper is produced here, in

Dr. Barnes talks to Mr. Larson about the Hazelwood case.

my school, using school computers and school paper and school printers and school electricity and school time."

Mr. Larson was quiet for a moment. He resisted the urge to start yelling. He wasn't looking for a big fight with Philip Barnes—never had been. In many ways he admired the principal. Doc Barnes looked out for what he thought were the best interests of the kids. He tried to keep everyone happy and working together—the teachers and the parents and the school board and the superintendent—not an easy thing to do. Dr. Barnes was a good principal, a good administrator. But Dr. Barnes was not a good teacher. And Mr. Larson was dead certain that if Dr. Barnes got involved in *The Landry News*, something important would be lost.

Clearing his throat, Mr. Larson stood up. "Well, it's happened before, hasn't it, Dr. Barnes? This is just one more educational matter that you and I disagree about. *I* say that *The Landry News* is a *classroom* project. The paper and printers and computers and time and electricity are being used as a normal part of my work as a teacher in this school, just like any other teacher and any other group of kids doing any other project."

Dr. Barnes stood up, too, and tapping on the newspaper sheet with his index finger, he asked, "Then you take full responsibility for this newspaper and whatever is printed in it?"

"I sure do," said Mr. Larson. "Absolutely."

"Very well then," said Dr. Barnes mildly. "I guess our meeting is over."

Mr. Larson bent down to pick up his briefcase and his red thermos, and as he did, Dr. Barnes stepped out from behind his desk and pulled open the door to the hallway. As Mr. Larson stepped into the corridor, Dr. Barnes said, "Mr. Larson, will you please be sure that I get one copy of each new paper as it comes out? I'd like to keep informed about the progress of your . . . *classroom* project."

"Next edition comes out this Friday," said Mr. Larson. "We'll be sure to get you a copy. Have a good evening, Phil."

Closing the door that exited to the hall, Dr. Barnes walked over and opened the other door that went into the main office. "Mrs. Cormier—I need you to take a letter for me."

Mrs. Cormier looked up at the clock. It was three forty-three. "Be right there, Dr. Barnes." She grabbed her pad and a ballpoint, walked in, and sat where Mr. Larson had been.

Dr. Barnes paced slowly behind her and said, "This is a memorandum to the personnel file of Mr. Karl Larson. I have just concluded a meeting with Mr. Larson. We discussed a newspaper being produced by students in his afternoon class. It appears to be a school newspaper, and I have asked Mr. Larson to show each copy to me before publication so that any objectionable material can be removed before it is distributed. Mr. Larson has insisted that the newspaper is a classroom newspaper and has taken full responsibility for the contents of each edition. He has agreed to supply me with one copy of each new edition that he and his students publish."

Stepping over to look over Mrs. Cormier's shoulder, he asked, "Did you get all that?" Mrs. Cormier nodded. "Good," said Dr. Barnes. "I'd like three copies for signature sometime tomorrow. Thank you, Mrs. Cormier."

As she left his office, Dr. Barnes sat down again and swiveled slowly back and forth.

His meeting with Mr. Larson had not gone exactly as he had planned. But Dr. Barnes was happy with the results—very happy.

Mr. Larson had accepted full responsibility for the newspaper and everything in it.

The more Dr. Barnes thought about that, the better he liked it. All he had to do was wait. One mistake would drop Mr. Larson right into the frying pan.

CHAPTER 14

LAW FOR ALL, ALL FOR LAW

WHEN THE AFTERNOON class came whooping into room 145 on Wednesday, the kids were surprised to see a TV and a VCR on a cart next to Mr. Larson's desk. Mr. Larson had never showed videos to them before.

When everyone had quieted down, Mr. Larson said, "I know you all need to get right to work on the newspaper, but first I want you to watch something I taped on TV late last night."

He pushed the play button, and a talk-show host told a joke about the president and the vice president telling lies to each other. The TV audience laughed and clapped.

Mr. Larson shut off the TV and pushed the cart aside. He pulled down a rolled up map of the world and tapped the black tip of a pointer onto different countries as he spoke. Mr. Larson said, "If that comedian lived in *this* country or *this* country or *this* country, and if he had told that joke about the president last night, today he would probably be in jail." Pausing dramatically, he moved the pointer to another country. "And if that comedian lived in *this* country and told that joke last night about the president, today he would probably be dead."

Moving the pointer to the United States, Mr. Larson said, "But, of course, that comedian lives in this country, and today he's not in jail, and he's not dead. He's probably sitting somewhere drinking mineral water and thinking of something else to make people laugh again tonight."

Mr. Larson rolled up the map and walked to the side of the classroom. Picking his way among stacks of magazines and a couple of book racks, he stood next to a bulletin board. The board was incredibly cluttered, but in the center there was a small poster printed in faded blue ink that had never had anything stapled over it. At the top it said:

The Bill of Rights
The Ten Original Amendments
to the Constitution of the United States of America

Mr. Larson put the pointer on the word *Constitution* and said, "Now I know we haven't studied the Constitution yet this year, so I'm going to get to the main point here as quickly as I can. The Constitution is like a list of rules, okay? It's a list of rules that tells how our country's government has to be set up. When the Constitution was first written down, some people said it gave too much power to the government and not enough protection to ordinary people. And these people said that before they would agree to the rules of the Constitution, there had to be a bill of rights, a *list* of rights that the government could never take away from people. They didn't want the government to start acting like a cruel king—they had already had one of those, and one was enough."

Mr. Larson tapped on the word *Amendments*. He said, "So they made some *amendments*. This word just means "changes." The Bill of Rights is contained in these ten *changes* that are now a permanent part of the Constitution.

"Now, this is the main idea I want you to get here. They made these ten original amendments even before anyone would agree to the Constitution itself. And the *First* Amendment is first for a reason. It promises that the government cannot get involved in religion—either for or against it. It promises that people are free to express their opinions and ideas—like that comedian last night. And it also says that there is freedom of the press, that the government cannot decide what a newspaper is *allowed* or *not allowed* to print."

Ed caught on right away and his hand shot up. "Does that mean we can print anything we want to in *The Landry News*?" he asked.

Mr. Larson said, "Good question, Ed. What do you think about that, Cara? Can you print anything you want to in *The Landry News*?"

Cara hesitated. "I . . . I'm not sure. I mean, I used to put anything I wanted into the paper because I made the whole thing from beginning to end. But now, I . . . I guess if someone didn't like what we wrote, they could keep us from using the printer, or the computer."

Then Joey said, "But if I used my own computer at home, and I bought my own paper and everything, like, then I could print whatever I felt like, right?"

Sharon's dad was a lawyer. She said, "Yeah, but if you printed a lie about me, my dad would sue you—and then your computer would be *my* computer!"

Mr. Larson said, "You've all raised some good points here. The fact is, when you publish a newspaper, you *do* have to tell the truth. If you get caught lying, someone is likely to sue you—take you to court—like Sharon said. And if a newspaper company publishes the newspaper, then the *owner* of the newspaper gets to decide what may or may not be in the paper."

It was quiet for a moment. Then Ed asked the question that was forming in everyone's mind. "So who is the owner of *The Landry News*? Cara, right?"

Cara shook her head. "Not really—not anymore. And I feel kind of funny having that still be the name of it. I think maybe we should change it to something different."

Joey said, "I don't. You started it, and you're still the

editor in chief, so I vote that we keep the name the same."

Cara blushed at Joey's little speech and blushed even more when the whole class clapped and cheered, agreeing with him.

Mr. Larson brought things back to order. "So that's settled . . . now back to Ed's question about who owns the newspaper . . . LeeAnn?"

LeeAnn said, "Well, the school owns *The Landry News*, right? I mean, like . . . the school buys the paper and the computer and all, so it's the school's, right?"

Mr. Larson smiled. "You could say the owner is the school, and that the head of the school is the principal. But the principal is hired by the school board, and the school board is elected by your parents and the other people in Carlton, and they are the ones who pay the tax money that pays the principal and the teachers, and buys all the paper and the computers and the printers, right?" After a long pause, Mr. Larson said, "There's a lot to think about when you're running a newspaper, isn't there?" And with that the lesson about the Constitution and the Bill of Rights and the freedom of the press was over.

Using the pointer like a gentleman's walking cane, Mr. Larson picked his way through the clutter back to his desk.

It was quiet for another moment or two, and Cara sat there, staring at the Bill of Rights on the bulletin board. She was wondering how much freedom of the press *The Landry News* really had.

A little suspicion formed in the back of her mind that, sooner or later, she'd find out.

CHAPTER 15

REF MAKES TOUGH CALL

ON THE FIRST Friday in December the ninth edition of *The Landry News* was distributed—over three hundred and seventy copies.

Sitting at his desk, Dr. Barnes read his copy carefully. And when he turned to page three, Dr. Barnes finally saw what he had been hoping for, week after week. Smack in the center of the page was the article of his dreams, an article that should not have been printed in a school newspaper. And Dr. Barnes was sure that a majority of the school board would agree with him.

A slow smile spread over his face, and in his mind, Dr. Barnes began planning Mr. Larson's retirement party.

Cara Landry was having the time of her life. *The Landry News* was growing and changing, and she was keeping up with it. By the fourth edition, Joey had to print on both sides of the sheet; and from the fifth edition on, *The Landry News* had needed a second sheet of paper—for section B.

Cara had to plan each edition. She had to read every story and every feature, plus she would help kids with their rewriting and revising. And on Thursdays, when Joey was assembling everything on the computer screen, Cara often had to cut articles or features that took up too much space.

Cara also had to reject whatever she didn't think would be right for *The Landry News*. Chrissy wanted to start a gossip column called "Hot Stuff" about school romances—crushes, rumors, and who was going to be dumped. When Cara asked if the information in her column would always be true, Chrissy had to agree that private notes passed among friends was the best place for this kind of news. And when Josh wanted to start a weekly ranking of the best fifth-grade athletes, Cara told him the list would have to include girls as well as boys. Josh decided to write a piece about ocean kayaking instead.

With all she had to do for the newspaper—not to mention her other schoolwork—Cara was barely able to find time each week to write her own editorial. The editorial was always the last item in the paper, and by the fifth edition that meant it went on page four.

The front page of *The Landry News* was the general news and information page—the main news stories, a summary of school and town events, and a weekly "Homework Countdown" that listed upcoming fifth-grade tests and project due dates. There was always a photograph, and if there was room, the front page also included the weekend weather prediction from the United States Weather Service, complete with little drawings that Alan made of sunshine, clouds, droplets, or snowflakes.

The second page was different advice and information columns that kids kept coming up with, like this question-and-answer column about pets.

Pets? You Bet!
by Carrie Sumner

Dear PYB:

I have a cockatiel bird named Dingo, and all he will say is "pretty bird, pretty bird, pretty bird," over and over again. I talk to him for an hour every day, and I have tried to teach him to say other words, but he isn't interested. No matter what I say to him, and no matter how many times I say it, all he says is "pretty bird, pretty bird, pretty bird." It's driving me nuts. Any advice?

From Crazy in Birdland

Dear Crazy:

I think your bird is mad at you because you named him after an ugly Australian wild dog. He wants to make sure that you know he's a bird, and a pretty one, too. Try changing his name to Wing-Ding or SuperBird or Flier, and see if it doesn't, maybe you should think about exactly why you want to be talking to a bird in the first place.

With deep concern, PYB

Alan Rogers had started a column where he interviewed kids about their favorite foods and how they got their parents to buy them.

Snack Attack!

Dedicated to life, liberty, and the pursuit of junk food

by Alan Rogers

AR: So, JJ, [not his real name] I hear you've perfected a way to get your mom to buy sugary cereal and Pop Tarts every time she goes to the store, even if you're not there to beg for them. Sounds too good to be true. Can you tell us about it?

JJ: Believe me, it's true. But it didn't happen overnight. These things take time and planning.

AR: What was the first step?

JJ: I asked my health teacher what meal is the most important one of the day.

AR: But didn't you already know the answer?

JJ: Of course. I knew she would say "Breakfast." And once she did, I went home that afternoon and told my mom that my health teacher said the most important meal of the day is breakfast.

AR: Ahhh! You were laying the foundation, right?

JJ: Exactly. Then I skipped breakfast for the next three days. Mom tried to get me to eat, but I just said, "I don't like anything we have in the house."

AR: Didn't you starve those mornings?

JJ: I had asked my friend ZZ [not his real name] to bring some toast to the bus stop for me, so I was okay. At the end of three days, I mentioned to my mom that I thought I might like some of those Cocoa Puffs, and that the chocolate and marshmallow Pop Tarts might be something I could eat, too. The next morning, there they were, like magic—right on the kitchen counter.

AR: Well, JJ, that's certainly an inspiring story, and I know our readers will appreciate your sharing it with us all.

There was a book review every week, a video-game tips column, a "Best of the Web" listing, and a "Best TV Movies of the Weekend" column. Since Christmas and Hanukkah were not that far off, there was a "Holiday Countdown"—a column listing the top ten presents that kids on the red and blue teams were hoping for.

Tommy read a lot, and when he was in fourth grade he had started collecting slang expressions that he thought were funny. He eventually discovered that there were whole dictionaries of slang. He asked Cara if he could have a column about slang, and the editor in chief said okay, as long as everything in the column had a G rating. Tommy agreed, and a column called "That Slang Thang" was born.

Section B—the second sheet of *The Landry News*— was a hodgepodge. If there were some good columns that wouldn't fit on page two, they ended up in section B. There were two regular weekly comic strips and usually a cartoon or two, as well as short stories and vacation travel stories about places kids had visited—like the Grand Canyon or the Field Museum. There were poems and jokes, and LeeAnn had surprised everybody with a completely creepy mystery story that had a new installment every week.

And then, on the Wednesday before Thanksgiving, Michael Morton came up to Cara after school at her locker and asked if he could give her a story that a friend of his wanted to have printed in the newspaper. Michael was a computer whiz, the kid who did the "Best of the Web" listing for the paper each week. He kept mostly to himself. Cara said, "Sure, Michael. I'll be glad to look at it." Cara stuck the sheets of paper in her backpack, grabbed her coat, and ran to catch her bus.

Late that night, Cara remembered the story, got it out of her book bag, and lay across her bed to read it. It was only two pages, written in black ballpoint. There were tons of cross outs and smears on each page, and the writer had pushed down so hard with his pen that the back side of each sheet reminded Cara of Braille, the raised alphabet for blind people.

There was no name at the beginning, just the title "Lost and Found." The story began with this sentence: "When I heard that my parents were getting divorced, the first thing I did was run to my room, grab my baseball bat, and pound all my Little League trophies into bits."

Michael Morton, computer whiz and loner.

Cara was hooked. The person in the story was a boy, and Cara was amazed at how similar his feelings were to the ones she'd had when her dad left. The same kind of anger, the same kind of blind lashing out. And finally, there was the same sort of calming down, facing facts. The story did not end very hopefully, but the boy saw that life would still go on, and that both his dad and his mom still loved him just as much, maybe more.

When Cara finished reading, she was choked up and her eyes were wet. She noticed that there was no name at the end of the story either. That's when it hit her that this was not fiction. It was real life. It was Michael Morton's own story.

Cara slid off her bed and went out to the living room, drying her eyes on the sleeve of her robe. Her mom was on the couch, watching the end of a show, so Cara sat with her for about five minutes.

When the show ended, Cara picked up the channel changer and shut off the TV. Then she handed her mom the story. "Would you read this for me, Mom? Someone wants me to put it in the next edition of the newspaper."

Joanna Landry took off her glasses and said, "Why sure, honey, I'd love to."

Cara watched her mom's face as she read, and she saw her mom's eyes fill up with tears when she got to the end.

Blinking back her tears, her mother turned toward Cara on the couch and said, "If I didn't know better, I'd have thought you wrote this sad little story yourself, Cara honey. I think it's *awfully* good, don't you?" Cara had brought a copy of each edition of *The Landry News* home, and Mrs. Landry had proudly taped them all onto the wall in the kitchen. She was thrilled to see Cara doing something so good—and good-hearted—enjoying herself and using her talents. Handing back the smudged pages, her mother asked, "So are you going to put it in the paper?"

Cara said, "I'm not sure. I think I'd better talk to Mr. Larson about it."

And after the long Thanksgiving weekend, Cara had her mom drop her off at school early so she could show the story to Mr. Larson before school.

Mr. Larson adjusted his reading glasses and took the pages over by the windows where the light was better. Three minutes later, he was finished, and his eyes were shining. "This boy has certainly caught the essence of a hard experience here," he said, reaching for his handkerchief.

Cara nodded and said, "So maybe I shouldn't put it in the newspaper, right?"

Mr. Larson looked down at the story again, then handed it back to Cara. "Tell me what *you* think about it, Cara."

Cara was quiet while Mr. Larson walked over to his desk, sat down, and picked up his coffee cup. "Well, first of all," she said, "I'm just sure this is a true story, so it's like telling the whole school about some family's private business. Someone might not like that—like the mom or the dad, for instance. Divorce is a pretty messy subject, don't you think? I mean, that part about him running away, and the police coming and everything—"

Cara paused, waiting for Mr. Larson's reaction. He took a sip of coffee, looked out the window, and then back to Cara's face. "You said you are sure this is a true story. Is it trying to hurt anyone?"

Cara shook her head and said, "No—in fact, it really helped me," and then she blushed at what she'd said.

Mr. Larson pretended not to notice and quickly said,

"Well, it helped me, too."

"So I should put it in the newspaper, right?" said Cara.

Mr. Larson said, "I appreciate your talking to me about it, but that's a decision that the editor in chief should make. I will say that whatever you decide to do, I will support you completely."

Four days later, the first Friday in December, in the middle of page three of the ninth edition of *The Landry News*, there was a story by an anonymous writer, a story called "Lost and Found."

It was the same story that Dr. Barnes was so excited about.

CHAPTER 16

SALVAGE CREW INSPECTS WRECKAGE

ON THE MONDAY after the ninth edition came out, Mr. Larson got a large brown envelope from Dr. Barnes, hand delivered to him before school by Mrs. Cormier—just in case he forgot to check his mailbox in the office. There were two items in the envelope. The first was a copy of a letter from Dr. Barnes to the school superintendent and each of the seven members of the school board. It requested an emergency meeting concerning "a disciplinary proceeding against Mr. Karl Larson." The letter stated that "Mr. Larson allowed the attached article to be published in a classroom newspaper under his supervision, and over three hundred copies were distributed throughout the school and community." Other phrases in the letter included, "lack of professional judgment," "disregard for individual privacy," "unprofessional behavior," "inappropriate use of school resources," and "insensitivity to community values." A photocopy of the third page of the ninth edition of *The Landry News* was stapled to the letter, with the story about the divorce circled.

The second item in the envelope was a letter to Mr. Larson from Dr. Barnes, informing him of the intended disciplinary action. The letter told Mr. Larson that this would be a public hearing and he might want to have his own lawyer present at the meeting. The secretary of the teachers' union at the school had been informed about the hearing. Dr. Barnes also reminded Mr. Larson that, if he wished, he could choose to resign. If he resigned, there would be no need for a disciplinary proceeding. He could quietly retire, and that would be the end of it. Dr. Barnes ended the letter by saying that publication of *The Landry News* must cease immediately.

Mr. Larson slumped back in his chair, his long arms hanging limp at his sides. He felt as if he'd been kicked in the stomach. The threat of losing his job was certainly real. Ever since Dr. Barnes arrived at Denton seven years ago, Mr. Larson had known that it was only a matter of time before something like this happened. And Mr. Larson thought, "Maybe I deserve this. I've been a rotten teacher, more like half a teacher, for a long time now. Maybe this school will be a lot better off without me. I've probably got this coming."

But Karl Larson was absolutely sure of one thing. The *kids* did not deserve this one little bit. *The Landry News* had become something wonderful. And the thing that hurt him the most was that because of *his* problems—not the kids' problems—Dr. Barnes was going to use this innocent little newspaper as the whip to send him packing.

But sitting there on his chair in his cluttered room, Mr. Larson turned a corner.

He forgot about his own problems. He began to think about how he could protect his students from the ugliness of this situation. He wanted to be sure that not one of them was harmed or upset in any way. As he began to think about the kids, all the heaviness and burden seemed to drop away. Then all at once, Mr. Larson got an idea, and he sat bolt upright in his chair.

And the thought that formed clearly in his mind was incredibly simple. It was a plan that would protect all the kids, and it would protect him, and it might even protect Dr. Barnes as well.

And one word summed up the whole solution: *teach*.

The newest copy of *The Landry News* lay there on his desk next to the letters from Dr. Barnes. Mr. Larson looked from one to the other, and he smiled. Everyone else could get as upset and angry and worried as they wanted to, but he was not going to worry. Why?

Simple. Because his kids were going to see this whole thing as one large, exciting, learning experience about the First Amendment and the freedom of the press.

And who was going to transform this mess into a thing of educational beauty?

Mr. Larson, Teacher.

CHAPTER 17

RESCUE SQUAD TACKLES CLEANUP

CARA FELT AWFUL. Mr. Larson had just told the class that *The Landry News* could not be published anymore—at least, not right away. He had made transparencies of the letters from Dr. Barnes and put them on the overhead projector so the whole class could see them while he explained what was happening. Then he showed a transparency of the story about the boy and the divorce.

Mr. Larson said, "Now, it's important for each of us to think very clearly about all this." Glancing over the twenty-three faces looking up at him from the darkened room, his eyes met Cara's for a moment before looking back at the screen. "Some of you might be tempted to think, 'Oh, if only we had not published this *one* little story, everything would be all right.' But is that true? No, it's not. Because if it wasn't *this* story, it would have been some *other* story or some review of a movie or a review of a book that someone does not like. You have to remember that publishing *this* story was the right thing to do. It's a wonderful story and a brave story, and I know that it was very good for a lot of people to read it and think about it—and a lot of people have told me that it's the *best* thing *The Landry News* has published so far. So that's the first thing—the paper just told the truth."

It *sounded* good—hearing Mr. Larson say it like that—but it didn't make Cara feel any better. She had a copy of the newspaper on her desk, and her thoughts went round and round. *I should have known better—I should have thought about Mr. Larson instead of the stupid newspaper. I should have just handed that story right back to Michael Morton. I should have known better.* The classroom snapped back into focus for Cara as Mr. Larson turned off the overhead projector and Sharon flipped on the lights.

As the kids squinted and blinked, Mr. Larson said, "So someone thinks that divorce is too personal to write about in a school newspaper. I'm the teacher in charge, so I'm the one responsible, so it looks like *I* am suddenly in trouble. But *am* I?"

Picking his way over to the bulletin board, Mr. Larson tapped the Bill of Rights poster and then rested the pointer on the First Amendment. "Am *I* in trouble here, or is something *else* in trouble?"

Mr. Larson could see by their faces that all the kids got the idea. It was Cara who said it. She said, "It's the

First Amendment that's in trouble—the freedom of the press is in trouble." Then she frowned and said, "But I still think *you're* in trouble, too."

Mr. Larson grinned, touched by Cara's concern. "Well, I am perfectly sure that there's nothing for any of us to worry about. We've all been doing good work here, and now, thanks to this situation, we're going to get to learn about the freedom of the press in a way that very few teachers or kids will ever get to. Besides, I've been in trouble before, and let me tell you—I think this is the *best* trouble I've ever been in."

A few of the kids laughed a little when Mr. Larson said that, but not Cara. Walking toward the front of the room, Mr. Larson glanced at her. She sat stiffly in her chair, glaring at her copy of *The Landry News*, biting her lower lip.

Back at his desk, Mr. Larson picked up a stack of stapled handouts and passed them around. "This is your study packet for this unit. Take a look at page one with me."

For the next ten minutes, Mr. Larson walked the class through all the steps in the process—things that would happen before the hearing, at the hearing, and after the hearing. He wanted to make sure there was nothing mysterious, nothing scary about any of it. He did not paint Dr. Barnes as a villain or himself as a victim. It was not us against them. It was just a contest between two different ideas of what was right, what was the greatest good for the greatest number.

As Mr. Larson calmly explained everything, Cara relaxed a little. He wasn't just pretending to be brave—Cara could tell he was truly excited about all of this. And when Mr. Larson squinted and rubbed his hands together and said, "It's like we get to mess around in our own private democracy laboratory!" even Cara had to smile.

She flipped ahead to look at the last page of the handout, looking for a clue about where this whole thing would end up. There was only one word on the last page: *Conclusions*. The rest of the page was blank.

That blank page was actually comforting to Cara. She was used to looking at blank pages, and she was used to filling them up with things that were true and good. To Cara, that final page looked like hope.

CHAPTER 18

CENSORSHIP+ COMPUTERS =NO WAY

JOEY SAT NEXT TO CARA on the bus that Monday afternoon. He was quiet, and so was Cara. Even after all the explanations, she still felt responsible for the whole mess, especially for what was happening to Mr. Larson. There was a lot to think about.

Joey broke the silence with a question. "So you're going to keep on publishing the paper anyway, right?"

Cara's ponytail wagged as she shook her head. "We can't, Joey. If we don't obey the rules, it will just make it harder for Mr. Larson."

They were quiet again, looking out the windows on opposite sides of the bus for the next two stops. Then as if a puppet master had rotated their heads at exactly the same moment, they faced each other and both started talking at once. "But the letter said *The Landry News*!" said Cara. "It didn't say stop making *all* newspapers!"

"I know, I know!" blurted Joey. "As long as we don't make a newspaper at school or pass it out there, we can publish anything we want to—as long as it's true!" Joey was practically shouting. "And why? Because it's a free country, that's why!"

Cara had hold of Joey's arm, squeezing it, and her voice had gone up an octave. "So you've got a computer, right?" she asked. Joey nodded, and Cara went on. "And you've got a printer, too?"

Joey nodded again and said, "It's not as big as the one at school, but it's a good one, and it even prints in color! We'll have to redesign everything for a smaller sheet size, but that's okay, because it's a whole new paper anyway!"

Cara stayed on the bus and rode to Joey's stop. LeeAnn and Alan and Ed had joined the conversation, and in four minutes they had already taken a unanimous vote on the new name that Ed came up with. By the time they got off the bus and had begun to walk the last block to Joey's house, the publishing committee had offered Cara Landry the job of editor in chief for a brand new newspaper, the *Guardian*. And she accepted, provided that the motto of the new paper could still be the same: Truth and Mercy.

Halfway through science class on Friday morning, Mrs. Cormier arrived with an invitation for Cara Landry. The principal wanted to talk to her.

A few minutes later, Cara sat across the desk from Dr. Barnes. She was glad she had experience in these matters. Cara had observed quite a few angry school administrators—at least one a week for most of fourth grade. She had developed what she called the Mad-O-Meter. It was a scale from one to ten, where one equals "mild tremor" and ten equals "erupting volcano." Judging from the color of his face, the rate of his breathing, the flare of his nostrils, and the fact that both doors of his office were closed, Cara thought that Dr. Barnes was probably at about eight—the "steaming mud slide" stage. She waited politely for Dr. Barnes to begin the conversation.

He slid a copy of the *Guardian* across the desk and turned it around so she could see it. The headline of the lead story was WHY THE FIRST AMENDMENT IS FIRST. The article laid out the situation involving *The Landry News*, Mr. Larson, Denton Elementary School, and the Carlton school board. Dr. Barnes had to admit to himself that it was a masterful piece of reporting. The story was honest, it was impartial, and it lived up to the newspaper's motto.

Dr. Barnes cleared his throat and said, "What is your connection with this newspaper, Cara?"

Cara disliked being treated like a baby. The masthead of the newspaper was on the front page, as plain as the nose on Dr. Barnes's face—and his nose was very plain from where Cara was sitting. The masthead listed all the workers on the paper. All twenty-three kids in Mr. Larson's afternoon class had wanted their names in the masthead, and each had done something to help get the *Guardian* pulled together in record time. Cara and Joey had gotten the idea on Monday afternoon, and the first edition had been ready to distribute today, Friday morning.

Dr. Barnes was a tempting target, but Cara didn't get snippy, and she didn't get angry. She didn't even get sarcastic. She pointed meekly at the masthead. "It says what everyone does for the paper right here in the masthead. I'm the editor in chief."

Dr. Barnes said, "I see. And weren't you the editor in chief of *The Landry News* as well?"

Cara nodded. "Yes, until Mr. Larson told us we had to stop publishing it for a while."

Cara already knew exactly where Dr. Barnes was headed with this. She did not want to suffer through a long and boring cat-and-mouse question session. Cara wanted to lay it all out on the table. And she also wanted Dr. Barnes to know right away that she saw what he was up to.

So before Dr. Barnes could ask his next question, Cara said, "You probably think that this paper is just *The Landry News*, only with a different name. But it's not, Dr. Barnes. First, *The Landry News* was written and assembled and produced during school hours on school property, using school equipment and supplies. The *Guardian* was written outside of school, and it was produced in a private home using privately owned equipment and supplies.

"Second, *The Landry News* was distributed to students by other students during school hours on school property. The *Guardian* is distributed by a group of kids to their friends on privately owned property before or after school hours.

"And third, *The Landry News* was supervised by Mr. Larson, and from the second edition to the ninth and final edition, Mr. Larson saw every copy of it. The *Guardian* was thought up and created independently by only the friends listed here in the masthead, without adults being involved at all."

Cara hadn't meant to push Dr. Barnes up toward the "erupting volcano" point, but the lava was starting to flow anyway. He glared at her and jabbed at the paper with his blunt index finger. "Young lady, do you mean to tell me that you did not intend to distribute these papers at school today? These papers are all over this school and all over the floors in all the buses."

Cara said mildly, "We didn't bring a single paper to school, honest. We have friends at almost every bus stop, and we had our newspapers ready this morning, so we handed them out. We even made sure that we stayed in someone's yard instead of on the sidewalk—because the sidewalk is owned by the town, and when kids are waiting for the school bus there, it's like school property. But after we handed the papers to our friends, where they took them—well, that wasn't up to us."

Cara leaned forward and pointed at the little symbol Joey had added to the bottom of the front page. "We even reminded kids to be sure to recycle the paper."

Cara sat up straighter in her chair and said, "Hey—I know! Next week, we'll add 'Please don't litter,' and see if that helps." Cara paused a minute, smiling absently at Dr. Barnes. Even his ear lobes were red now.

"And guess what?" said Cara brightly.

"What?" said Dr. Barnes, almost in a whisper.

"If you flip that paper over, down at the bottom you can see our Internet address—isn't that cool? By this time next week the *Guardian* will be online, and our Internet edition won't use any paper at all! No litter! Isn't that great?!"

Dr. Barnes disliked displays of emotion, especially anger. It wasn't professional. So in an abnormally quiet voice, Dr. Barnes said, "Yes, that's a fine idea, Cara. Well then. Please . . . go out to the front office now . . . and ask Mrs. Cormier . . . for a pass . . . to your class. And close the door behind you . . . please."

Two minutes later Cara left the office. Dr. Barnes's door was still shut.

If it hadn't been against the rules, Cara Landry would have skipped down the hall, all the way back to her science class.

CHAPTER 19

DECEMBER TO BE WARMER THAN NORMAL

MR. LARSON HAD not been a favorite among his fellow teachers in recent years. He was too standoffish, too solitary. Most of the other teachers disapproved of the wildness of his classes. To the teachers who had been around a long time, seeing Mr. Larson become less and less professional about his teaching had been especially sad, because they remembered the old Karl Larson.

But *The Landry News* had gotten everyone's attention. Every teacher had watched the newspaper grow from one sheet to two, then to three and four. They saw the quality of the writing and marveled at it. "Fifth-graders!" they said to each other as they passed the *News* around the teachers' room. "Larson's got *fifth*-graders doing this kind of work! Amazing!"

Most of the teachers had met Cara Landry. They knew that the success of the newspaper was due in large part to her hard work and energy. But they also knew that it was no accident that *The Landry News* had come out of room 145. Without the experience and the guidance and the understanding of Karl Larson, *The Landry News* could not have become what it was.

So, when the teachers' union representative was notified about the disciplinary hearing, the faculty rallied around Mr. Larson. There was a teacher's meeting, and the vote of support was unanimous.

Right away, Ms. Steinert wrote up a press release about the situation. A committee duplicated the eight copies of *The Landry News* and sent sets of them along with the information sheet to every newspaper, radio, and TV station in the greater Chicago area. They printed up handbills with the divorce story on it and mailed it to the home of every taxpayer in Carlton, asking the question, "Should someone be fired because of this?"

Mr. Larson's wife was active in the Chicago teachers' union, and each elementary, junior high, and high school in the metropolitan area received a copy of the press release about the hearing and the charges. The president of the union had made a statement on WGN about the case and the importance of supporting free speech and academic freedom.

Of course, all the parents of the kids in Mr. Larson's class already knew about *The Landry News*. Many of them had been making their own photocopies of the paper for grandparents and aunts and uncles, so everyone could see the wonderful things those bright kids in Mr. Larson's class were writing and thinking and learning.

A reporter from the *Chicago Tribune* followed up and learned that the kids were now publishing a different paper, the *Guardian*, on their own, including an Internet edition. Four days later, the online *Guardian* had a free link from the *Tribune*'s own homepage—and three days after that, the *Sun Times* followed suit.

Before the superintendent had even posted a notice on the town's cable TV channel to list the time and place of the hearing, there had already been articles about the situation in both of the big Chicago newspapers. Mr. Larson had even been interviewed in the Sunday *Tribune*, and a reporter from Channel Nine's evening news had come to the apartments at Edgewater Village to interview Cara Landry.

Cara hadn't liked the interview or the reporter, a woman with bright orange hair. It was a cold and windy afternoon, but the reporter wanted to talk outdoors. She said she looked better on camera in natural light. Barking orders, she got the camera crew and the sound guy in position next to some evergreen bushes.

After finding the best angle for the shot, she faced the camera, smiled, and said, "I'm Jordy Matlin, coming to you live from the Edgewater Apartments in Carlton. This is the home of Cara Landry, a young lady whose newspaper is at the center of a local controversy. Now Cara, tell our viewers, was it your teacher or your principal who got you in trouble about this newspaper?"

Cara wasn't expecting such a question. She froze up.

The reporter stopped smiling, lowered her microphone, and yelled, "Cut!" Bending so close that Cara could smell the acrid scent of her hair spray, Jordy Matlin said, "This is the part where I ask you questions, and you answer them, okay? All you have to do is listen to the question, and when I hold out the microphone, you talk. All right?" The camerawoman cued the reporter with a count of five, and then Jordy asked Cara the same question. "Now, Cara, tell us, was it your teacher or your principal who got you in trouble about this newspaper?" This time, Cara was ready. She had remembered that this was just like writing for the newspaper, only she'd be talking instead. All she had to do was tell the truth in a kind way. So Cara said, "Neither. And I'm not in trouble. The newspaper's not even in trouble, really. It's just a difference of opinion about what should go into a newspaper made at a school."

The reporter tilted the microphone back toward herself and said, "This story about a divorce that you published—didn't you think this would cause some problems? If this isn't just a story, say, if this really happened, then some family's business has been spread all

Jordy Matlin, reporter for WQRR in Chicago.

over town. And, of course, many churchgoers think divorce itself is bad. Didn't you think there might be a problem here?"

Cara looked into the camera and said, "I wasn't thinking about anything except giving someone the chance to tell a story— and it's a story that I think has been good for a lot of kids to read."

The camera stayed on Cara's face for another three seconds, and then the reporter said, "Cut," quickly shook Cara's hand, and turned on her heel and clicked off across the parking lot, talking with her producer. Cara heard her say, "Now we need a shot of the school, and fifteen seconds each with the principal, the superintendent, and the school board president. And we've got to find this teacher that they're trying to ax. We can lay out some copies of the kid's newspapers and get a collage shot back in the studio before we do the full mix. Ted tells me he's holding two minutes for us in the local segment, but we have to really hustle if we're going to make it." All the newspeople piled into two white vans and roared off toward the center of town.

Cara was disappointed. She thought there would be more to it than that. She'd only gotten to say about three sentences, and it was such a complicated story. Fifty or sixty words wasn't enough. And what had the reporter called Mr. Larson . . . "this teacher they're trying to ax"? Cara winced at that, wishing she had used her moment on camera to say something that would have helped take the heat off Mr. Larson.

Joanna Landry came over and put Cara's coat around her shoulders. Cara smiled up at her mom and said, "Now I know why I like newspaper stories better than TV news stories." Her mom nodded and smiled. "That reporter was kind of a tough bird. Still, you did just fine, Cara honey. Now let's get in out of this wind."

Based on the number of phone calls received at the superintendent's office, the location of the hearing was moved from the town hall to the high school auditorium so there would be enough room for everyone who was planning to attend.

During the ten days before the hearing, Mr. Larson and his afternoon class kept track of each development and how it related to the First Amendment. The kids saw the impact of the newspaper and television coverage. They studied Mr. Larson's interview in the newspaper and compared it to Cara's TV interview, and then compared them to other interviews of Dr.

Barnes and the superintendent. They split into teams and had debates, and they put a whole new layer of clippings and cartoons and news photos onto Mr. Larson's bulletin boards.

Mr. Larson was happier than he had been for many years. By the time the day of the hearing arrived, he was ready to walk in with his head held high. All of his students were planning to be there.

For most people, this was simply a disciplinary hearing. But for Mr. Larson and his students, it was the last lesson in a unit about the most interesting subject they had ever studied.

CHAPTER 20

HOME TEAM GOES FOR BROKE

SHORTLY BEFORE 7:30 on a Tuesday night in December, Mr. Larson straightened his necktie, kissed his wife, then turned to walk down the sloped aisle of the high school auditorium. A row of folding tables had been set up in front of the auditorium stage. After he sat down across from Dr. Barnes at the first table, Mr. Larson turned his head and looked out into the audience. It looked to him like there were at least four hundred people in the room.

His wife had settled near the back and was smiling at him, all warmth and support. The kids from his class were scattered all over the place, sitting with one or both of their parents. Cara and her mother were in the fourth row, and when he looked at them, Cara gave him a nervous smile and waved shyly. Mr. Larson felt self-conscious up there at the front of the hall, but he did not feel alone.

There was something that Mr. Larson had not discussed with the kids in his class. It was entirely possible that the freedom of the press would win *its* battle, and that *he* would still lose his job.

True, public opinion mattered. Newspaper reporters and camera crews from two of the three major TV stations were here. But at the end of the night, it would all depend on how the school board voted. Mr. Larson knew that out of the seven members, three would love to see him leave, and two others were not very fond of him. It was going to be an uphill battle.

At exactly seven-thirty, the superintendent called the meeting to order. The school board president, Mrs. Deopolis, read the call-to-meeting notice and then introduced Dr. Barnes. Since it was Dr. Barnes who had brought the complaint, he was required to speak first.

"Madam President," he began, "on Friday, December seventh, I read the newest edition of this student newspaper and found a story about divorce that I did not think was appropriate. As you know, I immediately brought the article to the attention of the board and the superintendent. You apparently agreed that the content was not appropriate, and since Mr. Larson had accepted responsibility for the content of the newspaper, you agreed that this disciplinary hearing was needed. Madam President, will you please explain to those present what the board found to be inappropriate in the story?"

As Dr. Barnes sat down, Mrs. Deopolis leaned closer to her microphone and said, "Yes, Dr. Barnes. We found that the subject matter and the description of the boy's suffering was too personal, and that the topic of divorce is too mature a theme to be treated in this way in an elementary school newspaper. The board feels that by allowing this to be published, Mr. Larson made a very serious error in judgment. In light of past complaints about Mr. Larson's abilities and practices as a classroom teacher, we agreed that this hearing was necessary." Turning to Mr. Larson, Mrs. Deopolis asked, "Mr. Larson, do you have a lawyer present or will you be speaking for yourself?"

Mr. Larson stood up stiffly, talking into a hand-held microphone. "I will be speaking for myself, Madam President." Stepping away from the table, Mr. Larson addressed the board members. "I see this issue of the story in *The Landry News* in very simple terms. Yes, Dr. Barnes made me responsible for the content of the paper, and I passed that responsibility on to the students. It is true that Dr. Barnes asked to see each copy of the newspaper before it was printed, and I refused that request. But Dr. Barnes did not *insist* on previewing each paper, which, as principal, he could have. Instead, he left the responsibility with me. He gave me no guidelines about what topics were not appropriate, nor does the school board have any clear policies regarding school newspapers. According to the *Hazelwood* Supreme Court decision, a school board must have a clear set of policies in force in order to censor a student newspaper."

Mr. Larson paused and looked around at Dr. Barnes. "So, as I see it, I am being accused of allowing something to happen that no one ever informed me I should not have allowed to happen in the first place. Either that, or the real issue here is those past complaints about my teaching practices that Madam President has mentioned."

Mr. Larson walked back to his place, opened his briefcase, and pulled out a copy of the article. "As part of my statement, I would like to read out loud the entire story from the newspaper so that all present and also all those watching at home on the town cable TV channel can judge for themselves its appropriateness or inappropriateness." The board members began hurriedly whispering among themselves, their hands cupped over their microphones.

The whispering stopped, and Mrs. Deopolis said, "Since it is a part of your defense, you have the right to read the story into the record, Mr. Larson."

A woman in the sixth row immediately stood up and raised her hand. Mrs. Deopolis nodded to her, and a Boy Scout trotted over to her with another portable microphone. "Thank you, Madam President. My name is Allie Morton, and my son Michael has asked if he may read the story aloud. He's the boy who wrote it, and it's about the divorce our family went through last year."

Almost everyone in the auditorium seemed to gasp at once. But Cara Landry didn't gasp. She had known this was coming. She had called Michael a week ago to ask him to read his story at the meeting. She told him it would help Mr. Larson if people could see that this was a true story. At first Michael said no. He thought he would be too scared. But after he talked it over with his mom, he called Cara back and said he would do it—for Mr. Larson. Cara sat up on the edge of her seat to see what would happen.

After another hurried conference among the board, it was agreed that Michael Morton could read his own words aloud for the record. He squeezed his way past knees and seat backs in the sixth row and walked down the aisle to where Mr. Larson stood. Mr. Larson handed Michael the story and held the microphone for him. Michael brushed the mop of brown hair out of his eyes, looked once at his mom in the sixth row, and then at Cara Landry in the fourth row. He focused on the page, gulped, and began to read, squinting because of the bright lights held up by the TV camera crews.

Lost and Found

When I heard that my parents were getting divorced, the first thing I did was run to my room, grab my baseball bat, and pound all my Little League trophies into bits.

I felt like I wanted to run away. I have a lot of friends who have divorced parents, but I never thought it would happen in my family. I felt like I was lost. This was going to ruin everything.

My mom told me that my dad was going to move out and live somewhere else. She kept saying things like "Don't worry" and "Everything will be all right" and "Things like this just happen." And she said that I would still get to see my dad and that I could talk to him whenever I wanted to. I didn't believe her.

My dad took me out to a restaurant. He wanted to talk to me. He said I wouldn't understand, but that he just didn't love my mom anymore. He was right—that was the part I couldn't understand. I mean, sometimes I yell "I hate you!" at my mom and my dad, and some days I feel like I hate everybody. But I don't really, and pretty soon everything's okay again. I know I could never stop loving my dad. And I could never stop loving Mom, either. So I couldn't see how my dad could stop loving her. And I thought that if my dad could stop loving Mom, then he could probably stop loving me, too.

When Dad went to pay for the food, I ran out of the restaurant and hid in the bushes by the parking lot. I saw him come outside and look for me, and he was yelling my name and he was really scared and worried. And I was glad. I watched until my dad got in the car and used his telephone, and then he drove off toward our house, really fast.

I walked over to my friend Josh's house, but

he wasn't home. Then I just walked and walked. It was way after dark when I got home. There was a police car in front of my house. When I walked in, my mom ran over to hug me, but I wouldn't let her. My dad said I was in big trouble, and that I was grounded. But I just said, "How are you going to ground me? You're not even going to be here to see *anything* I do." Then I went to my room and slammed the door as hard as I could.

That was about a year ago. My dad did move out, and now he's already married again. I never did really run away, not even for an afternoon. But I used to cry a lot, late at night. I know some kids will think that's a sissy thing, but I couldn't help it. And one day my mom was late getting home from work, and there wasn't a message, and there was no answer at her office, and I got so scared, and I ran to her room to look in her closet to see if her dresses were still there. It was stupid, but I was afraid that maybe she had moved out, too.

Sometimes I'm not as happy as I used to be, but I try not to show it. I think my mom is happier now, but if I get unhappy, it ruins things for her and then it's hard for both of us.

Things aren't so bad now, just different. I found out that my mom told the truth back at the beginning, because everything is mostly all right, and when she said "things like this just happen," that was right too. Now I know that something like this can just happen, because it happened to me.

And I also found out that my dad still loves me. And I even know that he still loves Mom, only not in a married way. It's not that I see him a lot or anything, because I don't. He's not with me every day, or at bedtimes, except one weekend a month. But I know he still loves me. I just know it, and sometimes just knowing something has to be enough.

Michael Morton, author of "Lost and Found," reads in defense of his teacher, Mr. Larson.

When Michael finished reading, people all around the auditorium were fishing around for tissues and handkerchiefs. There was a spontaneous burst of applause, and he made his way back to his seat. After Michael sat down, his mom put her arm around his shoulders and squeezed.

When it was quiet again, Mr. Larson said, "Thank you, Michael." Then he held up the story Michael had just read and said, "How could someone say that *this* is not appropriate content for elementary school children to read and think about? Parents and others who have very good motives—people like Dr. Barnes and all of us who want only the best for children—we may not like to admit that things like divorce create very real problems for children, but they do. And if children are honest enough to admit that, why can't we?

"My teaching style is unconventional, and Dr. Barnes and I have disagreed about that since he arrived here seven years ago. Could I have been a better teacher during that time? Yes. I admit that. But what has happened with this newspaper—and that includes allowing this story to be published—is some of the best work I have done in all my nineteen years as a teacher. If I am to be fired, please, let it be for something other than this."

Everyone, even Dr. Barnes, knows that in an auditorium with four hundred people on their feet and cheering, with the TV cameras rolling, and the reporters scribbling in their notebooks, it's not a good idea to fire the person the crowd is applauding.

In less than a minute, while the audience was still clapping and cheering, Mrs. Deopolis took a quick poll of the school board and announced for the record that the disciplinary action against Mr. Karl Larson, Teacher, was dismissed.

Cara Landry had done as Mr. Larson asked and stopped publishing *The Landry News*. But even though the *Guardian* had kept her busy, Cara had not stopped *writing The Landry News*, and she had not stopped printing it. As the crowd began to leave, Cara stayed in her seat in the fourth row and turned to watch.

Joey and Ed stood at doors on the north side of the auditorium; LeeAnn and Sharon took the two doors at the south side. They were handing out a special edition of *The Landry News*.

Cara reached into her coat, pulled out a copy, and carried it down to Mr. Larson, who was surrounded by reporters. He stopped midsentence when Cara put it into his hand, and looked from the paper to Cara's face and then back to the paper. Cara stood to one side and watched quietly as he read the whole thing.

The special edition was only the front side of one page. It had a single headline—**LARSON IS VINDICATED!**

And the only other thing on the page was an editorial.

From the Editor's Desk
The Heart of the News

When *The Landry News* chose the motto "Truth and Mercy," we did it to remind ourselves that a good newspaper must have both. A newspaper that is only filled with cold, hard facts is like an iceberg, crushing anything that gets in its way. A newspaper that only looks at the soft and gentle side of things is like a jellyfish, floppy and spineless. From the start, *The Landry News* has tried to be a balanced, good-hearted newspaper.

I have been going to school now for six years. Some of those school years were soft and gentle, and some were hard, cold years. It depended a lot on what kind of teachers I had. It also depended on me.

The best year so far is this year. This year has a good heart. And that's because the heart of this year is Mr. Larson.

The kids who work on the *News* noticed that about fifteen years ago Mr. Larson was chosen Best Teacher of the Year three years in a row. We are sure that sometime soon Mr. Larson will be Teacher of the Year again. For all of us who work on *The Landry News*, he already is.

And that's the view this week from the *News* desk.

Cara Landry, Editor in Chief

The heart of this year is Mr. Larson.

Here's a sneak peek at *We the Children*,
the first book in Andrew Clements's
new series, Keepers of the School!

Promise

As the ship's bell clanged through the school's hall-way for the third time, Ben ran his tongue back and forth across the porcelain caps that covered his front teeth, a nervous habit. And he was nervous because he was late. Again.

When she was being the art teacher, Ms. Wilton was full of smiles and fun and two dozen clever ways to be creative with egg cartons and yarn—but in homeroom she was different. More like a drill ser-geant. Or a prison guard. Still, maybe if he got to his seat before she took attendance, he *might* not have to stay after school. Again.

The art room was in the original school building,

and Ben was still hurrying through the Annex, the newer part of the school. But the long connecting hallway was empty, so he put on a burst of speed. He banged through the double doors at a dead run, slowed a little for the last corner, then sprinted for the art room.

Halfway there, he stopped in his tracks.

"Mr. Keane—are you okay?"

It was a stupid question. The janitor was dragging his left leg as he used the handle of a big dust mop like a crutch, trying to get himself through the doorway into his workroom. His face was pale, twisted with pain.

"Help me . . . sit down." His breathing was ragged, his voice raspy.

Ben gulped. "I should call 9-1-1."

"Already did, and I told 'em where to find me," the man growled. "Just get me . . . to that chair."

With one arm across Ben's shoulders, Mr. Keane groaned with each step, then eased himself into a chair by the workbench.

"Sh-should I get the school nurse?"

Mr. Keane's eyes flashed, and his shock of white hair was wilder and messier than usual. "That windbag? No—I broke my ankle or somethin' on the stairs, and it hurts like the devil. And it means I'm gonna be laid up the rest of the school year. And you can stop lookin' so scared. I'm not mad at *you*, I'm just . . . *mad*."

As he snarled that last word, Ben saw his yellowed teeth. And he remembered why all the kids at Oakes School tried to steer clear of old man Keane.

A distant siren began to wail, then a second one. Edgeport wasn't a big town, so the sound got louder by the second.

From under his bushy eyebrows, Mr. Keane looked up into Ben's face. "I know you, don't I?"

Ben nodded. "You helped me and my dad scrape the hull of our sailboat two summers ago. Over at Parson's Marina." He remembered that Mr. Keane had been sharp and impatient the entire week, no fun at all.

"Right—you're the Pratt kid."

"I'm Ben . . . Benjamin."

The janitor kept looking into his face, and Ben felt like he was in a police lineup. Then the man suddenly nodded, as if he was agreeing with someone.

He straightened his injured leg, gasping in pain, pushed a hand into his front pocket, then pulled it back out.

"Stick out your hand."

Startled, Ben said, "What?"

"You hard a' hearing? *Stick out your hand!*"

Ben did, and Mr. Keane grabbed hold and pressed something into his palm, quickly closing the boy's fingers around it. Then he clamped Ben's fist inside his leathery grip. Ben wanted to yank his hand loose and run, but he wasn't sure he could break free . . . and part of him didn't want to. Even though he was frightened, he was curious, too. So he just gulped and stood there, eyes wide, staring at the faded blue anchor tattooed on the man's wrist.

"This thing in your hand? I've been carryin' it around with me every day for *forty-three years*. Tom Benton was the janitor here before me, and the day he retired, he handed it to me. And before Tom Benton, it was in Jimmy Conklin's pocket for thirty-some years, and before *that*, the other janitors had it—every one of 'em, all the way back to the very first man hired by Captain Oakes himself when he founded the school. Look at it . . . but first promise that you'll keep all this secret." He squinted up into Ben's face, his blue eyes bright and feverish. "Do you swear?"

Ben's mouth was dry. He'd have said anything to get this scary old guy with bad breath to let go of him. He whispered, "I swear."

Mr. Keane released his hand, and Ben opened his fingers.

And then he stared. It was a large gold coin with rounded edges, smooth as a beach pebble.

Outside, the sirens were closing in fast.

"See the writing? Read it."

With shaky hands, Ben held the coin up to catch more light. The words stamped into the soft metal had been worn away to shadows, barely visible.

He read aloud, still whispering. "'If attacked, look nor'-nor'east from amidships on the upper deck.'" He turned the coin over. "'First and always, my school belongs to the children. DEFEND IT. Duncan Oakes, 1783.'"

Mr. Keane's eyes flashed. "You know about the town council, right? How they sold this school and all the land? And how they're tearin' the place down in June? If that's not an *attack*, then I don't know what is."

He stopped talking and sat still. He seemed to soften, and when he spoke, for a moment he sounded almost childlike. "I know I'm just the guy who cleans up and all, but I love it here, with the wind comin' in off the water, and bein' able to see halfway to England. And all the kids love it too—best piece of coast for thirty miles, north or south. And this place? This is a *school*, and Captain Oakes meant it to stay that way, come blood or blue thunder. And I am *not* giving it up without a fight. And I am *not* giving this coin to that new janitor—I told him too much already." His face darkened, and he spat the man's name into the air. "*Lyman*—you know who he is?"

Ben nodded. The assistant custodian was hard to miss, very tall and thin. He had been working at the school since right after winter vacation.

"Lyman's a *snake*. Him, the principal, the superintendent—don't trust any of 'em, you hear?"

The principal? Ben thought. And the superintendent? What do they have to do with any of this?

The sirens stopped, and Ben heard banging doors, then commotion and shouting in the hallway leading from the Annex.

The janitor's breathing was forced, and his face

had gone chalky white. But he grabbed Ben's wrist with surprising strength and pushed out one more sentence. "Captain Oakes said this school *belongs* to the kids. So that coin is yours now, and the fight is yours too—*yours!*"

The hairs on Ben's neck stood up. Fight? What fight? This is crazy!

Two paramedics burst into the room, a woman and a man, both wearing bright green gloves. A policeman and Mrs. Hendon, the school secretary, stood out in the hallway.

"Move!" the woman barked. "We're getting him out of here!"

Mr. Keane let go of Ben's wrist, and Ben jumped to one side, his heart pounding, the coin hidden in his hand.

The woman gave the janitor a quick exam, then nodded at her partner and said, "He's good to go—just watch the left leg."

And as they lifted the custodian onto the gurney and then strapped him down flat, the old man's eyes never left Ben's face.

As they wheeled him out, Mrs. Hendon came into the workroom and said, "I'm glad you were here to help him, Ben. Are you all right?"

"Sure, I'm fine."

"Well, you'd better get along to class now."

Ben picked up his backpack and headed toward the art room. And just before he opened the door, both sirens began wailing again.